MW00908679

PIECES of LOVE

By

PJ Sharon

Bon Voyage!

PJ Sharon

This book is a work of fiction. Names, characters, places, and incidents are the product of the author's imagination or are used fictitiously.

All rights reserved. Except for use in any review, or as permitted under the U.S. Copyright Act of 1976, no part of this publication may be reproduced, distributed, or transmitted in any form or by any means, or stored in a database or retrieval system, without prior written permission of the author. Thank you for respecting the hard work of this author.

Copyright © 2014 by PJ Sharon Books

Cover by The Killion Group

Edited by Judy Roth

Acknowledgements

The creation of a book is much like raising a child, filled with joyous moments, daily challenges, and more than a few heartaches, headaches and frustrations. Such a huge task could never be left to one person. Ultimately, it takes a village. My gratitude goes to my writing communities, both on-line and real time, who help me become a better writer with each critique, workshop, and word of advice.

To my editor on this project, Judy Roth. You're the bomb, sister! And to my eagle-eyed proofreader, Gina Beach. Love you like crazy.

A huge thanks to my family and friends, without whose support and encouragement I would likely never stick my head out the door. And to my husband, who I adore. I couldn't do any of this without you, darling.

A special thanks to beta readers Kenzie S., Melissa H-K., Collette W., Michelle T., and Ann A. Thanks for reading. I appreciate your feedback. To Myrna, who helped me find my voice and always "loves me the best." And a final thanks to Lidy, who blessed me with the opportunity to travel the Mediterranean with her. Thanks for showing me the world and sharing your story, Mom.

Dedication

For Mama and Papa,

World travelers bound to meet again one day.

And for all the teenagers struggling to find their way in this crazy world. Learn to say "yes" to the gifts life brings your way, and say "no" to anything that doesn't further your quest to be the "best you" that you can be.

It gets better. I promise.

Look for the PIECES of LOVE theme song, written and performed by PJ Sharon, with Ozone Pete on guitar, and Jim Fogarty of Zing Studios in Westfield, Ma. on keys & engineering

Now available for download on
i-Tunes

Other Books by

Award Winning Author PJ Sharon

Heaven is for Heroes

On Thin Ice

Savage Cinderella

Waning Moon

(Book One in the Chronicles of Lily Carmichael trilogy)

Western Desert

(Book Two in the Chronicles of Lily Carmichael trilogy)

Watch for Book Three, Healing Waters, in 2014

Chapter 1

I've heard it said it takes twenty-one days to make or break a habit. At least that's what the Medusa Lady said. Amanda and I called her that on account of her crazy, bleached blonde hair sticking up in all directions, and the icy glare she gave us when she didn't like something we said. Amanda had a way of pissing people off. In my opinion, a family therapist who couldn't see past a little sarcasm or a few swears was clearly in the wrong profession. But Mom made us go anyway. Until Amanda went off to college and acted like everything was cool. She was always better at pretending than me.

Almost a year without my sister and her absence still ached like a raw and bleeding ulcer. A wrenching sadness flooded my chest as my stepfather pulled into the airport parking lot.

"I'm sorry it has to be this way, Ali, but I can't handle work and dealing with you while everything is so...difficult with your mother." Mitch forced a smile past the worry on his face. "It'll be okay. I promise." He stood on the curb next to my luggage, holding the car door open as if he was a chauffeur and I was a rock star. Without my guitar and heading for exile, I felt more like a prisoner on death row.

"This sucks. I don't want to go." I slung my backpack over my shoulder, and with my hair tumbling over my eyes in a dark curtain of bangs, dragged my feet toward the check-in kiosk.

"I know kiddo. But your mom and I agree that this is the best thing for everyone." He slowed his pace, rolling my luggage beside him, his loafers squeaking on the polished concrete.

It seemed useless to argue any longer. Obviously, I'd pushed him and Mom too far. I knew it wasn't that he didn't care about me. He'd been my stepdad for four years, and he was nice most of the time, but he didn't understand me any better than he had understood Amanda. Mitch had some pretty strict rules about right and wrong, and the Hartman women seemed to see rules as being made to be broken. He had married Mom after only six months of dating. Even if he'd known he was signing on for heartache and tragedy, I couldn't blame him for wanting me out of his rapidly thinning hair. The little he had was gray, and the wrinkles around his eyes made him look older than his mid-forties. With a paunch starting around his mid-section, he looked more like an accountant than a cop.

I grabbed his arm for one last plea. "Can't I even talk to Mom?"

"Not yet. Her doctor wants to make sure she's stabilized before she has any contact with family." He patted my shoulder. "I miss her too. But this is only for a little while. She's going to get better and be home before we know it." His tone didn't sound so sure and my heart took another plunge. "As soon as she's feeling better, I'll have her call you," he finished.

Mitch slid his credit card into the machine and a moment later it spit out a boarding pass with my name and destination on it. I studied it, my eyes burning with tears. Alexis Hartman, flight 1242 to LAX. I had a sudden urge to bolt for the exit. I couldn't believe he was shipping me off to California to stay with my grandmother— a woman I hadn't seen since I was twelve. That was four years ago, and I could barely remember what she looked like. The only details that stood out in my mind were her dyed red hair and fancy jewelry, and the emptiness in her eyes at my grandfather's funeral. Since then, our contact had been limited to forced phone conversations on holidays. I also hadn't flown again and desperately hoped I'd outgrown my motion sickness. My forehead beaded with sweat and I gulped for a breath.

"I don't see why I can't stay here? It's not like I'm a danger to myself." I wanted to assure him I wasn't like Amanda, but I couldn't get the words out. My throat closed as he lifted my suitcase onto the scale and the woman at the desk checked it in.

"You can't stay here because I don't have time to supervise you this summer. I'm on rotating shifts at the precinct, and I want to be with your mother whenever I can." He gave me a stern look. "Besides, you've made it pretty clear I can't leave you alone without you getting into trouble." His dark eyes met mine with that cool cop reserve that probably worked great on suspects and felons.

"I promise I'll quit. You don't have to send me away. I'll stay out of trouble. Pleeeze?"

He glanced at the large screen up on the wall. "It looks like your flight is departing on time. C'mon, I'll walk you as far as security."

I pushed off the wall and trailed after him. "But…"

He cut me off and kept his voice low, forcing me to catch up to hear him. "I don't have any other choice, Alexis. You've been given every opportunity to prove yourself. Yet you've been busted for pot twice, and I don't have to tell you what comes next. There is only so much trouble I can sweep under the rug before it starts affecting my reputation as a police officer." As we approached the security booth, he pulled me away from the crowded line. People removing their shoes, being patted down by airport security officers and scanned with metal detecting wands, moved like cattle through the x-ray machine. We stood far enough away for him to lecture me privately. "You don't seem to grasp the seriousness of your actions. Your mother can't take one more…"

"I get it!" I stopped him before he could say the word, *tragedy, disaster, heartbreak…disappointment*. Whatever he meant to say, I didn't want to hear it. In a calmer tone I continued. "I just don't get why pot is such a big deal. They're decriminalizing it all over the place." A guard shifted his gaze to me. I pushed my hair out of my eyes and hoped the Visine and dark eyeliner hid any signs that I was stoned. I'd smoked the last of my stash knowing I couldn't bring it with me and hoping it might help my motion sickness on the plane. Trying a new tact, I glared at Mitch. "Besides," I added, "pot is like…medicinal."

He leaned in closer, almost whispering as he glanced at the security guards. "Marijuana is an illegal substance, and it's a long way from being good for you on any level."

We'd had this argument before. "It's not like it's addictive," I grumbled. "And it's not the stoners going around robbing liquor stores or beating people up. It's the junkies and alcoholics wreaking havoc on society." I dropped my backpack on the floor and untied my sneakers, aware I was both antagonizing my stepfather and stalling him to keep him from leaving me to go through security and board the flying death trap alone.

He let out an impatient breath. "I'll agree to disagree about the criminal activity of *stoners,* as you call them, but as for the addictive part—we'll see, won't we? And speaking of attitude— you'd better get yours in check, young lady." He folded his arms, aiming for the big bad cop stance he couldn't quite muster. Since he was only five foot-nine—an inch or so over my gangly height, and I'd seen him freak over a spider, it was hard to feel threatened. The "young lady" remark hit me though. I'd heard him take that tone and

4

say those same words to Amanda more than once. I shoved the memory into a dark corner and grabbed my sneakers.

Resigned to the countdown on the clock marking my imminent departure, I sighed. "Can I have my phone back now?"

"I suppose you'll need it. I've set it up for International calling, but don't go crazy phoning your friends and texting all the time. It's for emergencies and so we can stay in touch. Your grandmother has orders to take it away again should you choose to be irresponsible." His sharp tone made me grit my teeth.

As soon as he handed me my phone I checked the messages. There were two from D.D., my best friend since seventh grade when I first moved to Thomson Lake, one from Sami, my sometimes friend, who was a year older, played in a band, and had access to all the best parties—and one from Jay, my hook-up for weed. We were supposed to have met at the mall on Friday night so I could get a few joints for the weekend. But all hell had broken loose at my house, and Mom had taken my phone.

The scene crashed into my mind—my mother screaming, crying, falling apart before my eyes, crumpling to the floor in hysterics. Mitch calling an ambulance, and paramedics carrying her out of the house—the sound of sirens.

"Ali, are you all right?"

My attention shifted to Mitch's voice. "Um, yeah, I guess so. I just hate leaving Mom like this."

Mitch tugged me into a hug. As much as I wanted to resist, I fell apart, feeling like the over-tired three year-old I watched having a fit as his mother dragged him onto the plane—another reason to dread the flight. Tears stung my eyes and my shoulders shook as Mitch's arms tightened. He gave me a solid squeeze and I reveled in the brief connection to someone strong and safe.

"Your mother is going to be all right, and this was not your fault." He stepped back, the moment of closeness passing too quickly as I swiped at tears. At arm's length, he looked kindly into my eyes. "Do you understand? You aren't to blame. This has been coming for a while."

I heard the words, but I didn't believe him. I knew how fragile Mom was after what happened with Amanda. All of us seemed broken and un-repairable in some way—my mother most of all. Now, my two arrests for possession had pushed her over the edge. It didn't matter that it was only a couple of joints, or that I was still considered a juvenile when I got busted, so it wouldn't count on my permanent record. Mitch got involved and pulled some strings to get me off with community service and drug treatment classes. But being that I was sixteen, they were both coming down on me hard. No more chances. If I got arrested again, they threatened to have me locked up—either in juvenile detention or in a rehab facility. It was only pot for Pete's sake. They were blowing everything way out of proportion.

Mom and I had been fighting about it when she totally lost it. She'd already taken my guitar away after the first bust, and then when she tried to take my phone away, I went ballistic and argued with her like an idiot. She screamed about Amanda's death and how she refused to have the same thing happen to me. She became irrational, which escalated to hysterical, and then—total meltdown. It had happened before, but it was the first time I'd seen it with my own eyes and the first time I had set it in motion. How could he say it wasn't my fault?

I sniffled and wiped my face on my sleeve, my eye makeup leaving a dark streak up the arm. "I can't go without talking to her. I have to tell her I'm…sorry." Tears flowed faster and Mitch hugged me again.

"I know, kiddo." Sympathy softened his tone as he rubbed my back in soothing circles, reminding me why Mom had fallen for him. "The best thing you can do is let her know you're all right and that you're straightening yourself out. She knows you aren't trying to hurt her. She's just worried about you. Look, why don't you send her a postcard from California?"

The announcement for my flight echoed over the PA and we both pulled away. "That's me, I guess." I swiped at my cheeks, embarrassed about acting like such a baby in public.

"Don't worry, okay? Your mom will be fine. What she needs is some rest, and some time to work through her grief. You just focus on your own recovery."

I cringed inwardly. By that he meant the classes I would have to take when I got to my grandmother's place. So much for a summer vacation.

"Flight 1242 to Los Angeles now boarding at gate seventeen," a female voice droned over the loud speaker. Mitch handed me my passport—the only ID I had since I'd flunked my driving test—another reminder of my loser status. I tucked it into my bag as my stomach took another dive. The last time I had flown on a plane, I had puked my guts out for half the flight. My knees wobbled as I said good-bye to Mitch and shuffled into line. I stuck my sneakers and backpack into a tray and sent it through the x-ray machine. As I stepped into the human irradiator, a loud beep sounded.

A plump woman with dark skin and a tight bun gave me a tired look, waved a wand over my body, and then patted me down with the impersonal approach of a mugger. "Take off your bracelet," she said finally, a tone of impatience in her voice.

Since it never came off, even to shower, I'd forgotten to remove the charm bracelet that hung at my wrist, covered by long sleeves nearly obscuring my hands. The silver dolphin charm caught the light and I blew out a sigh, thoughts of Amanda slipping past my guard. I set the bracelet in the tray and walked back through the machine without further incident. Pulling my sneakers on, and snapping the bracelet back in place, I looked over my shoulder, all of my words caught helplessly in my throat. Mitch forced a smile and waved as I disappeared into the crowd herding toward gate seventeen. I had no choice but to get onto the plane. My life was about to take a sharp climb into an unknown world, and I didn't like the idea one bit.

Chapter 2

Six hours, three barf-bags, and a lay-over in Denver later, I stumbled off the plane and retrieved my suitcase from the baggage claim carousel. From the odd looks I was getting, my face must have been a pasty shade of green. If it meant hitchhiking all the way home, I would do it, but I never wanted to get on another plane again. I called my grandmother, who told me to meet her out front in ten minutes. Following the signs to the drop-off and pick-up zone, I plunked down onto a nearby bench and half-heartedly browsed through the Architectural Digest I'd confiscated from the plane.

The air was warm with a nice breeze, and palm trees swayed in a line across the road. People passed by, ignoring me and rushing off to their next destination. A lady with too much perfume sat beside me. My stomach rolled. Since breakfast had left me hours ago and the food on the plane had sent me running for the stinky closet they called a bathroom, my stomach growled from hunger. The strong floral fragrance assaulted my nose, and I knew from experience, dry heaves were next. I got up and moved away, clearly doomed no matter what I did.

Pacing, I waited until a dark blue Mercedes pulled up to the curb and my grandmother stepped out, a broad smile on her face. I recognized the red hair and jewelry as her trademark style, but I'd forgotten how much she looked like the pictures I had of my father.

9

She had his sharp nose and bright blue eyes. Even the shape of her lips as she smiled reminded me of him. She rounded the front of the car and threw her arms around me. "There's my little Ali Cat." She drew back. "My goodness how you've grown."

"It's just Ali, now." I turned away, recalling our last visit and shuddering at her use of the nickname *Ali Cat*, a name only my father and Amanda had used. I hefted my bags into the back seat and climbed in the front of the swank luxury sports car, the tan leather cool from the air conditioning. Not for the first time, I wished I had been able to bring my guitar. The summer would be unbearable without it.

"Of course. You've probably outgrown that silly name, haven't you? We'll have to come up with a new one. Ali is so plain." When she buckled her seatbelt into place, she had a revelation. "I know. I'll call you Lexi. That's much more suitable for a young woman." She fixed her hair in the mirror and pulled into traffic. The tires squealed.

I sighed, tightening the seatbelt across my shoulder. *This was going to be a long summer.*

We made small talk and covered all the usual bases—Mom's undetermined stay in a psychiatric hospital in Connecticut, my plans for college after high school, and whether I had a boyfriend—a big fat no on that front. She grilled me about Mitch and asked if he was a good father, and I wondered what she expected me to say. If I said yes, would I be insulting my real father—her son? And if I said no, would she judge my mother and blame Mitch for Amanda's downward spiral? Figuring there was no way to win, I replied, "I don't know, I guess."

"Well, let's get one thing straight. There will be no calling me 'Grandma,'" she said as she zoomed onto the highway, cutting off a tractor trailer truck and ignoring the blare of his horn. "You can call me Maddie like everyone else. I'm much too young to be a grandmother." She grinned.

She was almost seventy, but I didn't argue.

The conversation shifted to her plans for me for the next six weeks, and it suddenly felt like I had been shipped to a summer camp for wayward teens, which I guess in a way, I had. "…up by nine—no sleeping the day away. You'll have a few chores. Mitch said no more than two hours a day on the computer or phone. I suggest an hour in the morning and an hour at night. And don't forget, you have your classes three times a week."

She continued reciting the rules, but I tuned out her voice and watched the cars fly by on the coastal route. A sign ahead read *Malibu, 27 miles of scenic beauty.* Palm trees lined both sides of the highway, and the sky was a perfect cloudless blue. At least the weather was nice. I wondered what her new house would be like. The last time I had visited, she lived in a sprawling ranch style house in Monterey. After my grandfather died and left her a boatload of cash, she had closed up the old place and moved to the beach. It seemed the shoe business had been lucrative.

Petite, a little on the curvaceous side, with hair cut in a stylish bob and enough makeup to dull the lines in her face, my grandmother looked like senior Barbie or an ad for a retirement magazine. *Come to sunny Malibu and live out your golden years in comfort and serenity.* My assessment was confirmed when we pulled into the driveway of her Malibu beach house a half hour later.

"Wow," was all I managed as she gave me the tour. The house wasn't overly big—only two bedrooms, each with its own bath. Despite its outward appearance of being small though, it felt spacious with its high ceilings and full length windows overlooking the Pacific. Any place with this view must have cost a fortune. I stared out at the waves crashing onto the white sand beach, observing the hordes of bared bodies that lounged in chairs or on blankets a little further down. I dropped my bags in the bedroom and went straight to the refrigerator. Condiments, a half-gallon of outdated milk, a quart of orange juice, and a bottle of wine, nearly empty. Maddie didn't eat in much, apparently. I opened the cupboards, each one more sparsely stocked than the last.

"I didn't get a chance to shop," she said, noticing my disappointment. "I'll order us some lunch." She dug out a cell phone and hit a single key, speed dialing a local delivery place. She put her hand over the phone and glanced in my direction, "Burgers okay?"

"I'm a vegetarian."

"Oh? What on earth for? No wonder you're so skinny." She uncovered the phone and said, "Two burgers, two orders of fries and a salad. Yes. Thank you. Twenty minutes? Perfect." She hung up and grinned. "We'll put some meat on those bones and you'll feel much better."

I cringed and my stomach tightened at the thought of a greasy burger. Since the time I puked my guts out after eating a piece of bad ham and watching one too many documentaries about the treatment of livestock, I had a general rule about not eating anything that once had eyeballs and had started out as a baby. I wondered if it was too late to escape and take a train cross-country back to Connecticut.

"After we eat and you've unpacked, why don't you take a little walk on the beach and get a feel for the place. We aren't far from the pier. There are some shops and restaurants you should check out, and I see kids your age hanging out there all the time. Maybe you can meet some new friends." Her tone was full of encouragement, as if I were here on vacation rather than some sort of punishment. "I have some calls to make this afternoon, but I'm sure you can keep yourself entertained for a while." She eyed me curiously. "You do like the beach, don't you?"

Wish someone had asked me that before they shipped me off to Exile Island. "Yeah, I like the beach," I said politely. No sense in starting off on the wrong foot.

She let out a breath, a look of relief washing over her face. "Good. Make sure you use sunblock. Your skin is so pale. Don't they have sunshine in Connecticut?" She smiled, obviously trying to be amusing while simultaneously being critical. I remembered my mother complaining about her "lack of verbal filters." *She means well,* Mom would say after my grandmother cut her down.

∞∞∞∞

I ate salad and fries for lunch and changed into shorts, a "Razerbacks Rule" tee shirt from our high school football team's pep rally, and flip flops. Maddie was caught up in a phone conversation when I slipped out through the sliding glass door. She waved and caught my attention, covering the phone. "Be careful, have fun, and be back by five-thirty for dinner. I'll order Chinese…and stay out of trouble." She was already back to her conversation before I closed the slider.

I strolled out onto the beach, happy to be free from adult supervision for half a minute. The day was hot, but the breeze made it feel dry and pleasant—different from the beaches on the East Coast, where the humidity could make you feel like your face would melt off at any second. I walked along the beach toward the pier in the distance. Hot, white sand sifted through my flip flops and bunched under my arches, forcing me to walk like I was kicking some invisible dog at my feet. People lay sprawled on towels and beach chairs soaking in the cancer rays. Couples holding hands

13

passed by and little kids ran into the splashing waves with carefree abandon that filled me with sadness, envy, and a longing for a simpler time. A time when Amanda and I played and laughed together. It seemed like so long ago.

My mind was about to take a dive into the depths of self-pity and despair when a flying object flashed into my field of vision. I reacted and grabbed, catching the Frisbee before it collided with my face.

"Nice catch." A male voice caught my attention.

"Lousy throw," I snapped back, caught off guard and annoyed.

"Sorry about that." A deeply tanned, shirtless boy with Hawaiian style board shorts and bare feet approached, his hand held out for the Frisbee. Shoulder length, sun-bleached hair hung in his face, but he promptly tucked it behind his ears and grinned.

I handed him the flying saucer that had nearly decapitated me and returned a quick smile—friendly, but not desperate, I hoped. "No harm done, I suppose."

Then we stood there smiling stupidly and not saying anything.

He broke first. "You're new around here."

"Yep." Being that I was ghastly under-tanned and over dressed for the beach—the only teenage girl in the vicinity actually wearing clothes—I must have stood out. I shuffled my feet, dumping another pound of sand out of my flip flops.

"I'm Seth." He glanced over his shoulder at a bunch of kids who were impatiently awaiting his return and calling him names from a distance.

"I'm Ali."

"Well…Ali. Where you headed?"

"Taking a walk to the pier. I just got here so I don't really know my way around yet." Awkward butterflies fluttered in my stomach. I stared at my feet and avoided the pale gray eyes studying me.

"Why don't I walk with you, then? I'd hate for you to get lost on your first day." He didn't wait for me to answer. With an easy flick of his wrist, he turned and zipped the Frisbee across the beach to a brunette who looked none too happy that Seth was abandoning the game. "I'll catch you guys later," he called and turned his attention to me. "Let's go. I'll show you around."

Five minutes and I'd already made a potential friend. Maybe this summer wouldn't be so bad after all. Guys back home weren't this forward, or mature. Seth wasn't super good looking or anything, but he seemed nice enough and he was interested—which was more than I'd gotten in three years of high school in Somerville, CT. If I wasn't exiled because of my obscurity and my attachment to mediocrity, I was labeled as that weird girl whose sister died. Here, I had no history.

"That would be great. Thanks."

Seth turned out to be a great guide. We reached the pier where crowds of people strolled, skated, or boarded along, laughing and smiling like California life was all a big party. He showed me some cool shops along the boardwalk and the local burger joint where Maddie had undoubtedly ordered our lunch. I still couldn't believe she put away both of those burgers by herself. That couldn't be good for a woman her age. Seth drew my attention to an ice cream vendor and pulled out his wallet.

"What'll it be? My treat." His goofy grin was kind of nice—comfortable like he already knew me. Lucky him, since I felt totally clueless about that mystery.

I looked over the menu, still thinking of Amanda. I ordered her favorite. "Coconut chocolate chip…on a waffle cone."

The pretty blonde at the counter eyed Seth like he had rabies. "Anything else?" she asked, her tone as biting as a Doberman.

"I'll have the usual." Seth smiled sweetly at her. "You know what I like."

The girl rolled her eyes and spun off to fix our order. Seth stuck a thumb out toward her and whispered. "We used to date. It didn't end well…"

The girl returned and Seth paid for the cones. I dove into my ice cream as we walked away.

"That's what I like to see," he said, checking out my ice cream selection and taking an unexpected bite. "Someone who knows what she wants." Seth put his hand on my lower back to lead me off the boardwalk. An uncomfortable flutter hit my belly. Maybe all Californians were this touchy feely. I didn't want to seem like a prude or anything, but I wasn't used to any boy touching me in such a familiar way. Most of the boys I knew from school kept their distance. It wasn't like I was hideous, but no one wanted to be around the dark and twisty girl who always looked so sad. Other than a few close friends—all girls—I hadn't even had a real date yet. I shrugged off the shiver that crawled across my skin. What did I know about normal teenage *getting to know you* rituals?

"Where are we going?" I licked my melting ice cream and followed his lead.

"I know where there's a party this afternoon. A bunch of my friends are there." He glanced down at me. "You do party, don't you?"

Now he had my full attention. I shrugged and nodded, playing it cool.

Summer was definitely looking up.

Chapter 3

Seth dragged me through a crowded house, not too much different than Maddie's. Only this one was decorated in bright patterned Southwestern furnishings like something you'd see in a ranch house in Arizona or New Mexico, manly but chic—probably owned by some rich bachelor who hired out the decorating and rented the place while he was off traveling the world. Without an actual adult anywhere to be found, the place was loaded with half-dressed teens, packed shoulder to shoulder, drinking, dancing, and shouting over the bump and grind music pumping through some rad stereo speakers.

"Are you sure I can't get you a beer?" Seth pulled me along through the maze of bodies.

"I don't drink," I yelled above the noise, which garnered a few stares as we passed through into the kitchen and out onto a deck at the back of the house.

The pounding became muffled—enough to hear without yelling.

"I thought you said you partied." Seth eyed me with brows furrowed like he was sizing me up to determine if I was worthy of meeting his friends.

"I smoke weed, but I don't drink or do hard drugs." I tried to make it sound like I was the same girl who knew what she wanted.

The girl who knew her favorite ice cream without thinking about it, or the girl who hooked up with strangers on a beach two thousand miles from home. Brave and confident—that was me. I stared him down for a minute before a smile curved the edge of his mouth.

"I know exactly where to get what you're looking for."

Five minutes later, I sat in a wicker chair in a small courtyard behind the house, a hidden sanctuary surrounded by a tall hedge of fragrant flowering shrubs. Seth passed me a fat stogie. I took a hit and held it, the sweet herby smoke curling around me as my lungs expanded and a pleasant fuzz hit my brain. I passed the joint along to the guy next to me who took a huge hit and snorted back a coughing attack. Around the circle went the joint, several guys and a couple of bikini clad girls a little older than me, each taking a hit and passing it on. I didn't catch all of their names, but it didn't matter. I was in my element and the stuff we were smoking was awesome. A few hits already had me feeling good and stoned.

"Better than that crap you get back east, right?" Seth had his arm around me. I didn't really feel comfortable with the closeness, but I wasn't about to set conditions on our friendship when he was my new supplier and his show of ownership was keeping all the other wolves at bay. I figured I could manage Seth before things got out of hand. An arm around my shoulder was a small price to pay for this most excellent smokage. I took another hit and held it. My lungs burned and my head grew fuzzier.

A second joint came my way. I took it, wondering whose endless supply I was tapping and how I could get my hands on some for later when I would sneak out of Maddie's place at night to take a few hits here and there. Maddie…oh, crud. I pulled my phone out of my back pocket to check the time. Dead as a doornail. I'd forgotten to charge it.

"Hey, like, does anyone know what time it is?" I asked. Pot smoke filled the air and music thumped in my head, drowning out my words as another joint passed under my nose.

"It's party time!" A girl with streaky blonde hair and a killer tan squealed as she danced in circles, drawing stares and dopey grins from every guy within twenty feet. Everybody laughed, including me, and my concern about getting back to Maddie's for dinner faded into the haze of smoke and the rhythm of the drums pummeling the air.

It was some time later, after I'd smoked more than my fair share of ass-kicking weed, eaten a bowlful of chips and guacamole, and drank a half gallon of lemonade, that I found myself sprawled on a beach blanket in front of the house with Seth. All worries about time disappeared with a stunning sunset, the most beautiful shades of orange, pink and purple I'd ever seen, changing before my very eyes. The darkness slowly descended, the ocean swallowing the sun like deep blue quicksand. Within minutes, the stars shone brightly against a black sky and the party died down to a dull roar in my head a short distance away. While I was in this state of foggy bliss, Seth made his move.

"I really likes you," Seth said, laughing at his own slurred speech. He leaned up on one elbow and hovered over me, the stench of beer strong on his breath.

"I like you too, man. But I'm not really interested in…"

He didn't let me finish. He leaned down and planted a wet, sloppy kiss on my mouth, his tongue diving between my lips before I could squirm away. I pushed against his chest, but he resisted. He grabbed my hands and pinned me to the ground. His mouth on mine stole my breath and stifled my efforts to protest. Panic set in. I struggled against him and finally managed to bite his tongue. With a gasp, I broke free of his slobbering assault. "Get off of me!"

At that moment, a flashlight beam blinded us. "Everything okay over here?"

I rolled to sitting and shielded my eyes from the light. It only took a second to register that the flashlight belonged to a uniformed police officer.

Seth sat up and swayed, giving the cop a salute. "Yes, sir, occiffer, sir!" Then he busted out laughing.

The light shone on me again. "You wouldn't happen to be Alexis Hartman, would you?"

My heart jumped to my throat. I climbed to my feet, sobering immediately. "Yes, sir."

"Your grandmother is pretty worried about you." He flashed the light on Seth. "With good reason, I see." He spoke into a radio attached to his uniform. "I found her, Cummings. Call it in."

"Roger that," a voice crackled from the other end of the radio.

The music suddenly stopped and people poured out of the house, running in all directions like ants escaping the nest during heavy rain. I could hear police yelling inside. "The party's over, kids. Get home where you belong and don't come back."

The officer with the flashlight took my arm and escorted me to a patrol car, pushing my head down as he deposited me into the back seat. A half hour later he and his partner, the invisible radio voice, Cummings, drove me back to Maddie's house, lecturing me on the dangers of drugs and hanging out with the likes of Seth and his friends. It wasn't my first time hearing this lecture or my first ride in the back of a cruiser. But it was the first time I was glad to have been picked up by the cops. I didn't want to think about what might have happened if they hadn't shown up.

When the door opened, my relief fled.

"Thank you, Jerry. I knew I could count on you boys to find her." Maddie gave a tight smile to the cop without taking her eyes off of me. The look on her face made my stomach plummet to my feet. With her chin quivering ever so slightly and her eyes watery pools of unshed tears, I knew I'd gone too far.

"No problem, Maddie." Officer Jerry released my arm and glared down at me. "Don't hesitate to call if she gives you any more trouble."

"I assure you, she won't." Maddie drew in a deep breath, still staring at me like I had drowned a kitten. Then her face softened as she shifted her gaze to the brawny Jerry. "You tell your father hello for me, won't you?"

The cop touched two fingers to the visor of his hat in a half salute. "Yes, ma'am."

I dragged myself through the door and expected to hear it slam behind me, but worse, the latch clicked with a soft, defeated *clink*. I kept my back turned, not sure if I should run and hide in my room or turn and face the music head-on. Maddie decided for me by saying the most dreaded words an adult could say.

"Sit down, Alexis. We need to talk."

Chapter 4

My grandmother gave me an earful, half of which I was too stoned to hear or care about, until she brought up the inevitable topic…Amanda. "After everything your family has gone through with your sister, I would think the last thing you would want is to take drugs and cause any more trouble. I don't understand you kids. You've got your whole lives ahead of you, and you're throwing yours away, just like Amanda."

Knowing nothing I said would make anyone see I wasn't at all like my sister, I kept my mouth shut. Amanda and I had always been worlds apart in every way. She was pretty, I was plain. Her sandy hair and stunning dark eyes, her long legs, and her gorgeous smile put my straight mousy brown hair, brown eyes, and boyish build to shame. The only visible indication that we were sisters was in the subtleties. The round face, the curve of our lips, and maybe the cuteness of our tiny noses—my best feature. Otherwise, my sister was smarter, more athletic, popular, and socially more adept than me in every way. I couldn't compete with her when she was alive. I certainly had no intention of trying to compete with her in death.

While Maddie took in a deep breath, no doubt preparing for another tirade, I jumped in with my only defense. "It's not like I'm shooting heroin or smoking crack. It's only pot."

"Which will lead to more. Mark my words, young lady." I was about to argue that statistically speaking this wasn't true when she brought up a topic that made my insides squirm and my jaw clench shut. "Your father started with pot when he was your age. It didn't take long for alcohol to follow. Once he started drinking, he was never the same. And you of all people know what alcohol cost him."

My father's death from a drunk driving accident changed the landscape of my entire life. I was six and Amanda was nine then, and it was only a few years after that she started drinking. Secretly stealing a sip here or there at first, and then drinking daily by the time she was fifteen. I never touched the stuff. I hated the taste and even more, I hated the way it made me feel—out of control. By then, most of my friends were already smoking pot. It seemed like a good alternative at the time. At least with pot, I didn't do anything crazy or act like an idiot. My teeth ached from clenching and words bubbled to the surface.

"Look…Maddie. Ground me or take my phone away, or better yet, send me home, but please, please don't make me sit here and listen to you compare me to Amanda or my father. I'm not like them and I never will be, okay?" I pushed myself up from the cushy white sofa, my head spinning enough to make me wobble.

"I can see that this discussion is futile while you're under the influence. We will decide what to do with you in the morning." Maddie stood, her normally wrinkle free appearance looking worn and her eyes tired. As I turned to go to my room she stopped me. "Lexi, I know I haven't been a big part of your life the past few years, but I…do care about you. I only want what's best, and I can tell you, doing drugs is not the answer to your problems."

I resisted the urge to correct her on my name or to ask *what the answer to my problems was,* because I knew this would only lead to a longer discussion than my foggy brain wanted to deal with. Instead, I muttered good night and skulked off to my room. Curling up on the firm cool mattress, I stared out the long window at the moon hanging over the water. Light sparkled across the surface like a million fireflies dancing and winking as the crashing surf of the Pacific lulled me to sleep.

∞∞∞∞

I slept dreamlessly and woke with a pounding headache and a mouthful of cotton and sawdust. After brushing my teeth, showering, and drinking a quart of orange juice, I poured a bowl of stale bran cereal with raisins—the only box in the cabinet resembling breakfast food—and sat at the kitchen table wondering if Maddie had slept in or if she was even home. The place was eerily quiet other than the hum of the air conditioning. I pulled my hoodie over my head. *Did the woman have to keep the place so freaking cold? What was the point of living at the beach?* I chewed the semi-crunchy flakes, annoyed there wasn't even a slice of bread for toast, or a donut to be found, and decided a grocery list was in order. I grabbed a pen and notepad off the counter. With another bite, I cringed and added Choco-puffs and real milk to the list.

The slider opened and Maddie strolled in, her red hair tousled and windblown, her cheeks rosy from exertion. She had on track pants, sneakers, and a faded *Les Mis* tee shirt. "Nothing like a morning walk on the beach to wake you up and make you feel alive," she said, still a little breathless.

Chocolate and Red Bull would probably do the same, but who was I to argue. "Could we go pick up a few groceries today?" I slid my list across the table and she picked it up, frown lines creasing her forehead.

"We won't need any groceries." She dropped the list and poured herself a glass of juice.

"Are you planning on starving me to death as punishment?" I asked, immediately regretting the opening I'd given her.

"On the contrary, my dear. Where we're going, you'll have all the food you can eat." Maddie sank into the chair across from me, sipping her juice and studying me over the rim of the glass.

I eyed her quizzically, afraid to ask for an explanation. The bran flakes were beginning to expand in my stomach. I slid the bowl aside, waiting for her to continue.

She set her glass down and raised a thin brow. "Curious?"

"Maybe," I said, pushing my bangs out of my eyes.

Maddie grinned, obviously satisfied she had hooked my attention. "Well, I just got off the phone with my travel agent. I had a cruise planned before your stepfather called to ask if I could take you for the summer. I've been trying to cancel my reservations, but my agent said that unless it's for health reasons, I'm obligated to pay for the trip. So instead, I've decided to take you with me."

"You mean on a boat?" The cereal formed a large mass in my stomach, growing instantly to the size of a grapefruit.

"No, on a spaceship. Of course on a boat, silly—although technically it's called a ship."

"But I can't go on a boat. I get really motion sick."

"It's a ship and you'll be fine. Cruise ships are like floating hotels. You won't even know you're moving." She kept smiling as my heart rate soared and sweat broke out on my neck.

"Floating is the operative word there, Maddie. You don't understand. I get sick on bumper boats. I cannot go on a boat...on the ocean..." The lump in my stomach took a sharp drop to my lower intestines.

"They have motion sickness medicine. You'll be fine," she said again. "Besides, this is a once in a lifetime opportunity for you. Fourteen ports in seventeen glorious days on the Mediterranean.

25

You'll see Europe for the first time and one of the stops is Tunisia. That's in North Africa," she clarified, obviously mistaking my look of panic for one of cluelessness. "It will be a fabulous trip. I've been planning it for ages. Now I won't have to go alone with a bunch of old fogies. It'll be fun. You'll see."

Clearly, we had totally different ideas of what constituted fun. Dreading the answer, I asked, "And how are we getting to this…ship?"

"We'll fly from here to Rome and then catch the ship in Civitavecchia. From there we'll sail down the coast of Italy to France and then Spain, and…" her voice trailed off as the food in my stomach made a sudden reverse turn, and I dashed to the bathroom. A few minutes later I returned, still feeling queasy at the thought of another flight and the idea of days—weeks at sea.

"There is no freaking way you are getting me on another airplane." I dug my heels in, spouting a dozen reasons that this trip was a bad idea. Apart from my motion sickness, I cited several compelling arguments. "What about pirates and terrorists? Political unrest in Tunisia and Libya?"

Maddie rolled her eyes at me.

"Don't forget about the Titanic. And don't even get me started on the hazards of flying on the oversized tin cans they call airplanes—which have been known to plummet to the earth at speeds that will rip your eyeballs out of their sockets. If humans were meant to fly, we'd have feathers."

We were still arguing hours later when a limo arrived to take us to the airport, complete with a scary-looking driver standing outside the house. A guard—I couldn't believe it.

"I'm not taking any chances with you," she said as she introduced the big guy. Hank, a muscle-bound character with a square face, dark eyes, and chocolate brown skin, towered outside the door waiting for me to try to escape and looking seriously capable of stopping me from any sneaky maneuvers.

"What about my court-ordered classes?" Desperation kicked in and sweat beaded on my forehead as I struggled with my suitcase.

"Mitch said he could arrange for you to take them when you return home."

My grandmother had thought of everything, damn her. I kicked, screamed, whined and cried all the way to the airport, but none of it ruffled her for a second. She was much tougher than I remembered.

She loaded me up on Dramamine and picked up some stupid ginger gum and wrist bracelets that were supposed to stimulate an acupressure point in the wrist to stop nausea. It wasn't like I hadn't tried all of these tricks before. My mother knew how I felt about traveling, and yet here I was sitting on a plane for the second time in two days, wishing I were anywhere else. I knew a hundred other people who would probably kill for a chance to see Europe or go on a cruise, but for me this was the next closest thing to hell. Not for the first time, I thought my sister was the lucky one. If this was life, death had to be easier. I gripped the armrests, closed my eyes, and swallowed back the organs that rode up in my throat as we sped down the runway.

Chapter 5

After I threw up twice in the airplane toilet and once on a cute, and surprisingly understanding, dark haired boy in the back row, I finally fell asleep, waking only long enough to down some ginger-ale and catch the end of an intense Vin Diesel action flick. Eight hours had passed like Chinese water torture, and Maddie and I were dragging our suitcases through the airport in Rome, shuffling toward a bus that would take me to the floating hotel of doom. I was hot, exhausted, and miserable.

"I don't see what the big deal is about Rome. This airport doesn't look any different than any other one I've been in. It's as big and confusing as the rest, only in a foreign language," I complained as we followed a young Italian woman with a *Welcome to Rome* sign onto the bus.

"*This* isn't Rome," Maddie sighed as she climbed the steps slowly, short of breath after trekking through the airport at breakneck speed. "Trust me, Lexi. You are going to love Europe. When we tour the Vatican and St. Peter's Basilica, and you see the Sistine Chapel for the first time, it will bring tears to your eyes. You'll see…you'll be glad you came with me."

We settled into two seats at the back of the bus, and I stared out the window, unable to argue any longer. Even I had my limit and I had reached it hours ago. I watched as non-descript buildings and scrubby trees passed by, no signs that Italy was any more fascinating or beautiful than anywhere else on the planet. Cars whizzed past—

little foreign jobs that looked economical and far less intrusive on the roads than the SUV's back home.

When we reached the port an hour later there was another ridiculously long wait, another security and passport check, and I was starving. As we approached the humongous ship my stomach lurched. The thought of climbing on board and essentially living there for the next seventeen days with my grandmother made me as nauseous as the idea of said ship bobbing like a cork through the Mediterranean. A vision of me heaving over the side rails flashed before my eyes. I was already missing home, more worried than ever about my mom. Instead of seeing the upcoming journey as an adventure of a lifetime, I wanted to cry.

The whole experience felt like some kind of torture that Mitch had devised to scare me straight. I wondered if my mother even knew that I'd left the continent. Another wave of worry was followed by a surge of anger. Of course she knew. They had all planned this together. I pushed down the tears and sense of betrayal bubbling to the surface. I refused to give in to my urge to panic and run home crying—*as if I had the option*. Instead, I dragged my butt up the gangplank in a long line of other cattle-like humans, who all looked much happier and more excited than me.

A part of me wanted to be at least a little excited. After all, my friends back home would be green with envy that I had spent half of my summer vacation cruising around Europe. But thoughts of what my mother was going through, and all that we had lost, crept into my mind. I couldn't even muster a half smile when Maddie put her arm around my shoulder for the welcome aboard photo being snapped as we hit the top of the gangway. A joint would definitely have made the whole experience more fun—or at least tolerable—but who knew when my next opportunity to get high would come along. Another wave of panic set in.

We made our way down a long hallway and up a few flights of stairs, avoiding the elevators that were bustling with gray-haired passengers. "This will be quicker," Maddie said, tugging me along by the hand and taking the steps with more energy than seemed possible for a woman her age. Our cabin turned out to be bigger than I'd imagined. There were double beds, a suitable sized bathroom, and a balcony overlooking the port. I flopped onto the bed next to my suitcase, which was there waiting for me.

"I need a nap," I said. My head ached and my body felt wrung out. We'd been traveling for ten hours.

"Don't you want to explore the ship? There is so much to see and do. I know you're going to love this, Lexi." Maddie tossed her hat on the bed and began primping in front of the mirror that covered one wall above a glass-topped desk.

"You've got to be kidding. Aren't you tired?" I groaned and pulled a pillow over my face.

"I suppose I am a bit worn out." Maddie plunked into a straight-backed, orange chair—one of two that flanked a small table against the wall. She checked her watch. "We could change into our swimsuits, go up to the Lido deck, and nap by the pool. They're serving lunch up there until 2:00. Or maybe you'd like to take a little siesta out on the Promenade deck. There are usually lounge chairs set up and it's quiet. Did you bring a book to read?"

"No. Do you have to be so cheerful and energetic all the time?" My headache intensified. Peeking one eye out from under the pillow, I cringed as Maddie gave me a chilly stare.

"It beats being a sourpuss," she said, then added, "They have a library. I'm sure you'll find something there that interests you."

"I doubt it," I said. There were a few books I was supposed to read from the summer reading list for school, but I hadn't even thought about it as I packed to go to Maddie's. It seemed I'd barely had time to throw a suitcase together before Mitch was rushing me onto the plane. A pang of guilt twisted inside me, knowing I hadn't even said good-bye to my mom. "When do you think I can call home?" I asked, my voice soft.

Maddie smiled sympathetically. "We can check in with your stepfather in a few days." She came and sat next to me on the bed. "I know you're worried about your mother, dear, but there isn't anything you can do except pray for her and let the passage of time take care of things." She shook her head, her blue eyes growing misty. "You've all been through a terrible time since Amanda…well…I'm sure your mother will get through this. She has plenty of people taking care of her." She patted my leg. "What you need to do is concentrate on taking care of yourself." She began unpacking her suitcase, all the while humming some old ditty from way before I was born. She stopped abruptly. "I know. We can do the sunset Tai Chi class later. Tai Chi is wonderful for clearing the mind and calming the soul."

I rolled over and stuffed my head back under the pillow.

∞∞∞∞

I awoke some time later to the sound of the ship's horn blaring and the subtle sensation of movement. I looked around, disoriented, and found a note on the bed next to me. *Lexi, I've gone to play Bingo. I'll be back later to meet you for dinner. Tonight's dress is formal, so wear something pretty. No shorts or tank tops. Enjoy exploring the ship and please, stay out of trouble, Maddie.*

Formal? Crud. The only thing I had with me other than shorts were jeans or a bathing suit. I rummaged through my suitcase, dragged out a few articles of clothing that weren't shorts or tank tops. Since unpacking would only serve to remind me that I was trapped, I slid the case under the bed. Defeated, I threw on a pair of capris pants, a button down short sleeved blouse and a pair of sandals—the closest thing I had to a nice outfit. By the looks of the sun on the balcony, it was late afternoon. A trek around the ship to orient myself seemed like a good idea.

Within three minutes, I was hopelessly lost.

Mazelike hallways leading nowhere and elevators that all had identical silver polished floral designs had me turning in circles. Our cabin was on the upper promenade deck, which apparently only housed cabins. The same with decks five, six, and seven. I spent half an hour working my way up and down the long narrow corridors, feeling more lost with each turn. Frantically, I searched for a ship's map, which I had seen next to the elevators, but now it seemed that even the elevators eluded me. I bumped into a few people and would have asked for directions but everyone spoke a different language or was rushing to get somewhere. All I wanted was to find my way back to my room, but I couldn't remember what number cabin we were in and I'd forgotten the keycard anyway.

Frustrated, I determined I wouldn't venture out of my cabin again for the next seventeen days. Near panic, I turned another corner and ran headlong into—my eyes widened. Perfect—the cute guy I'd thrown up on in the back row of the plane.

Chapter 6

"Are you lost?" Deep green eyes with long dark lashes loomed before me.

I took two steps backward, totally flustered. Met with a cocky expression of amusement, my heart skipped and my cheeks burned. A crooked smile that seemed to light up his face caught me off guard—like he knew something I didn't know.

"No...I...um...I'm exploring the boat." *Could I sound less convincing?*

"Technically, it's a ship." He sounded just like Maddie. His grin widened and I was instantly annoyed. With his dark brown hair trimmed short, he could have passed for a military school cadet, the Mr. Perfect type I was so not into.

"Right." I tucked my hands in my pockets and shrugged. "Well, I'm going to keep...exploring." I turned my back, my face hot as I retreated down the hall.

"Hey," he called. "You know if you go this way, you'll find the forward elevators. They'll get you down to your room on deck four."

I spun to see him pointing down the other hallway and my face blazed hotter.

"Oh? And how do you know where my room is?" I sniped, walking back toward him and stopping a few feet away, my arms folded across my chest.

"Because I saw you and your grandmother go into room 4052 a couple of hours ago. You're right down the hall from me."

He held up his key card. "Room 4064," he said, grinning like I should be ecstatic about this news.

"Okay, so we're neighbors." I avoided eye contact by sizing him up. I didn't like how smooth, how confident, how crazy good looking he was. Boys of about eighteen—which is what I judged him to be—should not be that comfortable in their skin. It made me nervous, and I thought of Seth of the nasty beer breath, his clammy paws all over me. I squirmed in my sandals.

As if he was in my head, Mr. Smooth gave me an innocent look and said, "I'm harmless. I wasn't stalking you or anything. I was just wondering how you were feeling after that rough flight."

"Yeah...the flight...sorry about that." I stared down at my feet, my mortification complete.

"No worries. It's not the first time I've been puked on."

When I glanced up, he was still smiling and looking like a cross between the two brothers on *Supernatural,* Dean and Sam, all rolled into one. I wasn't sure how to respond to his comment. Should I be grateful that my puking on him wasn't that bad and say *thank you*? Or should I apologize again and skulk away before I said or did anything else to embarrass myself?

I decided on both. I couldn't be a total coward. "Thanks for saying that, but I *am* sorry. I don't travel well," I added lamely. It was hard to meet his eyes, which had an empathetic gleam to them. Dressed in Dockers and a collared polo shirt, he exuded a certain charm that made me feel like Thompson Lake was very far away and much less sophisticated than the world he knew.

"Try this." He dug in his back pocket and handed me a foil package. "It works great. Take one every night before you go to bed and the motion won't bother you so much." Noticing my doubtful frown, he added, "I can get more from the ship's Medical Officer. No worries."

I took the package, wondering if he might have something a little more potent in his pocket. The thought of being without weed for the next three weeks had me heaving a sigh.

"Thanks again. I should get going to dinner. I'm supposed to meet my grandmother there at five. It must be pretty close to that now.

He checked his watch. "You have fifteen minutes. Didn't anyone mention its formal night?" He looked me up and down for a moment, and taking note of my involuntary expression of horror at his scrutiny, covered, "You have plenty of time to change…" When my eyes grew wider he stammered, "I mean…I wouldn't worry about it. It usually takes me a couple of days to get my bearings when I travel." He smiled broadly, working his dimples to try to make me feel less self-conscious—and failing miserably. "It's not like they'll throw you overboard or not feed you."

I had to crack a smile at that. He was trying to be nice, and I couldn't make up my mind if I should be on my guard or accept his charitable gesture. He was obviously a rich kid with not a care in the world except to feel sorry for me—the lost, lamely dressed, motion sick girl who needed sympathy like I needed a fork in the eye. I stood up to my full height, squaring my shoulders so that I was only an inch shorter than this sweet, intimidating, captivating, and completely out-of-my-league guy. "You go on a lot of seniors' cruises, do you?" I asked coolly.

"This is my third cruise actually—although this is my first time in the Mediterranean and I don't usually travel with seniors."

"Are you here with a relative or did someone ditch you?" I asked, wondering if we at least had that in common.

For the first time, his face faltered, a tiny crack in his armor of self-assurance. "My dad is meeting me in France. Until then I'm on my own." He recovered and the crack closed up, but he knew that I knew it was there, and I could tell he didn't like me knowing.

Not one to miss an opportunity to prove the Medusa Lady right, I capitalized on his weakness so I could make my own inadequacies less glaring. "Does your dad make a habit of leaving you on cruise ships alone in the middle of the ocean?" My voice sounded both skeptical and sarcastic, exactly what I wanted in my effort to gain the upper hand in the conversation.

This time, however, he held his face in perfect composure, the cocky guy returning to the forefront, his lips curled into a condescending smirk. "Technically, the Mediterranean is a Sea, not an ocean. And not that it's any of your business, but the trip was a graduation present. My father is a cardiac surgeon. He was called for a consultation in Paris and this was the only ship arriving in France on the day we were supposed to meet."

"Oh…" I said, deflated. Not only had I insulted him, but I'd accused his famous father—who sounded like he might be up for a Nobel Peace Prize—of abandoning him. I shrugged, my cheeks growing warm again. "You're right. It was none of my business. Sorry."

We stood awkwardly for a minute, neither of us making eye contact. Finally, I broke the silence as I slipped past him toward the elevators. "I'll be going to dinner now. Maybe I'll see you around."

"If you're going straight to the dining room, you need to go the other way—toward the stern." He pointed down the hallway I'd just come from and gave me the abridged version of the crooked smile I'd seen a few minutes before. This one, forced and polite. So much for making friends. From the look on his face, I'd done a fair job of blowing any chance of fun on this trip—right out of the water.

Chapter 7

A half hour and several wrong turns later, I made it to the dining hall, a huge chandeliered room filled with bustling waiters delivering silver covered trays to what seemed like hundreds of tables. With the red tablecloths and everyone wearing fancy suits and ball gowns, my clothes completely set me apart. As the waiter assessed my apparel—likely preparing to remind me how underdressed I was—Maddie stood and waved.

The waiter bowed politely, showed me to our table, and pulled out the chair across from Maddie, gesturing for me to sit.

"Oh, dear…is that the nicest outfit you brought with you?" Without waiting for my response, she continued, "We'll pick you up a few things on our travels. Don't you worry."

I squirmed, trying to ignore the stares from the next table. Then I noticed we were one of the few tables for two and wondered why we weren't part of the larger seating arrangements like most of the other passengers, who—I noted—were all pretty much gray haired and old.

Maddie gave me a sympathetic smile. "I thought you and I could use a little one on one time to get to know each other. Besides, your grandfather and I always had a private table when we dined."

I stared at the menu, deciding on the Mesclun salad and the pasta something-or-other that I couldn't pronounce. "Aren't you sick of me yet? Everyone else seems to be." My tone came out snippier than I'd intended, but it was the first real thing I'd said to her since the trip started.

She lowered her menu and eyed me over the glasses she'd just slipped on. "No one is sick of you. Although, it seems your behavior is getting out of control, don't you think?"

I didn't want to get into defending myself at the start, but I couldn't let the comment slide. "I'm not *'out of control.'* If marijuana wasn't illegal, we wouldn't be having this conversation."

"Perhaps not, but the fact is, until the Federal Government decides differently, marijuana *is* illegal, and you've been caught twice breaking the law—three times if I choose to tell your mother about your little party incident on the beach."

I rolled my eyes and pulled the menu up in front of me again.

"Lexi…Ali…listen to me." My grandmother's face turned stony as she reached across and lowered my menu. "I remember what it was like to be young. I ran with a fast crowd in my day. Back in the sixties when I was modeling in New York and doing the Broadway circuit, I saw my share of parties. Don't act as if your generation invented getting high." She laid down her own menu and removed her glasses. "But if I hadn't been so caught up in my career and living the high life, I don't think…well, I don't think your father would have had such a hard time…with alcohol." Her voice was low and her eyes a sad and glassy blue.

"This isn't about my dad. Or Amanda," I said before she could throw my sister in the mix. "I don't know why everyone wants to blame my actions on someone else. It isn't a big deal."

I turned my attention to the waiter who arrived to take our order. He was young, and like most of the wait staff, appeared to be Indonesian, according to Maddie. We ordered our dinner and when the waiter left, the silence between us was somber. I hadn't thought about my father in a while, but being with Maddie, it was hard not to. I'd stopped wondering why he drank. I figured it was about some childhood drama that he never resolved. Maybe this was it. Maybe he felt his mom didn't love him. Or maybe there was more to the story. I wasn't certain I really wanted to know. Dredging up the past was a waste of energy as far as I was concerned. Besides, I barely remembered him.

Maddie broke the awkward silence. "What is it you want out of life, Lexi?"

The question startled me and I had to think for a minute. "I don't know. I just want to finish school and be out on my own…like every other teenager."

"What about college? Don't you have a dream? Something you're passionate about?" Maddie continued as the waiter delivered our first course—white plates adorned with a smattering of greens, sliced pears, glazed pecans, and what looked like feta cheese. "Don't you want to see the world?"

Her eyes took on a far-off look as she stared beyond me out the long windows to the darkening sky. I followed her gaze. As much as I was grateful I wasn't feeling sick, I still couldn't help but notice the subtle movement of the ship through the water and the horizon gliding by. I dropped my focus to my fork and plate as I considered her question.

"Well…I like playing guitar, but my grades haven't been that great this year, and Mom won't let me take lessons again until I pull them up. I don't really care, though. It wasn't like I was learning anything from my teacher that I can't figure out myself." I stuffed a forkful of greens, drizzled with tangy dressing, into my mouth.

"Guitar, huh? And I suppose you want to play in a band." Maddie folded her napkin across her lap, nibbled on a roll, and sipped her wine.

"My friends have a band…but…I don't really like playing in front of people." I picked up a pecan that slipped off my fork, and popped it in my mouth. The conversation was leading down yet another road I didn't want to go. I played for myself and no one else. How that could possibly translate into a career in music, I couldn't imagine.

Not that it mattered. Mom thought my guitar was one more thing distracting me from getting better grades. Math and science weren't bad, but I had let my English and history grades slide. It wasn't that I couldn't do the work, I just wasn't any good at being a student—having people tell me what to do all the time—tell me who I should be and how I should think. Mom would never go for music school anyway. *Too much money for too little return*, she'd say, more practical than ever since Mitch was basically supporting us. I dismissed the idea for the hundredth time.

"Your grandfather played guitar when I first met him." Maddie's eyes got the same misty, far-off look again. "He gave up on music all together once we moved to California and he started the shoe business. He didn't seem to play much after Nicholas was a few years old. I guess he got too busy. I was surprised when your father picked it up as a teenager. It must run in the blood." Her voice sounded strained.

I ate my dinner in silence, putting together the unfinished pieces of my father's life and listening as Maddie reminisced about Grandpa and the "good old days." All I remembered about Grandpa Henry was that he smelled strongly of cologne and gin. He was funny in an oddball sort of way, always cracking jokes and laughing at things that amused only him. We didn't see my grandparents much after Dad died, so I missed the opportunity to get to know my grandfather better. The one clear memory I had of him was that the light had gone out of his eyes after his only son died.

As far as my dad and his guitar, I vaguely remembered him showing me a few chords when I was small, but I'd all but forgotten the sound of his playing. Mom had given me his old Gibson when I turned ten and started me with music lessons to keep me from driving her crazy by plucking away at the strings trying to teach myself. I had an electric guitar I played unplugged when I didn't want to be heard, but his old acoustic was my favorite—the only piece of my father that still meant something to me. I tuned back in to Maddie's stroll down memory lane just as the waiter arrived to take our plates and hand us the dessert menu.

"Ahh, dessert. Henry's favorite part of the meal. Remember, we're on vacation, so order anything you like." Maddie's eyes lit up as she oohed and ahhed over the delicious choices on the menu. "I think I'll have the crème brulee," she said finally.

"Me too, I guess." I handed the menu to the waiter, glad not to have to come up with a decision on my own. As much as I was sick of everyone treating me like a kid, the responsibilities that lay ahead terrified me. The most money I'd earned was a few hundred bucks the summer before, cleaning stalls at the horse stables at Thompson Lake. Once school started, I'd had to give it up or flunk out. Time management and setting priorities were not my strengths. The Medusa Lady tried to convince me that my lack of focus was a weed issue. I wasn't so sure since I'd never been able to match Amanda's natural efficiency and ability to juggle everything at once.

"Tomorrow, we begin exploring the Mediterranean." Maddie's voice cut through my painful thoughts. "I can't wait for you to see Santa Margherita. It's such a beautiful little village."

Before I could ask what was on the agenda for the tour, a familiar face entered the dining hall. My new friend seemed to be following me. His gaze roamed through the crowded tables searching for someone. I wondered who he might be sitting with when his focus landed on me, and a smile stretched across his face. Crud…he was heading our way. I slid up in my chair and straightened my shirt, pulling it down lower to cover my midsection and the new post in my navel, still a bit red and itchy from the piercing. I kept my eyes cast down, hoping he would veer off toward another table.

"Hi again," he said as he approached.

I lifted my gaze and my face turned instantly warmer. Dressed in a sport coat and tie, and a pair of black slacks, complete with a polished belt buckle and expensive dress shoes, he looked like he'd stepped off the cover of Prep School Boys edition of GQ magazine. Maddie set down her napkin and turned to greet our visitor.

"Hello, young man." She glanced from him to me and back again. "I assume you two know each other." Then her gaze fell on me. "Lexi didn't mention she'd made a friend." Her eyes sparkled and her lips turned up into a suspicious but satisfied grin.

"Ethan Kaswell, ma'am. Nice to meet you." He shook her hand, meeting her grip for a moment and making eye contact, and then there it was—that thousand watt grin.

Maddie's eyes lit up. "Would you care to join us?"

"I'd hate to intrude," he said with a quick glance my way.

"Of course not," Maddie replied before I could object. She signaled to the waiter and asked him to bring another chair, despite the fact she and I had all but finished eating. The waiter complied and before I knew it, Ethan was sitting beside me, patiently enduring Maddie's interrogation. His ability to eat while being visually dissected, and simultaneously answering the onslaught of questions heaped on by my grandmother, was impressive. I ate my dessert in silence. As much as I felt bad for the guy, I couldn't help but appreciate Maddie's ability to get to the vital stuff fast.

It turned out that Ethan was from New York, he'd attended a prep school in Connecticut for the past four years, and had recently graduated at the top of his class. He'd been accepted to Columbia's Pre-Med program in the fall on a Lacrosse scholarship. As I fought not to choke on the crusty sugar coating on my crème brulee, I couldn't help but be impressed…and annoyed. He was exactly the kind of guy Amanda would have dated in high school, the kind she could pretend to be perfect with—the kind I steered clear of. My chest tightened, and I reached for water, unable to swallow past the scraping in my throat from the crystallized sugar.

"So where are you going to school in the fall?" Ethan asked, innocently turning his eyes toward me as he shoveled another bite of steak into his mouth.

"I still have a year of high school," I said, my ears heating up. "I haven't thought much about college yet." I eyed Maddie, who looked all too pleased with herself.

Ethan swallowed, set down his fork, and sipped his water. "Taking some time off for the summer to explore the world, huh?" Although obviously meant to make me feel better about my inferior status and lack of direction, there was a hint of longing in his voice. Maybe having your life mapped out wasn't as appealing as it seemed.

"Actually, I'm here as punishment for criminal behavior," I said. "You might want to keep your distance. My delinquency could be contagious," I added, sending a smirk in Maddie's direction.

He choked on his water and Maddie rushed to pat his back, glaring daggers my way. As the coughing fit passed, Maddie said, "Since you're traveling alone, why don't you join us tomorrow on our tour of Santa Margherita?"

"I'd love to, thanks." Ethan didn't take his eyes off me. "Here I was, thinking this trip was going to be boring and lonesome." My face flushed as his grin widened. "It seems I was wrong about a lot of things."

Chapter 8

Much to my relief the next day proved Ethan both right and wrong. I'd taken the twenty-four hour motion sickness medication he'd offered and slept like the dead, no remnants of the nausea from the day before remaining. A current of anticipation ran through the crowd, the enthusiastic murmurs promising the days' excursion would be anything but boring. Ethan met Maddie and me just in time to get his purple sticker that designated him as part of our tour group.

The morning was already hot at nine o'clock as we set out toward the mountain laden coastline of Portofino. White villas—interspersed with soft green, yellow, orange, and red buildings—painted the hillsides, creating a picturesque setting that made me smile in spite of myself. As the ship-to-shore tender approached the docks, we passed sailboats and yachts ranging from comfortable day cruisers to opulent floating hotels and high-tech speedboats. Locals lounged along the gray sandy beach and swam in the blue green water, attempting to stay cool.

I pulled my hat over my eyes, glad I'd heeded Maddie's insistence on sun-block. She had also nixed my flip-flops in exchange for my sneakers and suggested shorts and a tank top when I'd held up jeans and a tee shirt.

Ethan helped Maddie step down onto the dock once the boat was tied off. When he reached for my hand, I reluctantly allowed him to help, though we both knew I didn't need it. An unexpected shiver sent my heart racing as he held my hand a little longer than

44

necessary, and my cheeks ignited when he flashed me a grin. The deep green polo shirt and khaki shorts he wore suited him, and the warm colors brought out the gold flecks in his eyes. I avoided his lingering gaze by taking in the amazing scenery. We boarded a second boat, which took us around a small peninsula and into Santa Margherita. My jaw dropped as the ferry docked. One of the most beautiful places I'd ever seen lay stretched before me.

"Back when these houses were built, home owners were only allowed to paint them if the taxes were paid," said the tour guide, a white-shirted man with olive skin and a round face, named Pietro. His bulbous nose and Italian accent gave him away as one of the locals. "Those who could afford to pay their taxes had the most colorful homes," he explained. "So, it eventually became a way of distinguishing the classes." We followed along in a crowd of a dozen other passengers.

Clearly smitten with our new companion, Maddie sent a devilish grin my way, stepping around me to put Ethan between us. "Isn't this heavenly? Henry and I came here for our third anniversary…or was it our fifth?" Maddie continued to ramble on about Portofino and how it had been a hot spot for old Hollywood stars back in the fifties and sixties, the likes of Frank Sinatra and Rex Harrison frequenting the village in the heydays after World War II. Most of Portofino had been spared during the bombings due to the pleading of wealthy German women who loved to travel to the idyllic locale for holidays.

Scooters, bicycles, and foot traffic passed us by in spurts as we made our way through the village and up the hillside trail toward the turreted remains of a coastal fortress located at the top. Maddie was quick to notice the painted on shutters adorning the houses we passed—a way the villagers who couldn't afford windows, used to create the illusion they had them.

"Saint George's church was rebuilt after the war," said Pietro, as he walked backwards up the trail between the buildings, his orange flag overhead. He pointed out the simple but lovely stone church that overlooked the Mediterranean in all directions. "From here you can see the Gulf of Tugullio, the Gulf of Paradiso, and the Castilla del Brown. Feel free to rest inside the church where it's cool, or explore the surrounding vistas. But be back here in fifteen minutes."

My gaze swept the breathtaking panoramic view in awe. The village of Portofino lay below, as perfect as a post card, stealing my breath and making me wish I had my phone with its camera, though it would do me little good since I'd forgotten to charge it…again.

I followed Maddie and Ethan inside the old church, determined not to spend much time there. Though the cool air offered relief from the scorching sun, churches and I didn't get along. Other than my early memories of Mom and Dad dragging us to Mass once in a while on Sundays, my only experiences in them were the funerals I'd attended. The wooden cross that hung at the front of the church reminded me of the polished wood of Amanda's casket, making my throat ache and my eyes fill. I excused myself and left Maddie resting in the shaded sanctuary, her eyes closed in prayer and a peaceful smile on her face.

Ethan followed me outside. "You okay?"

"Yeah. I'm not one for churches and religion." I headed up a narrow trail toward the cliffs to catch the bay side view.

"At school, we had to attend services every Sunday unless we were going home to be with family." Ethan gazed out over the water, his eyes far away and his face having lost its usual good humor.

"I take it you spent a lot of Sunday mornings in church then."

46

His brow furrowed. "I mostly only went home on holidays. With my dad working so much, there was really no point."

"Where's your mom…if you don't mind me asking?" I sat on a stone bench and he settled beside me. The warmth of his shoulder touching mine scattered my thoughts.

He answered slowly, as if unconvinced of the truth in his own words or uncertain if he wanted to share the information. "She died," he said finally. "When I was eleven. She had cancer." He studied his sneakers and I noticed the uniformity of the laces, still clean and white.

"I'm sorry," I said, not knowing what else to say to ease the tension of the moment. I wasn't at all prepared to tell him about Amanda, but I could definitely relate to losing a parent. The words spilled out before I could stop them. "My dad died when I was six…drunk driving accident." Just saying it out loud ripped open the old wound. He didn't need to know that my dad was the drunk driver, or that he'd taken a twenty-year-old kid with him in the head-on collision. The name Jake Connelly jumped to mind, indelibly imprinted in my psyche. I kept my gaze focused on the horizon where the sea met the clear blue sky.

Ethan's eyes widened. "Man, that sucks…sorry."

We sat quietly for several minutes, each lost in our thoughts and nothing to say that could make life less tragic for either of us. The call from the tour guide below finally broke our silence.

"We'd better get back," I said, rising from the stone bench.

Ethan grabbed my hand. I turned and met his gaze, those green depths shimmering like bottomless pools in the sunlight. "Thanks for telling me about your dad. It's nice to know that someone gets it, you know?"

Not sure how to react to the closeness or the igniting presence of his fingers wrapped around mine, I slid my hand free and turned away, capturing one last memory of the incredible view. "You have no idea," I whispered.

∞∞∞∞

Back in Santa Margherita we had Sicilian Romano pizza at the Ristorante Palma, waited on by a gorgeous Italian guy who was tall and lean and had the face of a sculpted bronze statue like I'd seen in the village square. Later, I ate my fill of gelato, which I had to admit was the best ice cream I'd ever eaten. As we stopped to enjoy fresh squeezed orange juice on the café walkway, I noticed Maddie looked tired, her face flushed.

"Are you all right?" I asked, concerned to see my grandmother's characteristic energy drained.

She fanned herself with her hat, a lemon yellow, wide-brimmed straw monstrosity she clutched in her hand. "I'm fine, dear. Maybe I've had a little too much sun. I can't wait to get back to the ship and lie by the pool in the shade. A good book and a little nap will perk me right up."

I looked her over doubtfully. Ethan touched her red cheeks, one after the other with the back of his hand. He frowned.

"Your face is hot and dry. That's a sign of heat stroke. I think we'd better get you back to the ship." Before she could protest, he was already signaling our tour guide.

"Don't be silly. I'll be fine."

Despite her resistance, Pietro insisted Maddie accompany him back aboard the ship. She continued to argue, adamant Ethan and I stay behind and finish the tour.

"You have to go shopping in the market. I'm sure you'll find some lovely outfits you'll be able to wear to dinner." She handed me a wad of Euros and retreated, Pietro leading her gently by the arm. "Be careful and stay together," she called. A new guide, a pretty young blonde woman named Pamela, reassured her as she took over the orange flag.

Concerned about my grandmother, but knowing she was in good hands, I did as she suggested and hit almost every shop in the village. The cash she'd given me turned out to be a good sum of money and the shopkeepers were quick to show me around and get me outfitted. Ethan haggled and bargained like a pro with the locals, something I had no clue how to do, or any idea it was customarily expected.

After trying on armloads of clothes, I picked out two colorful and flowery skirts, a pair of chunky heeled sandals, and several tops. I felt like Julia Roberts in Pretty Woman. Ethan easily took on the Richard Gere role, amused and charming as I admired my new look in the mirror.

"You'll need this when you go into the churches," the girl in the next shop said in broken English as she draped a beautiful silk shawl over my shoulders. "It is disrespectful for so much skin to show." She eyed my skimpy shorts and bare midriff, a gleam of envy in her eyes as she gaped curiously at my belly piercing.

"I'll take it. Thank you," I said, grabbing another gauzy top off the rack. I usually hated shopping, but here in this foreign land, so far from the expectations and pressures of home, and no one looking over my shoulder to tell me what to do, it actually seemed kind of fun. I felt funny spending Maddie's money so frivolously, but she hadn't hesitated to assure me she could afford whatever I might need and the prices were dirt cheap compared to back home.

Ethan made silly faces when I tried on something outrageous and his goofy commentary only made the experience more memorable. When I emerged wearing a flowing skirt and a halter top baring my shoulders, he grinned broadly and said, "You look awesome." And then with the next outfit he said, "I like that one," his eyes lighting with sincerity as I spun around. His comment about me having to *"beat off the Italians if I wasn't careful,"* made me laugh out loud it was so ridiculous.

As much fun as I was having, I almost hated to show it, let alone relax and enjoy it. I realized I'd had a scowl on for days—maybe even months—and that this was the first time I'd really enjoyed a day since I couldn't remember when...since before Amanda.

Maybe I was setting myself up for a huge let down, but for the first time in a long time, I felt special—and precariously happy.

Chapter 9

"I'm much better this morning," chirped Maddie as she opened the door for room service. She insisted on ordering breakfast at the crack of dawn so we could make it on time for our shore excursion, and of course, that's what she and Grandpa Henry always did.

I sat on the bed playing with the bath towels, attempting to re-create the octopus configuration I'd found on my pillow when I returned to the cabin the night before. Maddie was thrilled with my purchases and had gushed over how nice I looked at dinner, causing endless embarrassment in front of the others at our table. She'd decided to try sitting with a group so Ethan could join us—since the table for two was overcrowded with a third person. It seemed she had taken to Ethan even more quickly than I had, and overnight, he'd become a perfect addition to our motley duo.

A mix of emotions conjured a list of reasons why this was a bad idea—not the least of which was that getting attached to someone I'd never see again after this trip sent warning signals to my brain telling me to keep a cool distance—a message my heart was clearly ignoring.

"It's a shame Ethan won't be joining us in Cannes. The Boulevard de la Croisette is one of the loveliest promenades to stroll. Do you know that Gloria Swanson, Grace Kelly, and even Jaqueline Kennedy Onassis walked along the French Riviera back in my day? There's no telling who you'll see now. Maybe even that handsome Johnny Depp fellow. Doesn't he live in France these days?" Maddie squinted into the mirror and applied a liberal dose of eye liner, patting her crow's feet and frowning.

"Ethan is supposed to meet up with his dad today," I said, ignoring her question about Johnny Depp's residency status. If living in a foreign country was the only way famous people could find some peace, being in the spotlight didn't seem like a great idea to me. I considered what it would be like to have a famous cardiac surgeon for a father, and then wondered if Ethan ever had a choice as to whether he'd follow in his dad's footsteps, and if walking in such a huge shadow was as awful as it sounded. I knew what it was like to have other people's expectations weigh me down, and suddenly I felt bad for him.

Maddie sipped her coffee and nibbled a croissant, then pulled a white, short sleeved shirt on over a sleeveless top and stared into the full-length mirror. "Will you look at these baggy arms?" She lifted her arm and pinched the fold of skin that hung loose underneath, a scowl of disgust clouding her expression. "I really need to get back to the gym and start working out again. Walking the beach isn't enough anymore. I just hate that everyone at the fitness center is either young and gorgeous, or as old as dirt."

I grinned inwardly. "You look great for…."

"Don't you dare say, 'for a woman my age'. I've never heard a more backhanded compliment." She fluffed her red hair, grabbed yet another floppy hat—this one fuchsia—and turned to me. "Are you ready to go?" Then she noticed I hadn't touched my food. "Really, Alexis, you are skin and bones. Eat something."

Did she not see the irony? I grabbed a sticky croissant and stuffed half in my mouth, then chugged my orange juice. She shook her head and raised a light brow, her frown deepening the creases around her lips.

PJ Sharon

It wasn't long before we were once again climbing from a transport boat they called a tender, onto shore. Cannes (pronounced *Con*, according to Maddie), home of the famous Cannes Film Festival, I learned, was named after the slender reeds which once grew along its shores. The air was scented by lavish gardens and natural flora, but high-rise condos and crowded resorts had sprouted up alongside the plants. I stared in awe at the endless beaches dotted with white umbrellas. The Alps Maritime beyond the village rose up and created a majestic amphitheater of hills that dropped sharply down to meet the blue sea. Having finally remembered to charge my phone, I flashed my camera every time I turned around, each site more beautiful than the last. What had once been a little fishing village was now a booming high-end resort.

Elegant boutiques and outdoor restaurants lined the wide street. Violin music floated from a café not far off, and the lyrical sound of the French language filled the air. I couldn't understand a word, but hearing it sent my heart soaring nonetheless. Maddie caught my arm as I captured another picture on my phone, this time of a street performer with a white painted face, miming at the passing tourists and holding out his hat.

"Isn't that Ethan?" Maddie pointed in the opposite direction through the crowd. I turned to see Ethan talking with a man in front of a boutique. A hard expression covered Ethan's face and he avoided meeting the man's stare. Whatever they were discussing, it didn't appear as if Ethan was at all happy about what was being said. Maddie headed in their direction before I could stop her.

As we approached, Ethan caught sight of us, and I watched his expression change to one of quiet acceptance and stoic calm. He interrupted the man—presumably his father judging by the similarities—and smiled stiffly. "Hi, Mrs. Hartman. Hi, Lexi."

I bit my lip and didn't correct him. Although I still preferred the name Ali, when he called me Lexi, it seemed to fit.

Maddie stepped between us to face Ethan's dad, interrupting the awkward silence.

"I told you to call me Maddie. Mrs. Hartman was my dear departed husband's mother, and God knows I don't want to be associated with *that* old battle axe." She smiled and stuck her hand out to Ethan's father, who was staring from me to Maddie and back, obviously confused. He was tall and broad-shouldered, older than I expected, with graying hair and green eyes that sparkled when his lips curved into a charming grin, not unlike his son's, I noted.

He took Maddie's hand and held it as if he were addressing the queen herself, giving her a slight bow of his head as he met her gaze. "I'm Martin Kaswell. Nice to meet you."

Maddie's face glowed. "And it's lovely to meet you as well. Your son has been a darling to keep us company on our voyage. He mentioned you'd be joining him for the rest of the cruise."

Subtlety not being one of my grandmother's strong suits, and Ethan's immediate shift in energy ratcheting the tension up a notch, I interjected, "I'm sure Dr. Kaswell has more important things to do than entertain us, Maddie. Why don't we take that walk up to the church and museum at the top of the hill? Didn't you say you wanted me to check out some antique musical instruments?"

Ethan glanced my way, a grateful but tight-lipped smile edging his features. His father, however, still wore the expression of a condemned man. His gaze fell back to his son. "Unfortunately, I've run into some problems with the case I was working on in Paris. I have to get back, so I won't be able to join you for a few more days. I'll try to catch up when the ship docks in Rome at the end of the week."

Maddie's face fell. "Oh, dear. What a shame." She glanced at Ethan, understanding finally dawning. "Well, don't worry. Lexi and I will take good care of Ethan. He truly is a wonderful young man—a credit to your outstanding parenting, no doubt." Her cool gaze held a challenge, and my chest tightened.

Ethan stuffed his hands into his pockets and stared at the cobbled street.

His father cleared his throat and deflected the barb. "Any good manners he has I'm sure are attributed to his mother." Now both men fidgeted, an uneasy silence settling between them. "I hate to be rude, but I must get back to my patient." He turned and laid a hand on his son's shoulder. Raw emotion rolled off of Ethan, but he stood rigid and squared his shoulders, stiffening further as his father hugged him. "I'll see you in a few days, son. Try to have a good time." Then he gave Maddie and me a polite nod and turned to walk briskly down the Boulevard, hailing a cab as he went.

Ethan stood staring after his father, a strained expression making his jaw twitch.

Maddie touched his arm and drew his attention. "Would you like to join us for the day? We're taking the tour to Grasse and St. Paul-de Vence."

"I don't think a perfume factory is really my thing," Ethan said, honest disappointment showing for the first time.

"Of course not," Maddie said, pursing her lips. She gazed up the long hill at the far end of the Boulevard, and a revelatory grin spread across her face. "Lexi wasn't too keen on the excursion either. Tell you what. Why don't you two stay with the walking tour of Cannes and really get a feel for the French Riviera while I take the bus tour to Grasse. I love the perfume factory and seeing all those lovely lavender fields. Besides, I'm not anxious to make another hike today in this heat. Let's meet back on board the ship for dinner. What do you say?"

Ethan's expression lightened and I wanted to hug Maddie.

"You mean it? Are you sure you don't mind?" I had been secretly dreading the perfume factory given my aversion to most fragrances. I imagined the bus ride back would be sheer torture after everyone on board had sampled the flowery French concoctions. Maddie cornered the tour guide and exchanged a few words with her, pointing toward us and nodding, a determined look on her face that pretty much guaranteed any irregularities in procedure would be overlooked. She returned a moment later.

"That's settled, then. You two stay with the walking tour, and I'll head off with the old folks." She glared at the bus driver, who, with exaggerated watch checking, impatiently waited for his last passenger. Grateful beyond words, I hugged Maddie, and Ethan and I headed off in the opposite direction, leaving her standing on the sidewalk smiling and waving cheerfully. "Stay out of trouble, young lady!"

"That was really sweet of your grandmother," Ethan said as we walked along side by side up the hill toward Saint Anne Church, which, according to the brochure, had been preserved as Musee de la Castre, a museum filled with archaic relics, historic photographs, and antique instruments.

"She has her moments." We fell in line behind the other tourists plodding up the wide stone steps. "So what's with your dad?" I asked boldly, taking a lesson from Maddie's interrogation style.

"Let's just say, I wasn't surprised the plan changed."

"Depending on someone who doesn't keep his promises must suck."

"Being a doctor isn't like a regular job," he stated in defense. "When you're dealing with people's lives, everything else has to take a back seat. It's the job. I'm used to it."

"You almost sound convinced," I said, shooting him a wary smile.

"I only hope that when I have kids someday, I can learn to balance being a doctor with being a dad better than mine has." His tone was more sad than bitter, and I had the urge to stop and hug him. Instead I hesitantly slipped my fingers through his and gave his hand a light squeeze.

"I have no doubt you'll be amazing at both."

His mood shifted and a genuine grin lifted the corners of his mouth, revealing straight white teeth and a perfect set of dimples. My heart skipped with relief when he hung on tighter and let our hands swing together all the way to the top of the hill.

The church turned out to be crowded but worth the hike. I learned that the building was originally a fortress erected in the eleventh century. The structure was both offensive and defensive, providing a base from which raids could be launched, as well as offering protection from pirates and invaders. Now, the beautiful stained glass, a fresco painting of Jesus being baptized, and the boat models sitting at the feet of the saints gave the place a sense of sanctuary. Historic photos of the church, from days past, lined the interior wall leading to the museum section, where the antique instruments were behind glass and off limits to touch.

"That's a cool one." Ethan pointed to an ancient stringed instrument propped on its side in the case.

"It's a lute," I said. "They were some of the earliest string instruments and what eventually became today's guitar." We continued browsing the cases, stopping to admire what appeared to be a lap harp. "This one is called a dulcimer."

"You sound as if you know a lot about musical instruments."

"I used to take guitar lessons."

"I always wanted to learn music, but with school and sports, everything else took a back seat. Are you any good?" Ethan eyed me sideways, a curious grin on his face. Warmth crept up my neck and into my cheeks.

"I don't know. I like to play, but playing in front of people...makes me nervous, so I've never had anyone tell me if I'm good or not."

Other than my music teacher and a few close friends, no one had heard me play for some time. At home, when Mom and Mitch were around, I practiced on my electric guitar—the one that made little sound without being jacked in. I didn't want to drive them crazy with the noise, nor did I want any kind of critique of my playing or my music choices.

At least that's what I told myself. But I knew there was more to it. Down deep, I wasn't interested in having people make me feel like more of a freak than I already did. Or maybe I just didn't want to share the part of my soul that came out when I sang or played. Whatever the reason, my being good or not didn't really seem the point. Ethan's voice drew my attention again.

"What kind of music do you play?" asked Ethan, the one question I'd hoped he wouldn't. He led me away from the tour guide, apparently more interested in talking than listening to her tell us the history of the place. Her melodic French accent faded as Ethan tugged me out of the cool church and into the hot sun.

I took a breath and answered the question. No use stalling. "My music teacher insisted I learn classical, but I really like playing the classic rock stuff and even some...well...don't laugh, but I kind of like folk...and country. It's soulful, you know? Some of it's twangy and irritating, but some of it has real depth and emotion behind it. And every song tells a story."

"A sad, twisted story." Ethan laughed. Seeing me cringe, he recovered quickly. "Sorry. You did ask me not to laugh. But I can't see you playing country music. You look more the type to play in some alternative rock or punk group."

I couldn't blame him for thinking so with the row of ear piercings I had on each ear and my signature dark eye liner. "I have a few friends who play hard core stuff. They're always bugging me to join the band, but it's not my thing."

"You being so reserved and all," he teased.

I glanced away, my cheeks likely flushing pink again—an effect I hoped would be mistaken for the heat of the day.

Then he stopped an caught himself. "Oh, I forgot something inside. I'll be right back." He jogged the short distance to the stone chapel, giving me time to reclaim my senses.

Whatever power he had to make me feel simultaneously awkward and completely awesome was beginning to fray my nerves. I wanted to relax and give in to liking him, but warning bells clanged in my head louder than the noontime bells from a village cathedral below. In less than three weeks, Ethan and I would say goodbye and likely never see each other again. It seemed beyond stupid to allow myself to develop any attachment that would surely lead to heartache and misery—something I had more than enough of already. Thoughts of Amanda crashed in on me. An instantaneous knot formed in my throat and my eyes filled. The rush of emotions snuck up on me when I least expected and always at the most inconvenient times. I sighed and pushed the tears back down, wiping my cheeks with the backs of my hands.

I was close to the top of the hill so I continued on. When I reached the high point, I took in the breathtaking sight. Below lay the ancient village with sweeping views of clear blue water and the Lerins Islands not far off.

"This was definitely worth the hike up," said Ethan, coming to stand beside me, a little breathless. We settled onto an empty bench.

I took in the scent of the sea and the fragrance of aromatic flowering shrubs wafting up from below. The smell of baked goods and bread reached my nose and a twinge of hunger ignited a low growl. The intrusion was a welcome distraction, but I wished I'd taken Maddie's advice and eaten more breakfast.

"I suppose we should join the tour. It's almost lunchtime and we don't want to get separated," I said, hoping my shift in mood didn't show.

"Wait," Ethan said as I stood. "Not that I wouldn't gladly fight through the stampede of elderly ladies heading for the French bakery for some buttery croissants, but…" a shy smile came across his face, different from his usual confident grin. "I have something for you."

I sat back down and he handed me a small, flat box. I stared blankly. "What is it?" I turned the box upside down.

"You'll have to open it to find out."

Slowly I lifted the lid, my heart pounding unreasonably hard. Inside was a tiny silver charm. I dropped it into my hand and studied the design. It was a tiny replica of a lute—like the one we'd seen behind the glass case in the church. When I didn't say anything, Ethan spoke up.

"It's nothing big, but I noticed your charm bracelet. I thought you might want to add a charm to remember your trip to France."

I stared at the bracelet dangling on my wrist. It had been the one item of Amanda's I hadn't allowed Mom to pack away—a gift I'd given my sister two Christmas's before, having spent a month's worth of allowance and babysitting money. It had come with a single charm—a dolphin—her self-ascribed totem. The heart, the dancer, the tennis racquet, and the peace sign charms she'd added on her own clinked together—pieces of herself she'd left behind. My throat all but closed and words stuck like I'd swallowed peanut butter. Before I could stop them, tears flooded my eyes.

Chapter 10

Ethan's apology and confused expression did nothing to calm me down. I wasn't ready to talk about Amanda—not with him. Not with anyone. I pulled myself together and gave him a lame explanation—how I'd never gotten a present from a boy before. Unless I counted the silly Valentine's cards we exchanged in grade school or the rabbit my neighbor Billy tried to give me when I was six, trying to make me feel better after my dad died. Another sharp stab hit me deep in the chest. Why did so small a gesture of condolence or a heartfelt gift bring on an ocean of grief and pain?

I didn't want anyone feeling sorry for me. Or maybe, as the Medusa Lady had said, I didn't feel deserving of love. She'd said that Dad's death at such an early age was perceived in my child's mind as if he'd abandoned me—as if he didn't love me enough to overcome his drinking. She was also quick to point out that his death being surrounded with so much tragedy and guilt was an added burden for family members left behind. But it wasn't like I'd caused his drinking, or that I had contributed to his driving drunk and killing himself and someone else. He'd been drinking since he was in his teens according to Mom. Medusa Lady said that alcoholism was a hereditary disease and that Amanda and I were susceptible. Somehow, I'd been spared that genetic trait as far as I could tell. Even the smell of alcohol turned my stomach. Amanda hadn't been so lucky.

The rest of the day was uneventful as I was lost to my grim thoughts and wanted nothing more than to be alone, get high, and play my guitar—none of which was likely to happen. My foul mood when I returned to the ship was evidence enough that at the very least, some alone time was called for. After ditching Ethan with another lame excuse of needing to rest up before dinner, I retreated to the upper deck, a swanky spot called the Crow's Nest that I'd found was pretty much deserted in the middle of the afternoon.

The bartender nodded as I wandered into the spacious lounge, the only inhabitant other than the waiter who was prepping for the before dinner crowd to show up for cocktail hour. I grabbed a booth and stared out the bank of windows overlooking the port.

Provence's gorgeous Mediterranean beaches lay stretched out in front of the modern city and its suburbs sprawled upward into the hills beyond. Several other cruise ships of various sizes floated nearby, situated among the smaller yachts and sailboats that bobbed along the coastline. The crystalline blue sea sparkled in the afternoon sun.

"Can I get you anything, Miss?" A short, mocha-skinned man with the trademark Indonesian accent pulled me out of my daydream.

"Ginger ale, please."

The waiter raised a brow and disappeared.

Ethan and I had eaten a hearty lunch at a sweet little café on the Boulevard after our tour of the church and my stupid meltdown. Now, in spite of the motion sickness pills he'd given me, I felt a little queasy. To distract myself I gazed around the room at all the plush red chairs, polished brass, and deep burgundy carpeting, and noticed an entertainment area set up for the musician who was currently nowhere to be seen. A piano and bench sat on one side and a guitar stand and mic were set up nearby. My pulse quickened at the site of the acoustic guitar leaning enticingly on its stand.

The waiter returned with my drink.

"Do you think it would be okay if I played the guitar a little?" I asked tentatively, fully expecting to be told the notion was out of the question.

He scoped out the empty room and exchanged a quick glance with the bartender who smiled and nodded. "I don't see why not. No one will be coming in for another hour or so, and I don't think Tommy would mind." The man set down a fresh bowl of peanuts and walked away.

I grabbed a handful and popped them in my mouth, following it up with a long pull off my soda as I geared up for the thrill of playing a guitar for the first time in weeks. I wiped my hands on a napkin and slipped out of the booth. Excitement and apprehension warred within me. What if someone came in? I assumed Tommy was the musician who owned the instrument, and knowing how I felt about my own, I doubted he would be too thrilled to find some kid shredding on what was likely his prized possession. I darted another glance at the entrance as if I were about to commit some criminal act.

As I settled onto the stool, the curve of the guitar rested on my thigh and my fingers found the strings. It was a beautiful instrument—a vintage Martin with a deep mahogany back and sides, a traditional maple bridge-plate, and an East Indian rosewood fingerboard. I tuned it by ear and strummed lightly, a sense of peace washing over me like warm surf. Playing transported me out of the world and deep inside myself in a way nothing else could. It took me to happy places, sad places—lonely places. But it always took me where I needed to go at any given moment. The words to a song

I'd written right after Amanda died, rose to my lips. A song I had titled:

Pieces of Love

To hear this song, go to <u>http://www.pjsharon.com/pieces-of-love/</u> and type in *Pieces of Love* as your password. (Case sensitive and include spaces.)

Or purchase the song on i-Tunes for .99 cents
<u>https://itunes.apple.com/us/album/pieces-of-love-single/id848325918</u>

When I was just a girl
Playing in the sun
My sister chased after me
She taught me to run

Then the clouds grew dark
And the air turned chill
The rain came down
When my sister lay still

Tears fall down from the heavens above
Til they wash away
All the pieces of love.

I cried with the clouds
But no one heard
Not one whisper
No, not one word

Tears fall down from the heavens above
Til they wash away
All the pieces of love.
Pieces of love, pieces of love, til they wash away
All the pieces of love

A life cut short
She threw it all away
Now I cry with the clouds
Most every day

Tears fall down from the heavens above
Til they wash away
All the pieces of love.
Pieces of love, pieces of love, til they wash away
All the pieces of love
Til they wash away all the pieces of love

As I finished the refrain, my voice drifted soft and low through the empty room, carrying my pain on the notes and filling my heart with longing for my sister. I continued to strum the chords, imagining myself in a time and place beyond the hell that my soul was determined to inhabit. It wasn't like I wanted to wallow in self-pity and suffering. I'd been doing everything I could think of to evade it. But nothing helped, really. Agonizing heartache and perpetual tears that lay just beneath the surface seemed inescapable. I blew out a long, slow breath, picking away at the strings as if trying to pluck the pain from my heart.

"That was beautiful."

My head shot up. Startled to see Ethan standing a few feet away, I stopped playing. "I didn't see you come in."

"I'm not surprised. You were pretty lost in your song. You sounded awesome. Did you write it?"

Heat crept up my neck. "Yeah, I did. I know it's probably not very good, but putting words to the music in my head helps me get all the crap out, you know?"

Ethan sat down on the piano bench.

"Why would you think that wasn't any good? It was better than most of the stuff I hear on the radio. It was fantastic actually...and so...real." He studied me carefully, sending an uncomfortable shiver across my skin. "You didn't mention you had a sister."

"I don't," I said too quickly. "Not anymore."

"Um...do you want to talk about it?"

"Not really," I snapped. I took another deep breath, afraid the emotions I'd stuffed down for so long would bring a flood of embarrassing tears screaming to the surface. "Sorry. Amanda..." I started, then stopped, suddenly unable to sit still. I set the guitar on its stand and began to pace like a cornered cat. A few people wandered in. If I was going to spill my guts to Ethan, now was as good a time as any, but the Crow's Nest wasn't right for such a painfully serious discussion.

"Why don't we go to the Loft?" Ethan suggested, sensing my unease. "Since you and I are basically the only non-seniors on the ship, the spot is pretty much always empty." He raised a conspiratorial brow so I let him take the lead, wanting nothing more than to find a place where we wouldn't be disturbed. If I was going to tell him the whole sad story, I needed privacy. My heart thundered as we passed a group doing tai chi on the upper deck. Sweat lined my upper lip as the sun beat down on us, and I wondered how I was going to explain my sister's death in a way that wouldn't make Ethan see me differently. The way my friends in school had—like I was damaged or broken somehow.

Ethan and I ducked into the Loft, a cool, funky space dedicated to teens, complete with video games, a karaoke machine, and a small library of books and music to choose from. Computer screens lined one wall, and a Ping-Pong table filled the center of the room. I crashed onto an overstuffed chair in front of a window with a view of the open sea.

"So what was she like?" Ethan started.

Grateful for the introduction to what would likely be an excruciating conversation, I let out a sigh. "She was…everything I'm not." A sad smile took over. "That about sums up my whole life story in a nutshell." I hugged a throw pillow and tucked my feet under me, letting my flip-flops drop to the floor. "Amanda was smart, funny, pretty, and notoriously popular in school. You know the type. Cheerleader, class president, voted most likely to succeed. She was three years older than me and I was like her shadow. All I ever wanted was to be like her," I said softly as I stared blankly out at the quiet expanse of water.

"So, what happened?"

My gaze shot to his, the green depths drawing me in as powerfully as the sea. I swallowed hard. Then the words tumbled out. "She started drinking in junior high school. Typical party type stuff. Sneaking booze from the liquor cabinet, hooking up with older guys who could always get their hands on a case of beer. Somehow, she kept up her grades, but I knew she was drinking…and doing other stuff, too. She hid it from everyone…and I helped her do it. Mom was kind of wrapped up in her new relationship with Mitch at the time." I turned away to escape my guilt and paused to organize my thoughts, unwilling to place all the blame onto my mother.

"When Amanda went off to college," I continued, "I guess the pressure got to be too much for her. She almost flunked out her freshman year. Mom totally freaked about it and tried to force her to come home and go to the community college in town, but Amanda refused. She promised she would do better, try harder…whatever." By now, my throat ached from dryness and the pain of holding my emotions in check.

Apparently seeing me struggle, Ethan asked, "You want something to drink?" He pointed to a vending machine in the corner.

"A water would be great," I said, relieved for the break. When he sat back down a minute later, I took a long swig off the cold drink and recounted the story as I'd replayed it in my mind a thousand times. "One night, Amanda went to a party with a couple of friends at a house off campus. They said she was playing some dumb drinking game and then wandered away from the group. Her friends didn't know it until hours later when they found her behind the house where she had passed out. By the time they got to her, it was too late…. The Medical Examiner's report said that there were no other drugs in her system, but her blood alcohol was .4…something like twenty times the legal limit." I raised my head to see Ethan's eyes filled with concern and sadness—just the response I didn't want. I turned my gaze out the window again.

"That's rough…I'm sorry."

"Not as sorry as I am," I said, bitterness rising. I looked back, expecting to see hurt in his expression, but instead, there was understanding. "I didn't mean to be…"

"It's okay. I get it. Nobody wants to be pitied. I hated how people treated me after my mom died. Everyone walked on eggshells expecting me to fall apart at any minute. There is nothing anyone can say or do to make it better, so it seems it would be easier if they said nothing. All those stupid sayings, *they're in a much better place,* or *time heals all wounds,* are just crap people say to make themselves feel better."

I nodded agreement since I'd had the exact same thought myself more than once. I took a deep cleansing breath and released it slowly, noticing that it came easier than it had in a while. A lightness spread through me as if a dark cloud had been lifted. Maybe the Medusa Lady was onto something when she'd said that talking might help. But it was more than talking about Amanda. It was sharing her story with someone who understood the pain of grief and loss. Someone who wouldn't see me as being as broken as I felt. Someone who saw the me no one else knew.

Chapter 11

"Hurry, Lexi. We don't want to be late for the tender to shore." When I came out of the bathroom, Maddie was stuffing sunblock into a giant floral bag. "You are going to love Barcelona. It's one of my favorite cities in Europe. The art, the history, the people—it's simply too much to take in in one day." Her exuberant grin turned to a frown as she got a good look at me. "You're not wearing that, are you?"

I examined my shorts, tank top, and flip-flops. "I was going to."

"You have all those lovely skirts you bought in Portofino. And I know you have more supportive shoes than those ridiculous flip-flops. This is a walking tour, my dear. Did you put on any sun block? Here, you'll need this." She tried to hand me a baseball cap that said Ocean Pacific Cruise lines on it. I stared at the black and yellow cap and made a face, hoping I wouldn't have to follow with an actual refusal. She rolled her eyes and dropped the hat on the bed. "Suit yourself. You're as stubborn as your father was. He never listened to a word I said."

The barb caught me in the chest and my jaw tightened. I bit back a sarcastic remark and instead asked a question I'd wanted the answer to for a long time.

"What was my dad like…besides being stubborn and being an alcoholic?" Two things I'd heard repeatedly from my mother, who refused to talk about him in any other context. Eventually, I'd stopped asking.

Maddie's face twisted into a pained expression, making me wish I could take back the question. "Are you sure you really want to have this conversation now?"

I shrugged. "Now's as good a time as any, but if you don't want to…"

"It's not that. I'd love to talk to you about Nicholas. It's just…well, I'm a little surprised you want to. Your mother said it was a sore subject with you. She asked me not to discuss him." Maddie's face turned stony when she mentioned Mom.

My ears perked up. "You talked to her?"

"Yes," she said carefully. "I had to get her written permission to take you on this trip, so I phoned the hospital before we left. She seemed glad you were coming with me, but she did ask that I not…burden you with reminiscing about your father."

A choked laugh spilled out. "Sounds like her. Always trying to hide the truth from me."

"She only wants to protect you."

"I don't need protecting," I grumbled. "I'm not a little kid anymore. Besides, I'd like to have more to remember my dad by than only the bad stuff, you know?" My voice sounded small. I sank onto the edge of the bed, twisting a finger into my hair, and then tucking it behind my ear.

Maddie sighed and sat down beside me. "You are so much like him."

"Yeah, I've heard about the stubborn part most of my life."

Maddie flashed a sad smile. "It's more than that. You have his soulfulness. Like you, he loved music. And there was a kindness in him. He hated to see anyone in pain. I can't tell you how many wounded birds, stray kittens, and lost dogs he brought home when he was a boy." She shook her head and stared off as if seeing into the past. "He was a sweet and passionate young man with a bright future ahead of him, but…I was busy with my career, your grandfather was busy with the shoe store. Perhaps Henry expected too much of an only son." Maddie studied her crooked little finger, the joints knobby and swollen with arthritis. "He could be a hard man, my Henry. He was a strict disciplinarian when Nicholas was small—rigid about church-going and quick to anger."

I had a moment to wonder if that meant my dad got his fair share of beatings when he was a kid. That seemed the way old school parents did things back then. Before I could muster the courage to ask, she went on, "Your grandfather believed that once a boy reached his teen years, he should be old enough and mature enough to make his own decisions and to live with the consequences. I'm afraid we just weren't paying attention to Nicholas and he…slipped away from us. Before we knew it, he was drinking himself into oblivion and there was nothing we could do to stop him." She sighed, the wrinkles around her eyes deepening. "I wish I'd been a better mother. He was a good boy and he deserved so much more…" By now, her eyes were tearing up and her voice shook, making me regret dredging up the past.

"Don't blame yourself." I patted her hand. "Most alcoholics are hereditarily predisposed," I recited the Medusa Lady's lame reason for not taking responsibility for someone else's drinking. She used to pound home the credo *you didn't cause it, you can't control it, and you can't cure it,* a notion that hadn't helped me in the slightest when it came to feeling less guilty that I hadn't done more to help my sister.

"You sound as if you've studied up on the topic." Maddie collected her bag and stood, clearly ready to move on from the conversation. She hung a sweater over one arm and checked the mirror one last time, wiping away a smudge of eye liner. "Henry did like his gin, but that was the way of it back then. A cocktail after work, one before dinner, a glass of wine at the table, and maybe even one more after dinner drink. In my day, it wasn't called alcoholism if you got up and went to work and supported your family. We were social drinkers."

"I'm not interested in blaming anyone for my dad's drinking. At some point everyone has to take responsibility for who they are and what they do." Another of Medusa Lady's lessons that finally made sense when I thought about it in the context of my dad—a lesson, ironically, I'd refused to hear in regards to myself. I cleared my throat, uncomfortable with the realization. "I just wanted to understand him a little better. Thanks for filling in some blanks."

Maddie turned back to me and smiled, blotting moisture from the corner of her eye with a tissue. "Let's do this again when we have more time."

To smooth over the tension, I changed into my sneakers. We silently made our way down to the lower deck to catch our boat into port, both of us ruminating on our own memories of Nick Hartman, a man I barely remembered, yet one who had left an indelible mark on my life.

If my dad was abused or neglected as a child, and he saw his own parents burying their problems in booze, it would explain why he turned to alcohol as a teenager. But I wasn't willing to hold all of his failings against Maddie, especially since she obviously carried enough guilt to sink a ship. I let go of the painful thoughts attached to memories of my father, a man who used to say he loved me so much he would hang the moon and the stars in the sky for me. The man who tucked me in at night and read me stories and taught me to pray. A memory I'd almost forgotten. I wondered if I even remembered the words anymore.

Ethan was waiting in the crowded auditorium as we entered. Being the only male passenger in the room under the age of fifty, he was easy to spot. His face lit up when he saw me, and he waved us over to join him. The sight of his grin, his dark hair, and even the preppy polo shirt he wore had a grin spreading across my face. My mood lightened instantly.

"You ladies look lovely, today." Ethan smiled his best Ashton Kutcher at Maddie.

"Thank you, my dear boy. And you're looking handsome as always." Maddie did the unthinkable and pinched his cheek. To his credit, he tolerated the embarrassing display, but a red flush crept into his ears. When he grinned appreciatively, I couldn't help but wonder if he was as starved for attention as my father had been.

∞∞∞∞

Barcelona was as amazing as Maddie had promised. We toured the city with stops at such famous places as the Cathedral de la Sagrada Familia—arguably Gaudi's finest and most spectacular creation, with its dozens of spires piercing the sky. Afterward, we stopped to have lunch at a small bistro where Flamenco dancers entertained us with music and dancing like I'd never seen.

A young woman with a long, thick braid and stunning blue eyes, tapped her booted heels to a feverish beat. Several men on stage played drums and guitar while she whirled her black velvet skirt as if trying to entice a raging bull. The red ribbon in her dark hair matched the festive colors woven into her ruffled top. Each player on stage came to the forefront, showcasing his talents and entertaining us with song and dance that brought to life my inner muse. The guitarist strummed mercilessly on the strings, his fingers moving too fast for me to even begin to try to memorize the chords for later. Finally, the show came to an end, and I was left breathless and totally envious of the skillful musicians and dancers who seemed so at ease performing their art for the enjoyment of an audience.

Later as we stood in the square, only yards away from medieval buildings and an original Roman wall built around 100 AD, I had a chance to take pictures. Maddie and Ethan posed in front of an old stone palace where we were told Columbus himself had visited the royal family. Ethan insisted on snapping shots of every door and archway we passed.

"What is it with you and doorways," I finally asked.

"Every door is different." He turned his camera on me, walking backwards to capture Maddie and I making faces at him, neither of us keen on having our picture taken up close. "You never know what's behind them. The possibilities are endless," he said as he spun and captured another shot of a huge set of ancient wooden doors carved with intricate designs. I smiled inwardly at his child-like enthusiasm and his contagious optimism.

"I'll never look at a door the same way again," I said, and the three of us laughed. We took turns making up stories to go with each of Ethan's pics, imagining who and what might be behind each door. Whether it was a modern day family sitting down to a meal or a long forgotten medieval knight hanging his armor on a wall after a hard fought battle, the infinite possibilities gave the doors on the buildings and houses an air of mystery. Each one symbolized a different past, present, and future, representing in my mind at least, a sense of hope that time and life goes on. A surprising feeling of comfort and wonder washed over me as I snapped several shots of huge ornate wooden and wrought iron doors.

The narrow streets, cobblestoned and unfit for automobile traffic, were lined with shops and outdoor markets, brimming with designer clothes, leather goods, fine jewelry, and Spanish porcelain. Artists displayed beautiful sculptures and paintings on every corner and the local people called to us to stop into their stores as we passed by. The brightly colored clothes, fascinating architecture, and hidden gardens filled with greenery and fragrant flowers scattered throughout the village held me captive at every turn.

"This place is amazing!" I said, twirling around to take everything in all at once and feeling dizzy with excitement. I wanted to stay forever—become a part of this new and different culture that seemed so full of music, life, and passion.

"I knew you would love it," Maddie gushed. As if reading my mind, she added, "Wouldn't it be wonderful to go to school here for a semester? You could study art, literature, history. If I had to do it over, this is where I would have attended school. They have some excellent exchange programs."

My mood shifted and I caught Ethan watching me curiously. I avoided thinking about college, which immediately brought up images of Amanda. I still had another year of high school, and the idea of being set adrift to tackle all the pressures of adulthood froze my insides—although I'd been told by my guidance counselor at year's end to start considering my options. I figured with Mom sick, my lame grades, and Mitch on the edge, I'd be lucky to make it to community college anyway. The possibility of studying abroad seemed terrifying and way beyond reach.

Ethan spoke up. "There are plenty of awesome schools not far from where you live. You should check out the music programs in New York. Or there's a great one right in Connecticut. It was close by where I went for Prep School. You might even be able to get in on a scholarship. You play well enough. Have you ever heard her play?" he asked Maddie.

"No, I haven't. But I'm sure she's very good." Heat rushed up my neck as Maddie studied me with a quizzical eye. "Music is in her blood. I was quite the crooner in my day. Did I tell you about the time I sang back up for Bob Hope's USO tour?" She stopped to poke her head into a gallery filled with exquisite sculptures made of metal and iron. "It didn't pay much but boy did we have fun." Then as if realizing she wasn't helping her case, she cleared her throat and continued. "Pursuing a career in music, or any of the arts for that matter, is not for the faint of heart. It can be a tough and demanding business. I'm not sure I would wish it on anyone—let alone my granddaughter," she added as she smiled at the store clerk and examined the price tag on a modern art piece. "The lives of artists, performers, and musicians are destined to be fraught with heartache and disappointment. Music is a lovely pastime, but it's better to be practical when considering a profession," she finished.

My heart skipped when Ethan interjected on my behalf. "But think of all the incredible art, literature, and music the world would be missing out on if people didn't take the risk and commit their lives to their passion."

"That's true," said Maddie as she ducked back out into the bright sunshine, Ethan and I at her heels. "But you're smart to follow in your father's footsteps and choose a medical education. There will always be a need for doctors, and you'll have the means to make a comfortable life for yourself and your family one day." Maddie fanned her face with the beautifully painted Spanish fan she'd picked up in one of the artisan shops.

Ethan and I exchanged a look. It wasn't worth arguing with adults who thought they knew best what kids should do with their lives. It didn't matter that she had followed her dream regardless of the impact it had on her family. Maybe she was speaking from experience, but I couldn't help but wonder if her advice had more to do with what she hadn't done than what she had.

Chapter 12

After a full day in Barcelona, we returned to the ship, showered, and dressed for dinner. I wore a long, colorful skirt, my flat sandals, and a plain red top with puffy, three-quarter length sleeves with peek holes along the seams, happy to look more like one of the locals than a tourist on a cruise ship.

Dinner consisted of five courses of decadent gourmet dishes, opulent desserts, and entertainment from the crew throughout. Men hustled out in single file lines, singing and dancing as they served our meals, their happy expressions a contagion among the passengers, as if not a care in the world existed beyond the chandeliered dining room. As amazing as it all was, I couldn't see it as a lifestyle I would want to adopt. I couldn't help feeling like I was staring through a window, looking in on a world where I didn't belong.

Ethan joined us again—a relief, seeing that Maddie's constant nit-picking about my straight hair, thin eyebrows, and slouchy posture was seriously getting on my nerves. She couldn't seem to stop herself from commenting on the exterior faults of others, so at least it wasn't only me.

If she saw people who were overweight, she pointed out that they should spend a little time at the gym and less time at the buffet. If she noticed a couple bickering, she would comment on how they should keep their quarrels private and consider themselves lucky to have one another. More than one passenger turned an evil eye our way. Her lack of social filters was embarrassing at the least and totally superficial and annoying at worst. I kept my mouth shut though, and let Ethan distract her with his charming smile and easy conversation.

"What would you like to do after dinner, Mrs. Hartman...Maddie," he corrected, clearly uncomfortable calling her by her first name.

"Well, I thought I might catch a game of blackjack in the casino." She eyed Ethan and me, a conspiratorial grin curving her lips. "I hear there's a good action movie playing in the theater tonight—something with that hunky Rock fellow. Why don't the two of you go? I'll be fine on my own. You know, I'm quite a card shark. Those blackjack dealers won't know what hit them." She dabbed her mouth with her napkin and set it on the table, pushing away and checking her watch. "I'll expect to see you back in the room right after the movie, Alexis. Is that understood?"

"Yes, ma'am." I hated being treated like a child, but I guessed I'd earned her mistrust after my party-going stunt back in Malibu. It wasn't like there was any trouble I could get into here on the ship. Unless one of the young staffers had a stash of weed somewhere on board, the worst I could do was get caught naked with Ethan. Tingles skittered up my arms and I stared at my empty dessert plate.

Where had that thought come from? I hardly knew him, though it felt on some level like I'd known him my whole life. He was sweet and cute, funny and sensitive—in a manly sort of way. His overall kindness and ability to understand me when I didn't really even understand myself put him in what Maddie would call a "keeper" category for boyfriends. He seemed so different from any boy I'd ever met before. Most of the guys at school were jerks, only looking for an easy hook-up or some arm candy to make them look cool. I wasn't the type to jump into relationships, but being so far from home in such an exotic location made me feel...reckless.

Ethan rose from the table when Maddie stood up. "I'll deliver her to her room personally." The tone of possessiveness in his voice sent another warm tingle to new parts of me I was trying desperately to ignore. I cleared my throat and gave my grandmother a smile and a nod before she turned and followed the crowd.

"You really know how to handle her," I commented as Ethan's gaze locked on mine with a mischievous glint. The hair on my arms stood up and heat crept into my cheeks.

"She's no different than any other adult. If you figure out what they want to hear, you can pretty much have them eating out of your hand." He pulled my chair out, his hand coming to rest on my elbow as I stood. My pulse escalated and the heat in my face intensified.

"Wow, you sound kind of diabolical. Should I risk sitting in a dark theater with you?"

He laughed. "C'mon. I'm only kidding...sort of." He raised a brow and walked alongside me as we exited the dining room and headed for the stairs. I had no idea where the movie theater was, but Ethan negotiated the twists and turns as if he'd lived on board forever. "Besides, there's no sense in doing things the hard way," he finished as we rounded another curve.

"I know what you mean," I said. "It's just easier to say *whatever*...no one really wants to hear the truth, anyway. I'm tired of playing the game, aren't you?"

"Believe me, I hear you. I don't think I've ever had a real conversation with my dad." His voice sounded sad and I sensed he was genuinely hurt.

"What would you say to him if you could tell him the most honest thing about yourself?"

Ethan stopped and turned to me. "Do you really want to go see the movie? I thought maybe we could walk around out on the Promenade deck and talk instead."

"Sure. That sounds great."

We pushed through a set of double wooden doors and out onto the deck. A balmy breeze lifted my hair, the straight wisps floating around my face and tickling my skin. I ran my fingers through it and tucked the strands behind my ears. The ship had left port a few hours before, and the only evidence of land was the far off lights that twinkled along the distant shore. A deep purple sky melted to a salmony pink along the horizon where the sun had dipped below the water. The first stars danced above us.

"So are you planning on answering my question?"

"Hm? Oh, what I would say to my dad if I was being totally honest?" He leaned on the railing and looked down at the water rushing past.

I kept my distance from the edge, not ready to test my motion sickness. Ethan looked out over the sea. "I guess I would tell him I'm not all that sure I want to be a doctor. I mean, it sounds good in theory, and it's not like I have a burning desire to do anything else, but it kind of feels like I've never really had a choice." He turned and faced me, bravely leaning back on the railing as if we weren't at cruising speed out in the middle of the Mediterranean.

"You're making me nervous, Ethan. Why don't you come away from the edge?"

He grinned and pushed off, taking my hand like he'd done it a thousand times. "Okay, scaredy-cat. Let's walk while we talk."

We strolled around the Promenade deck a dozen times, holding hands and sharing our fears, hopes, and dreams. He was into

White Snake, some retro eighties band, which was cool with me since my own taste in music was in constant question by both my parents and friends. We decided on the same favorite food—lasagna with garlic bread. And when it came to movies, we agreed on action and sci-fi/fantasy. For the first time since Amanda had gone off to college, I felt like part of a twosome again—as if I weren't alone in the world. But more, I felt for the first time, like part of a couple. My heart warmed at the thought.

Elderly, white-haired couples, smiled as they passed us by, making me wonder what it would be like to grow old with someone I loved. There seemed to be a comfort in it, but at the same time, knowing that one of them would have to outlive the other, my insides felt hollow. I thought of Maddie and Grandpa Henry—how they'd been married for better or worse for over forty years and how hard it must be for Maddie to be alone now. A new appreciation for her general state of orneriness settled into my heart. The realization sank in that maybe she needed to find fault with others because she was so unhappy with the aching emptiness inside herself. I shared my observation with Ethan, who concurred, his usual compassionate expression showing as we spoke about my grandmother.

We talked about school, and sports, movies, and music until we'd walked and talked for almost two hours and my feet finally gave out.

"What do you want to do now?" I asked, flopping onto a lounge chair. I hiked my long skirt up over my knees and planted my feet firmly on the deck on each side, raised the back of the chair from a reclining position, and settled myself in, the excess cotton material gathered in front of me. Unconcerned about my un-lady-like image, I gazed out over the dark water. The half-moon had risen and its light cast a shimmering glow on the sea, turning the sky above a soft twilight blue.

"That depends on what you're up for." Surprising me, Ethan straddled the lounge chair and sat facing me, blocking my view so that all I could see was him with a backdrop of sparkling moonlight dancing on the water beyond him. He took my hands and I shivered.

"Are you cold? We can go in."

"No. I'm okay. I was just thinking about how the moon makes you look a little ghostly."

He smiled and then his expression grew serious. He chewed his lip for a moment and then his features softened. "And I was thinking that you look like an angel in the moonlight. You're really beautiful, Lexi."

I studied our entwined fingers, my heart thundering in my chest. "My name is really Ali…Alexis. Maddie thought Lexi was a more grown up name."

"You seem more like a Lexi to me, too." My gaze was drawn to his full lips, which had turned up into a crooked grin, revealing a deep set dimple in one cheek.

"I guess it doesn't matter. Lexi is fine. Maybe Maddie's right. Maybe it's time I grow up—start acting more like an adult." Uncertain of where I was planning to take my new found boldness, I slid closer, my heart racing. Our knees touched, and I leaned in, half expecting him to back away or tell me he wasn't interested. Instead, he met me half way, closing the distance and settling his lips on mine.

Warmth surged up my neck and heated my face, but I didn't care. All I could focus on was the feel of his mouth, warm and inviting. His fingers slipped through my hair and gripped the back of my head, holding me steadily against him. Every nerve ending in my body came alive, making me wonder if he was having the same thoughts about me that I was having about him.

I'd heard that teenage boys thought about sex something like seventeen times a minute. If that was true, he and I were definitely on the same page.

Chapter 13

The kiss grew. Soft at first, then more. Oh, God, I wanted more. I instinctively licked across his lower lip and was instantly met with a firm grip, pulling me closer. I reminded myself to breathe through my nose when his tongue found mine and we fell into the most perfect French kiss I could have imagined. I had nothing to compare to, but this was…excellent. I took in his sweet, spicy scent, absorbed his warmth, and groaned as my whole body responded to the heat that fled through me.

Just as I considered inviting myself to his room, he pushed me away with hands on my shoulders, disconnecting us abruptly. "We shouldn't be doing this." He drew in a sharp breath and let it out in a rush, his chest heaving. "I mean…Maddie wouldn't appreciate me…" He released my shoulders and leaned back.

The chill of the air raised the hairs on my arms. I hated the sense of loss I felt as he slipped further away, and my heart squeezed. I swallowed and sat up straighter. "Maddie isn't here right now and I don't plan on telling her we kissed. It's none of her business. I'm almost a senior in high school and I can kiss anyone I want." My jaw ached from holding back what would either be tears or a toddler-worthy fit.

"We're only going to be on this ship together for the next two weeks and then we'll each go our own way. It doesn't seem like a good idea to start something. You said it yourself. You're only a senior and I'm going off to college. It's probably not the best time to start a relationship."

I narrowed my eyes at him. "I know what you're saying. I thought that too. But...if not here and now, when?' My cheeks burned but I couldn't stop the flood of words. "Look, I've never...felt like this. Like I wanted to get to know a guy...better. Besides, you and I both know life is way too short to turn away the good stuff that decides to show up once in a while. I'm not saying we should run off and get married." A small grin slid across his face and his eyes softened. The pulse in my throat sped up. "We can either try to fight it and make both of us miserable, or we can see what happens and try to enjoy our time together. Two weeks of trying not to kiss you again would be very damaging to my psyche." I pressed my lips together in a pout to keep from smiling as his eyes lit up and his grin widened.

"When you put it that way, I can totally see your point." He slid forward and our knees touched again. This time, after running a finger down my cheek, he moved slowly toward me, his eyes capturing mine in the moonlight. I drew in a breath as if readying myself for a dive into deep water, which is exactly how it felt to give myself over to the enticing sweetness of the kiss. Ethan was slow and gentle, his hands exploring my hair, the contours of my jawline, and then my neck. His fingertips felt tickly and hot, and left a trail of fiery sparks wherever he touched.

It seemed a long time passed, both of us completely enjoying the moment, and neither of us ready to come up for air, when a shrill voice tore us apart. "Alexis Jean Hartman!"

My head spun to see Maddie approaching with a stern expression, her arms waving.

Ethan pulled away and created a cool distance from me, his face the picture of guilt. "Mrs. Hartman...I'm sorry..."

"I don't want your apology, young man. I want your assurance this won't go any further." She came to a stop and stood her ground, giving me a scowl that would have made convicts turn righteous. "You can't stay out of trouble for two minutes without supervision, can you?" She glared at me and fisted her hands on her hips. "Get to the room now. Ethan and I have a few things to discuss."

"Maddie, don't do this..." I pleaded, my embarrassment complete when she countered.

"Don't Maddie me! It's bad enough you've gotten arrested twice for possession, nearly flunked out of your junior year of high school, and now you're following in your mother's footsteps and looking to get yourself pregnant!" Her face contorted with anger, and then she stopped, clutched her shoulder and staggered to the next lounge chair over, lowering herself down. Even in the dim ship's lighting I could see her face turn ghostly pale. I jumped to my feet.

"Maddie! Are you okay?" I dropped to my knees next to her. Ethan came to her other side, guiding her to lie down.

Maddie closed her eyes and heaved in a deep breath. "I'll be fine. It's nothing, really." Her words came in stops and starts between gulps for air. "I just need to rest for a few minutes. These spells usually pass quickly."

"Should I go find the ship's doctor?" I asked, my voice shaky.

"No. Don't," Maddie protested. "I told you I'll be fine. Let me stay here for a few minutes."

"How long has this been happening?" Ethan glanced my way, his face filled with concern as he focused back on Maddie. "Your pulse is racing." He held her hand, his fingers poised on her wrist.

It took her several seconds to answer. "A few months I guess. I have an appointment for a physical when I get home." Her voice sounded stronger and relief swept through me. After a long and silent few minutes, Ethan helped her up.

"We need to tell the ship's doctor," I said.

"I don't want to be a bother. Help me back to the room, and I'll be good as new by morning. If I don't feel better, I'll go see him then." She walked on her own, but with Ethan and me flanking her at either side.

"I'm sure it wouldn't be any trouble," said Ethan. "Ship's doctors are on call at all times. Besides, you'll probably make his night since you're not calling on him for seasickness pills or an ice pack for some sprain."

For the first time tonight, Maddie smiled, sending a sideways glance at Ethan. "Are you trying to play me, son? Because you're wasting your time."

Ethan gave up, but I sensed his full attention focused on Maddie, as if continually assessing her condition. Regardless of what he'd said about not being sure about medical school, it was clear Ethan would make a great doctor. He was calm and cool, and naturally good with people.

By the time we reached our room, Maddie's color had returned. She slid the pass key through the scanner, and then turned to lay her best laser blue glare at me. "Say goodnight you two. And make it quick. Ethan and I will have our discussion tomorrow." She disappeared inside, and I heard the fan go on in the bathroom.

"I feel awful that I nearly gave my grandmother a heart attack." I stared down at my feet, unsure of what this turn of events would mean for me and Ethan.

"Maddie is obviously not well. She needs to see a doctor as soon as possible." Ethan took my hand. "It wasn't your fault." When I didn't respond, he lifted my chin and captured my gaze. "Did you hear me? Anything could set off an episode. You heard her. This has been going on for a while now."

"Obviously, my upsetting her didn't help." I drew my hand away from his, folding my arms across my chest and staring at the buttons on Ethan's shirt. "I think we probably shouldn't see each other." As much as the words wanted to stick in my throat, along with the tears I refused to cry, I forced myself to say them. "It was never going anywhere anyway, right?"

Ethan stuffed his hands into his pockets. "Right. That's going to be kind of tough though, when we're stuck on this ship together for the next two weeks." When I remained silent and he caught me biting my lip, he added, "But I guess it's a big ship, huh?"

"Yeah." A lame response was all I had. "I've got to go," I said, avoiding the hurt expression on his face and the sad eyes that would no doubt draw me back into his arms and into another kiss if I didn't turn away. But he was already ahead of me. He turned his back and strode down the hall. I slipped into the room and leaned against the door, aching as I heard the click. My head dropped back with a hard thump. Grateful that the sharp pain took the focus off the crushing sadness in my heart, I sucked in a deep breath and faced Maddie as she came out of the bathroom.

Chapter 14

As Maddie had promised, she woke acting like her old self and lectured me until I made my break for the shower. Since we were at sea for the day, she insisted we go to breakfast on the Lido deck and spend the day together, *catching up.*

"I still think you should see Dr. Bowman." I'd taken the liberty of looking up the doctor in the ship's directory and now knew exactly where the Medical Officer was located.

"I'm fine. Stop worrying about me. I was simply overtired and when I got upset..." seeing the guilt wash over my face, she stopped mid-sentence. "Look Lexi, I know I was the one to push you and Ethan together. I just wanted you to enjoy some of this trip. He seemed like such a nice young man."

"He *is*..." I realized my voice had ratcheted up to a shrill whine as other passengers stared. "It wasn't Ethan's fault," I said more calmly.

"Clearly." Maddie eyed me suspiciously. "The way you two were going at it, I have to assume you've had some experience with boys."

My face grew hot and I set my fork down. Embarrassment be damned, I resented her insinuating I was a slut. "Actually, it was my first kiss...ever."

Her gaze softened and she shook her head. "I'm sorry, Lexi. Maybe I overreacted, but I am responsible for you while you're with me, and I can't risk having you get into *that* kind of trouble. It could destroy your life and ruin Ethan's plans for medical school and a future." Her comment the night before about my mother getting "herself" pregnant hit me squarely. Amanda and I had figured out long ago that Mom was already pregnant when she and Dad got married, but hearing the resentment in Maddie's voice, it finally made sense why she never liked my mom. It seemed she blamed her for getting pregnant and ruining her son's life.

"It almost sounds like you're saying it would have been better if Amanda and I hadn't been born."

Maddie's eyes went wide. "Of course that isn't what I meant at all. Your mother and father were thrilled to have you both. I'm simply saying that it wasn't easy, and you and Ethan are too young to have to make those kinds of sacrifices. Besides, you barely know each other."

"It's not like we're sleeping together or having sex!" Another curious glare from the lady next to us—a woman with enough wrinkles to look like a state highway map—reminded me again to lower my voice. "And it looks like we won't be getting to know each other any better. I told Ethan last night that I can't see him anymore. Does that make you happy?" My voice may have been softer but there was no less edge to it.

Maddie let out a sigh. "No. It doesn't make me happy. Contrary to what you may think, adults do not enjoy making teenager's lives miserable. I'm only trying to protect you. I thought it would be nice for you to have a friend your own age to hang out with on this trip, but clearly, your feelings have gone beyond friendship."

I threw my napkin on top of my half-eaten plate of food and sighed, frustrated. "I haven't had time to even think about how I feel." I slumped in my chair. "All I know is that it felt...good to be close to a boy, to like him in that way. I've never met anyone like Ethan before—someone I wanted to be with." Confusion mingled with a deep ache in my chest, bringing tears to the surface before I could stop them. I looked away and stared at the clear blue water of the outdoor pool glistening in the sun. It was early morning and already seniors were staking their claim to lounge chairs and dipping into the pool for a few laps.

"I hate to see you so unhappy, sweetheart. I know how tenderhearted the teen years can be. I was a girl once too, you know. I understand what it's like to fall head over heels in love. It's the most wonderful and terrifying feeling in the world, and everyone should have the chance to experience it at least a few times in life."

I kept my gaze locked on the pool, determined not to let my tears fall in front of my grandmother. Instead, I plastered on a fake smile.

"I'm *not* in love. I'll be fine, Maddie. Don't worry about me, okay?"

Her face morphed from concern to relief, and then her lips curved upward. "I know. We'll have a girl's day. What do you say to a mani-pedi, a new hairstyle, and a little ship-board shopping? Then we can take in a round of shuffleboard, play a game of Bingo, and try one of those cooking classes this afternoon."

"Sounds great," I lied through the tightness in my jaw. I would have rather had a dental appointment, but I didn't want to run into Ethan, and I wanted to keep an eye on Maddie to make sure she had no further episodes. Besides, I would have done anything to change the subject and stop talking about my feelings. A painful ache had taken up residence in my chest after my hasty good-bye with Ethan, and I couldn't imagine it going away any time soon. The sad and hurt expression on his face was etched into my brain, and part of me longed to replace it with an image of him smiling and happy again.

I followed Maddie around all day, humoring her and trying to act like I wasn't miserable. *Fake it til you make it*—a common mantra in a grief group I'd been forced to attend as part of my counseling—came to mind.

As it was, the mani-pedi turned out to be a good idea. Tension melted out my toes as the young woman massaged my feet and calves. I relaxed a fraction and let my guard down, recalling the Medusa Lady's suggestion to be in the moment and appreciate the "good stuff" in life. She was big on not letting the pain of the past or fear of the future keep me from discovering the *miracles in all the little moments.*

Thoughts of Ethan pushed through, and I shoved them back, determined to stay strong and focused on the now—without him in the picture. I even risked sitting in the hairdresser's chair and having her give my shaggy mop a "fresh look." Styled in a short messy cut with dark strands fingering out along my neckline and others feathering forward to frame my face, I had to admit, the look suited me, and the bangs hung low over my brow just the way I liked.

Next, we headed to the shops on mid-deck. Maddie picked out a new outfit for her and after some minor begging, I convinced her to let me try on the short skirt and boots I'd been admiring in the window all week. The boots were uber-expensive, but once I had them on, Maddie insisted she get them for me, if only to see me smiling. She seemed hell-bent on making up to me for ruining my blossoming romance. When she saw me admiring a beautiful silver bracelet with a dolphin inlaid with some kind of New Zealand seashell material called Paua, which looked like polished abalone, she came up beside me.

"Dolphins always remind me of Amanda," I said. "They were her favorite," I added with a small smile, a rush of warmth seeping in for the first time in connection with the memory.

"Can I get that for you?" Maddie wrapped an arm around my shoulder. "Maybe the dolphin can have some new meaning to you—a reminder of our trip to Europe—a new beginning."

"A new beginning," I repeated, staring at the sparkling shell. "That would be nice." It was all I could say without tears welling in my eyes. Was there such a thing? The idea that I could somehow start over—do things differently this time around—make the right decisions when it came to hard choices. I slipped the bracelet onto my wrist next to Amanda's charm bracelet as Maddie paid the cashier. Adjusting the cool metal so the two bracelets sat together, I wondered if somewhere, Amanda was experiencing a new beginning.

As we left the store, Maddie handed me a small box.

"It's the necklace that goes with the bracelet and an extra set of earrings for all those holes in your ears."

Chuckling, I grinned. "Thanks, Maddie. I love them."

"And I love *you*." She laid her palm against my cheek. "I hope you'll always remember that, sweetheart."

I hugged my grandmother, grateful not only for the cool gifts, but for the opportunity to get to know her, spend time with her, and remember that my dad had once been her little boy. I could see him in her eyes and when she smiled a certain way, warm memories of my father's laughter touched my heart, bittersweet but welcomed. I pulled back and swallowed past the lump in my throat, anxious to lighten the mood again.

"I love you, too...Grandma." My lips twitched.

Maddie turned a mock glare on me and tugged on my cheek with enough pinch to make me squirm. "Don't call me Grandma."

After we dropped our bags in our room, we walked arm in arm to the upper deck and joined in a mean game of shuffleboard with several other seniors. Maxine and Joel Hirschman from L.A and a mousy couple named Carl and Mitzie Jones from Austin, Texas, turned out to be formidable opponents. But with Maddie's determination and my unparalleled shuffleboard skills, we took the lead and won both games.

Maddie high-fived me. "Way to go, darling! Who knew you inherited the Hartman competitive spirit?"

"It's nice to finally be good at something. Maybe I have a future in shuffleboard. Isn't it an Olympic event somewhere?"

Maddie laughed and set down her cue, saluting the elderly couples who shuffled off to their next event. "I've got a hundred bucks that says I win at Bingo."

"I have nothing to bet with."

"Don't worry, I'll think of something I want." Maddie's cryptic remark and confident tone made me wary.

We strolled past the smoky casino and headed for the piano bar lounge where today's Bingo would be held. People passed us by several at a time. The pulse in my temple pounded. I half-expected to see Ethan somewhere in the crowd. I wondered where he was and what he was doing, and wished I could be with him…wished I could tell him I was sorry and kiss him again.

My thoughts were interrupted when we entered the bar a few minutes early for the game and stumbled upon the pianist entertaining the crowd with old American Standards. Maddie and I settled into chairs set around a small cocktail table. Everything on board the ship managed to be comfortable and elegant despite being bolted to the floor. As much as I tried not to think about it, I was reminded again that we were at sea and my stomach gave an involuntary roll. To my endless gratitude, I hadn't really suffered from seasickness since we'd been on the trip, but it was clear to me that I would never really have my sea legs under me. I ordered a club soda and focused my attention on the pianist, an older gentlemen in a black tuxedo and bow tie who was playing a sweet rendition of "Someone to Watch over Me."

The gathering crowd applauded as he played out the final notes and bowed his head. He spoke into the mic, "Here to entertain you all with his brilliance in calling out the Bingo winning numbers is one of our volunteer guests, a young man all the way from the lovely state of New York, Ethan Kaswell!"

My stomach dropped and my gaze shot to the side of the stage where Ethan made his entrance. Simultaneously, Maddie and I muttered, "Oh, dear God."

Chapter 15

"Did you know he was going to be there?" I asked Maddie in a low whisper as we herded out with the crowd.

"I had no idea."

Ethan had appeared as surprised to see us as we were him, but he recovered enough to call out the numbers and focus on making the game fun for the room full of seniors in attendance. His quick glances my way had the effect of me missing several of the numbers and thus blowing the game, giving Maddie the advantage. I dreaded finding out what I owed her for our little bet. I'd been looking forward to cashing in that hundred dollars when I got home, figuring I could score some good weed and it wouldn't have to come out of my meager allowance. Oh, how I wanted a joint. The tension between Ethan and me had vibrated across the room, and I wished I were anywhere else.

Before I could beg Maddie to let me spend the rest of the day in our cabin and skip dinner altogether, Ethan's voice came from behind, spinning Maddie on her heels.

"Do you still want to have that talk?" He glanced nervously from me to my grandmother, who raised a brow and nodded.

"Brave boy," Maddie commented coolly. "Actually, what I have to say should be said to both of you." She glared at the nearby Mrs. Epstein who had stopped to adjust her undergarments. "Let's go somewhere private where we won't be disturbed." Maddie swung around and Ethan and I followed, each of us keeping a notable distance from the other.

Maddie led us to—of all places—the Sports Bar. We grabbed a table in the corner. She responded to my nervous glance at the backs of several men sitting at the bar. "Don't worry," she smirked, "most of them need hearing aids, and once a man is focused on a game of *any* kind, he pays no attention to anything said in the vicinity. Now, you're both going to listen carefully to what I have to say, and I hope you'll respect my experience in these matters." She sounded as if she was about to discuss stock market tips or recipes. Ethan and I nodded feebly, both aware refusal wasn't an option.

"I understand how feelings can develop very quickly, especially at your age. Given the fact you are the only youngsters on this ship, it doesn't surprise me in the least you're smitten with each other." She caught my mortified expression and put up a hand. "No use in denying it, and it's nothing to be ashamed of or embarrassed about. It's as natural an attraction as a bee to a flower, and teenagers have been swapping spit since the dawn of time." She waved off the waitress before the young woman neared the table. Then she grinned, apparently enjoying my discomfort.

As flames rose up my neck, I covered my face with my hand so Ethan couldn't see my reddened cheeks.

Maddie continued, "The problem is, you two are at very different points in your lives. I'm sure you can see that. I understand what I saw last night was a...somewhat innocent kiss. But don't think I don't know what comes next."

I fought the urge to crawl under the table. "Do we really need to do this?" My stomach had curled into a ball and my nails bit into my palms.

"It's okay, Lexi. I get why your grandmother is concerned. She doesn't want to see you get hurt. Neither do I," he added, shifting his gaze back to Maddie.

"I'm glad you understand the consequences, Ethan. It shows a lot of maturity on your part. But have either of you even thought about birth control? I already know you aren't on the pill, Alexis. I asked your mother specifically, since I've never met a sixteen-year-old girl who doesn't attract every testosterone saturated male within a hundred yards."

"Maddie! You are so…" I was climbing out of my chair, but Ethan grabbed my wrist and drew me back down.

"I'm not going to say you're wrong, ma'am. The truth is, I don't know what would have come next if you hadn't stopped us. But I can tell you I care about your granddaughter, and I would never do anything to hurt or disrespect her." Ethan met Maddie's steady gaze.

"Good to hear, my boy. I think we have an understanding then." She stood as if that ended the conversation. "I don't mind if you two want to hang out together, as they say." She waved her hand in the air. "But none of this 'friends with benefits' business. Mark my words, kissing will lead to more. And with all those raging hormones going on between you two, remaining in control of yourselves will become impossible. Trust me, I was the queen of raging hormones in my day." Leaving me with an image I would have to scrub from my brain with steel wool, she turned and strode away, calling over her shoulder. "I'll see you back in the room in an hour to prepare for dinner, Lexi. We're eating with that nice Jewish couple again and those two gay men. It should be very entertaining." She laughed as she turned the corner and disappeared.

"That was horrifying," I mumbled, rubbing knuckles across my forehead. A dull throb had taken up residence behind my eyes.

Ethan grinned, his shoulders relaxing. "I don't know. I thought it could have been much worse. I half expected her to lay out a package of condoms or something."

My cheeks heated another degree, and my eyes stayed focused on the door where Maddie had just made her grand exit. "Please don't joke about it. My grandmother would obviously rather die than see me lose my virginity to a guy I'm never going to see again—" the words tumbled out before I realized what I'd said. "Oh, God…" I sighed, my mortification complete as I melted into the chair.

"If it makes you feel any better, I haven't—" Ethan studied the pepper shaker in his hand. "—done it, either." Our gazes met and I saw the truth behind his words.

My mouth dropped open. "How is that possible?" A stupid question I immediately wanted to take back.

"There weren't exactly many dating opportunities in my prep school. Unless you're gay." He grinned. The smile faltered when my eyes grew wide. "Which I'm not," he added quickly. "Not that there's anything wrong with…listen," he said, setting the pepper shaker next to the salt and taking my hand. "I really like you. But I have to respect what Maddie said. As much as I'd like her to be wrong, getting in deeper would be a bad idea for both of us. I'm all for us hanging out and just being friends for the rest of the cruise. Maybe we can keep in touch when we get back and see where things go, you know?"

The hopeful look in those deep green eyes made my chest ache. I wanted to believe that we would keep in touch. There was always e-mails, texts, and Instagram, but I had my doubts that a college guy would have any interest in pursuing a long distance relationship with a high school senior. A lump formed in my throat and I drew my hand away.

"I don't really see the point, Ethan. You're heading off to college, and I'm going to be stuck in Somerville, doing community service for the next year while I finish school and figure out what I'm going to do with my life."

"About that," he said, his eyes narrowing. "What was Maddie talking about? Did you really get busted twice for possession?"

My jaw clenched. I totally didn't want to have this conversation with Mr. Perfect. "It was no big deal. I got caught with a few joints. My stepdad is a cop, and with what happened to Amanda, things got blown way out of proportion."

"So you're here instead of at home on lock-down?"

I nodded.

"Not a bad gig, if you think about it. Seeing Europe for a few weeks is a pretty cool punishment—if you could call it that."

His amusement came across as self-righteous and suddenly annoyed me way more than Maddie's proclamation that we were to keep our friendship on the up and up. Maybe keeping my distance wouldn't be as much of a problem as I'd thought.

"Spending my summer on a boat with my grandmother in the middle of the ocean with no weed available is not my idea of a good time." I folded my arms across my chest and stared at the big screen in the corner, a rabid game of soccer reminding me how good it would feel to kick something right then.

"It's a ship—and we're at sea—not the ocean..."

"I don't give a f..." I started as I shot out of my chair, and then stopped. I huffed out a breath. "I don't need your judgment, or anyone else's for that matter. What I need is a good buzz!" Heads turned and I felt my face flush. "I'm out of here." I turned my back and headed for the exit.

"Lexi, wait up." Ethan was out of his chair and at my side before I reached the elevator. He grabbed my arm and spun me around. I glared at his hand on my arm and he let it drop. "I'm not judging you, Lexi. I want to understand…talk to me, okay?"

I punched the elevator button. "What's to talk about? I like to smoke pot. It's not like I'm a meth addict or shooting heroin." I hit the button again, cursing under my breath. My heart raced and my head pounded. All I wanted to do was disappear, be left alone to my irritable mood, and shed another bucket of tears over my pathetic life.

"I've smoked weed a few times. It never really did much for me." Ethan shoved his hands into his pockets and stared at the arrows above the elevator door.

"Good for you. Now your father won't have to worry about you tarnishing his reputation or his good name." I recalled the lengthy lectures I'd endured from my mother and Mitch who seemed more worried about how my embarrassing behavior affected them, than about me. I pounded a fist on the elevator door. "Open, dammit!"

The door slid open and an elderly woman with a walker, and her husband—who looked like he was a hundred years old—ambled out, gaping suspiciously at Ethan and me as they passed. I forced a tight smile as I stepped into the elevator and turned to face front. No sense in giving the old people reason to worry they might be cruising with a psychopath. Any remnants of amusement disappeared when the doors closed. As the elevator ascended I took a deep breath and stared straight ahead.

"Why are you still here?"

"No place else to be." Ethan leaned casually against the railing and studied me. "What's got you so pissed? Is it that Maddie put the brakes on things between you and me?"

"Don't flatter yourself."

"Okay." He cleared his throat and an awkward silence filled the elevator.

I gloated inwardly, glad to see a chink in his armor, and then immediately felt like a bitch. He didn't deserve my wrath. Especially since my mood probably had nothing to do with him. The truth was, I didn't know what was bugging me. I was irritable and totally jonesing for a joint. The doors opened and we stepped out onto our floor. I turned down the hall toward my room and he watched me go, apparently uncertain of whether to follow or leave me to my lunacy. I ran my key card through the scanner and pushed open the door. Looking back down the hall, I saw Ethan standing in front of his cabin watching me, his face full of hurt, confusion, and frustration.

"I'll see you later," he called down the hall.

"I doubt it," I grumbled. I shoved my way inside and shut the door tight behind me, disappearing into the cool, dark room. I tossed my key card on the table and tumbled onto the bed. Grabbing the dog-shaped towels lying on my pillow, I whipped them through the air, rattling the blinds.

Great—now I was the freaky girl who had a public meltdown, abused defenseless towel puppies, and broke the heart of a sweet, cute guy who was only trying to be a friend.

Chapter 16

I'd convinced Maddie to let me skip dinner and stayed in bed, hiding in the dark until sleep finally overtook me. Before I knew it, bright sunlight streamed through the long blinds. I stretched and yawned.

Maddie was already up and dressed. "I guess you needed to catch up. I've never seen anyone sleep so soundly."

The smell of coffee and bacon brought me to sitting and I ran my hands through my hair, shaking off the sleepiness. My stomach rumbled. "Are we in port already?"

"We put into Tunis about an hour ago." Maddie opened the curtains and drew back the blinds, forcing me to shield my eyes. "Hurry up and get dressed. You don't want to miss our welcome from the locals."

I dragged myself out of bed and followed Maddie onto our balcony, still in my pajamas. A blast of desert heat took my breath away. My eyes widened as I took in the ancient city port of La Goulette, Tunisia. A band of several men and women in brightly colored outfits, all of them with dark faces and heads covered, danced, sang, and played drums in greeting. A half a dozen camels lay with their long legs folded beneath them waiting for their masters to put them to work. A photographer was taking pictures of a tourist petting the camels and posing as if he in his Red Sox baseball cap and plaid golf shorts belonged in the exotic setting.

I ran to wash up and dress, chowed my breakfast as if I hadn't eaten in a month, and rushed to the auditorium to get our sticker and join our tour of the North African cities of Carthage and Sidi Bou Said. Maddie let go of the events of the day before, but I noticed Ethan's conspicuous absence from our tour group.

As we walked down the gangplank and stepped onto the dock, Maddie insisted I pose with one of the camels. As silly as I felt, the experience seemed surreal. I petted its soft nose and reveled in the crazy long eyelashes that gave the creature an awkward and gentle beauty. Captivated, I looked into her eyes and saw my reflection, which drew me even closer. When the trainer offered to have me sit atop the saddled hump on her back, I eyed Maddie, who smiled and nodded approval.

"Go ahead, darling. Seize the day! You may not have another chance to do something like this again."

Her words struck me and as much as I wanted to remind her of how she'd just put the kibosh on my budding romance, I immediately thought of Amanda. If she were here, she wouldn't hesitate. She wouldn't let anything stand in the way of what she wanted. And she wouldn't let a good time pass her by. My sister was all about living life to the fullest, experiencing everything she could.

I wondered if somehow she'd known her life would be cut short. Or if maybe her adventurous spirit was what had made her so reckless. I'd probably never know for sure, and the truth most likely lay somewhere in the middle. Torn between my apprehension about climbing onto the large animal and the excitement of trying something so out of the ordinary, I decided it was now or never.

I climbed aboard the camel and clung to the saddle horn as it rose to its feet. My heart beat faster as the man led me around the dock. The rocking motion was disconcerting, but I quickly adjusted and soon I relaxed into the seat. A wide grin spread across my face.

"This is amazing, Maddie! Don't you want to try it?"

She laughed. "I'm afraid my days of camel jockeying are over, sweetie. I'll just stay down here and enjoy taking pictures." She snapped another shot of me waving over my shoulder as the trainer led the camel back to its station. Her front legs folded down like an accordion until she settled to the ground. I slid off and joined Maddie, the two of us falling in line with the other tourists headed for the buses.

"I wonder where Ethan is," Maddie said.

I shrugged, settling into a seat next to the window on the air-conditioned bus. I hated to tell her how badly I'd messed things up with him the day before. He probably wouldn't want to see me again for the remainder of the trip. My heart sank. I hadn't meant to take out my frustrations on him. Maybe I'd just been jet lagged or PMS'ing. Or maybe, as the Medusa Lady had warned me, without my pot habit, I'd have to face my feelings. Her voice rang in my ear. "*An addiction is anything that comes between you and dealing with your feelings.*" Whatever my issue, I felt better after a good night's sleep and some time alone.

I thought about how much I missed my friends, my guitar, and hanging out getting stoned at Thompson Lake with D.D. and Sami. They always had plenty of drama to keep things interesting, and they knew where all the best parties were. Twelve more days and I'd be that much closer to being home. Then, things could get back to normal—whatever that meant. An edgy sensation moved through me as the bus pulled away from the docks. So much hinged on how my mother recovered from her breakdown and whether Mitch would put up with me for another school year while I figured out if I wanted to go to college or simply get some minimum wage job and bum around for a year or so—an appealing alternative to dealing with real life.

The bus ride to Carthage was uneventful, with Maddie "resting her eyes" and leaving me to take in the sights and listen to the tour guide. The buildings we passed were mostly white with sky blue roofs, many of them homes and businesses with Tunisian people stationed outside their shops waving the tourists in out of the bright sun. Beyond the villages the desert loomed, everything in its path a dull, sandy brown. Flat-roofed buildings of the same color, some in disrepair and others modern and sturdy but equally as non-descript, dotted the roadway, making the scenery appear monochromatic and desolate. When we reached our destination, I woke Maddie.

"Oh, I must have dozed off." She stretched and pulled herself together. "Sylvio—the lovely man playing at the piano bar," she clarified while adjusting her hair, "kept us all up until past midnight singing old Broadway show tunes." Viewing herself in a compact mirror, she fixed her lipstick and laughed. "I haven't had such fun in eons."

We shuffled off the bus and out into the hundred-degree day.

"Are you having any fun on this trip, Alexis?" She asked, her tone serious.

"I guess I am...sure." I hated to sound ungrateful. I wasn't so dense that I didn't realize how much it must have cost to take me with her on the cruise. I'm sure I had Grandpa Henry to thank, but she could just as easily have sent me packing back home to face the firing squad after my little party detour in Malibu. I took the high road and kept my attitude in check. "It was really nice of you to bring me, Maddie. And, well...thanks."

A smile curled her ruby red lips. "You're welcome, darling. I'm glad we've had this time together." She tugged her floppy hat lower and slid a pair of large sunglasses on. "Now, let's go see where the Carthaginians practiced human sacrifice."

108

∞∞∞∞

Carthage as a city, it turned out, had been around for three thousand years or so, and they did indeed, practice human sacrifice—according to the tour guide, a deeply tanned man with dark shaved hair, large, deep set blue eyes and an amiable expression.

"During the Punic era when the Phoenicians inhabited the land, they would routinely sacrifice women and children to appease their gods." Muhammad, aka "Mike," said as he led us into another world. An eerie energy pervaded the mazelike structures. Long tunnels between buildings and large pieces of stone lay in columns, the rubble of an ancient city that had seen many wars. "The Romans finally conquered the city around the time of Christ when they were taking over most of the rest of the European empire. Six hundred years or so later the Muslims took over and ruled for many centuries." Mike turned his back and headed for the next destination on our tour, his words echoing off the stone walls on either side of us.

As I followed the other tourists through the archways and down the long narrow paths, it struck me again that nothing lasts forever. Even these thick walls and this once powerful and rich city had been beaten down by time and erosion, defeated by battle wounds and death.

After a few hours of wandering the ruins of Carthage in the desert heat, Maddie looked wilted. "I think you'd better rest here in the shade," I said, concerned she would have another episode and wishing Ethan were with us.

Maddie plunked into a plastic chair next to a table at a snack bar not far from the buses. A large umbrella overhead offered shade.

I brought her a bottle of water. "Stop fretting over me, Lexi. I'm fine." She fanned her face with her hat. I frowned, unconvinced, and sat beside her, struck by the signs of her age.

"Why does life have to be so hard all the time?" I asked, kicking back in my chair and sipping on my own bottle of ice cold water.

"It gets easier, trust me," Maddie answered. She smirked and arched a brow at me. "Then it gets harder again. Life is full of ups and downs, darling. That's what keeps it so interesting." Maddie gazed out at the brilliant blue sea beyond the walled tower overlooking the harbor. "You must miss your sister." She reached over and patted my hand, a sympathetic expression deepening the lines around her eyes.

"And Mom," I said, reluctance in my tone.

"That's perfectly understandable."

After a slight hesitation, I added, "I hate that I didn't get to say good-bye."

"To your mother or Amanda?"

"Both," I whispered, the words caught in my throat.

"Your mother knows you love her." A sad smile drew her red lips into a tight line and then she added softly, "I'm sure Amanda knew it too."

"Did she? I don't remember the last time I told her." Tears welled below the surface as I focused on the tower at the end of a narrow strip of land. The gray turrets against the clear sky appeared unyielding and cold, like sentinels set to keep intruders at bay.

"Of course she knew. Just as you know how much she loved you." Her certainty drew my attention and our gazes met, the blue in her eyes warmer than I'd ever seen.

"I still wish I'd done things differently."

"We all do, sweetie. Regrets are an unfortunate consequence of youth." She winked and peeled a red curl away from her sweat soaked skin. "Sometimes even old folks screw up. Look at it this way. You have an opportunity to learn one of the hardest lessons in life, and learn it early."

"Really? What's that?" I asked, unsure if I wanted an answer.

"There are consequences to all of our actions…and inactions. But we can't blame ourselves forever. There comes a time when we have to accept that we are human and move on—forgive ourselves and others, and let go of the things we can't change."

"Is that followed by having the courage to change the things we can, and the wisdom to know the difference?" I rolled my eyes. "I've had enough lecturing about the consequences of my actions to last me a lifetime, and the rest sounds like something out of an AA brochure." A wry smile quirked my lips. "How did we go from me asking why life is so hard to a preview of a recovery meeting?"

She released a lyrical laugh—one that was slowly growing on me. "I'm not lecturing you, dear. And those AA people might know what they're talking about. Letting go and letting God, and all that." She shook a bony finger in my direction. "We all need to stop holding onto the past and focus on the future." She closed her eyes, tilted her face to the sky as if hoping for a breeze, and then fanned herself again.

I wasn't sure I could ever let go of Amanda—or the guilt I carried over having failed her in so many ways. I swiped a hand across my forehead as a bead of sweat trickled from my hairline. The sun's rays peeked over the edge of the umbrella.

"I just wish the sand would stop shifting under my feet and life would stay the same for a while." But I knew that wasn't possible and that it wasn't what I truly wanted anyway. I wanted things to be different, I wanted not to hurt anymore, and I wanted my mom to be better. I wanted to be done with high school and off on my own, and I wanted Ethan to be a part of my life. I wanted it all...but uncertainty had me paralyzed.

Maddie's voice pulled me to attention. "Isn't life such a miraculous journey?"

I raised a sweaty brow. "I can't wait to hear this."

Undeterred, Maddie flashed me her best stink-eye and continued, "Don't be fresh with me. I'm making a point. One person dies, another is born. We age and die, but that isn't the end. The journey continues. I can't say with any certainty that there is a heaven, but I have come to see every part of life as a transformation. It's all part of a beautiful plan, Lexi. You simply have to believe there is a reason for everything and trust that someday you'll understand."

"I don't think I can." Unwilling to see my sister's death as part of a grand plan, or accept the idea that it would someday make some kind of sense, I snapped. "Nothing about Amanda's death seems miraculous or beautiful. Death is ugly and life is...painful." Not for the first time, a spike of anger toward God ran through me.

Maddie touched my hand. "I'm not talking about your sister. I'm talking about you...and yes, life in general. Lexi, running away from painful feelings isn't the answer. You can't fight change...or death. Both are inevitable. What I'm saying is we can make choices that will bring about positive outcomes so we can make the best of the journey while we're here. And all we can do is try our best to be happy." She gave my hand a final squeeze. "You won't know unless you try."

I stared out at the water, my eyes brimming with tears. I'd made a mess of my own life, hidden my sister's secret—which ultimately led to her death—and I'd sent my mother over the edge.

Now, there was no going back, no fixing anything, and no getting past the fallout of my choices. Happiness amid the chaos and fallout seemed fleeting at best. "I just wish it wasn't so hard to let go," I whispered.

Maddie sat back, sliding her sunglasses over her eyes and resting her hat back on her head as if her duty was done in trying to shed some light on the mysteries of the universe for me. She took one more sip of her water and capped the bottle. "Someday you'll see that as painful as it is to let go, holding on is infinitely worse."

Chapter 17

Later, as I sat on the promenade deck, lounging in a comfortable chair and sipping on a fruity umbrella drink, the faces of the kids I'd seen in the marketplace in Sidi Bou Said weighed heavily on my heart.

Maddie had haggled over a silver bracelet and new pair of *Hand of Fatima* earrings for me with a surly Tunisian in the bustling little village that was crowded with tourists and vendors. The *Hand of Fatima* was a traditional symbol of good luck and protection from the "evil eye." Having them dangling from my ears gave me a weird sense of connection to the local culture and an uneasy confidence that maybe my life was about to take a turn for the better.

From the simple life they lived, it appeared the people of Kusadasi could have used some of that luck. When children approached to offer maps at a premium, I'd had a hard time passing them by. Their bare feet and sunken eyes behind plastered on smiles screamed poverty and need. Though they seemed to take it all in stride, my heart hurt for them nonetheless.

I wrote a few poems which I thought I might later turn into songs. As impossible as it was to capture the souls behind the weary expressions, and how they made me feel, I had to try.

Nameless Faces

Hearts race behind nameless faces,
No traces of prosperity.
Eyes filled with hopeless rage,
They turn the page of destiny.
Masks of happiness they put in place,
A merry chase, they sell their plea.
I in turn, turn my back
Ignore the attack of morality.
If I could change just one life
Ease their strife, would it set me free?
Or would I finally see…it's not about me?
It's about humility.

Inadequate as they were, the words brought me some level of comfort. Giving the children a voice somehow seemed to ease the sting of Amanda's silence. Maddie's view on life being a transformation and a journey for us all gave me hope that their souls would find some kind of peace. An image of Amanda, smiling and happy flashed in my mind and an explosion of gratitude filled me.

My life back home, as tragic and painful as it was most days, was filled with things to be grateful for. Maddie's words came back to me. *You can't fight change…or death. Both are inevitable.* The words sliced deep with their truth. But maybe if I stopped clinging to the torment of the past and spending so much time fearing the future, I could enjoy the present and fully appreciate that I was on a cruise ship in the Mediterranean with a cute boy and an opportunity to get some questions answered about my dad. A new determination crept into my bones.

I put the final touches on another poem, this one with the object of my inspiration in mind, and stuck my pen inside my notebook. I rushed to change clothes and headed for the dining hall, hoping to run into Ethan, and have the opportunity to apologize for the night before.

When I joined Maddie for dinner, the table was already steeped in conversation. We sat with Benjamin and David, the guys from New Hampshire who were in their fifties and on their honeymoon, and a spry but elderly Dutch woman who was there with her two daughters, both about middle-aged. They'd apparently gotten smart and learned to tag-team their mother and share the responsibilities of entertaining her. As Maddie liked to say, *she took up a lot of space in the room.* The woman monopolized the dinner conversation, and I tuned out half-way through a thickly accented diatribe about the soup.

I searched the dining room for Ethan, who I was sure was avoiding me. I couldn't blame him after I'd been a total snot. But after I apologized, then what? Go back to hanging out, only being friends, and ignoring the gigantic magnet of attraction that we were being asked to ignore? I sighed. Not the ideal situation, but better than living with the gnawing ache of knowing I'd hurt his feelings and left things broken between us.

"May I be excused?" I dropped my napkin on the table, my stomach flopping when they brought the main course of petit fillet and lamb chops. The soup and salad had been enough for me, and the sight of red meat juice on a plate made me shudder.

Maddie eyed me desperately, as much in need of rescue as I was, but trying to be compassionate and patient with the woman, who had moved on to discussing the remoulade dressing for the lamb.

"Of course, dear. Will I see you at the show? I hear the magician is quite good."

I cringed. "I think I'll take a walk around the deck and then head up to the room early."

"Oh, do you want me to come with you?"

"No. You go ahead to the show without me. I could use some time alone." The last thing I needed was her chaperoning me and Ethan when I finally found him.

David, an attorney with dark, close cut gray hair grinned. "You're welcome to join Ben and me, Maddie. We're going to the show." Ben, a little round-faced with obviously dyed brown hair and rich, soft brown eyes, grinned and nodded agreement.

Maddie nodded and winked at me. "All right. I'll see you later then. Be careful," she said. I almost hated to leave her in the clutches of the animated woman who was now discussing the plight of the Euro as she dug into the dripping meat, but David and Ben shooed me along, full of assurances that Maddie would be well taken care of.

I quickly made my way to the upper deck, certain I would find Ethan playing video games in the Loft or watching a game of some sort in the Sports Bar. I checked the Crow's Nest and lapped the Promenade, a sense of dread taking over. I wondered if he was intentionally making himself scarce or hiding in his room. Finally I poked my head into the fitness center—and there he was, alone and looking hotter than ever.

Feet pounding on the treadmill and a hard, focused expression on his face, Ethan ran at a brisk pace. Sweat dripped down his temples and his shirt was soaked. I swallowed through a dry throat as I entered and tucked my key card into my back pocket. He saw me coming and slowed, punching buttons on the controls and stumbling slightly as I approached. The sweaty smell of him should have bothered me, but instead, I found myself taking in a deep breath and memorizing the scent.

"What's up?" I asked lamely.

"Really? You're starting there?" he huffed out, keeping his eyes focused forward.

My stomach twisted. "I came to say I'm sorry. I was a jerk yesterday, and I shouldn't have taken my bad mood out on you." I batted my lashes for good measure. "Forgive me?"

He glanced my way, but kept running, his breath uneven. "What do you want me to say, Lexi? You made it clear you didn't want to be friends."

"I know what I said…but that's only because I didn't think I could be 'just friends.'" I stared at the floor, my hands busy with the lacy edge of my top. "This is new territory for me. I'm not very good at this relationship stuff. I've never had boyfriends—or many boys that were friends for that matter." I raised my gaze to meet his, glad to see pools of deep green that showed a spark of empathy.

He hit the button and the treadmill wound down to a brisk walk. Grabbing the towel on the console, he wrapped it around his neck, and wiped the sweat from his face. Drenched, the light blue Lacrosse tee shirt clung to his body, outlining a nice solid chest and lean, six-pack abs.

"So you still want to hang out, or what?" he asked. Despite his chilly tone, a hopeful cadence rang through. I took it as a good sign he was ready to forgive me, but I got why he was keeping himself in check. Probably the smartest approach given that I had ruthlessly stomped on his feelings. Another pinch of guilt tightened my chest.

"I'd like that," I said. "Maybe we can go check out a movie later?" A movie seemed harmless enough, and a good starting point for our renewed friendship.

"Okay," he replied cautiously. "I'll meet you up at your room in about a half hour." He shut down the treadmill and stepped off.

"Great." I backed away and banged my shin on a weight bench as I left him in mid-hamstring stretch. A small smile curved his lips when I stifled an *ow* and my face flushed with heat. I had a feeling the throbbing in my shin was nothing compared to the beating my heart was about to take. Between the scent of his sweat acting like a drug, and the solid lean muscles that defined his frame, this 'just friends' thing wasn't going to be easy.

∞∞∞∞

The movie ended up being some sappy romance. Ethan tolerated it well, but I sensed him zoning out occasionally—possibly contemplating jumping ship during the steamy bedroom scenes.

I considered the possibility of joining him, the two of us lost at sea and immortalized as star-crossed lovers, forbidden to be together and forced to choose death in order to spend our eternity as one. It would have made me laugh but I immediately thought of Amanda, her death still too close to see any humor in dying young. The pervasive question that had been plaguing me resurfaced.

"Do you ever wonder if your mom is in heaven?" I asked as Ethan and I made our way out of the dark theater headed for our respective rooms.

"Yeah. I believe so." I liked how Ethan never blinked an eye at my stupid questions. He would simply think for a second and answer thoughtfully and truthfully.

"But what if there really is no heaven?" I asked. "What if when we die, everything just...stops? We get buried in the ground, decay into dust, and we're...done?"

Ethan let a grin slide across his face. "Then we're done and we never know the difference." He punched the elevator up button and turned to me while we waited. The elevator doors opened as he responded. "But I don't believe that's how it works. I don't think our spirits die when our bodies do."

A passenger I recognized as Mrs. Lowenstein stepped out of the elevator. Bulging eyes stared through thick glasses. "Quite right, young man. I'm planning on a long afterlife." She bared crooked and yellowed teeth at us and teetered off.

Ethan and I stepped onto the elevator, breaking into laughter as the doors closed. When we exited a moment later and headed down the hall, I resurrected the conversation. "What makes you so sure?" A long silence followed until we reached my room. "C'mon. It's not like you've seen the *other side*. Have you?" I added, curious when he took a moment to respond.

"I was with my mom when she died. In the last few minutes…there was a peacefulness that came over her face. Right at the end, I remember her saying she wasn't in pain anymore. She told me I shouldn't be afraid and that she wasn't alone. When she…passed on, I had a strong sense of her spirit leaving her body and moving upward." He shook his head. "I can't explain it, but I just know there's *something* after." Lightening the mood, he added, "Besides, I can't imagine God would let a perfectly good soul go to waste."

"I like the way you think," I said, smiling in spite of myself. "But you're assuming there *is* a God."

"You don't believe in God?" He asked, surprise in his tone.

"I don't know what to believe. This world is so messed up. If there is a God, why would He…or She," I said, eyeing Ethan with a grin, "let all this bad stuff happen?"

"Free will makes it kind of impossible for God to control everything. That would mean He...or She," he returned the grin, "would have to force us to make right choices. You can't pin everyone's stupidity on God. It's people who are messing up the world, not Him...or Her." Long dark lashes batted at me as if he were imitating a female, causing a giggle to escape my lips.

I considered his logic. "Maybe. But I wish things were different—not so complicated."

"Me too." Those deep green eyes studied my face, finally settling on my lips, which sent an instantaneous flutter to my belly. "We should probably say good night. We have an early day in Palermo."

He was right but I didn't want the night to end. "When is your dad joining the cruise?" I asked, stalling and outlining the curve of his jaw with my gaze.

"Day after tomorrow when we reach Rome. He said we could do the Vatican and St. Peter's Basilica tour together, but I'll believe it when I see it." Bitterness infused his tone, drawing my attention back to his eyes. The sadness behind them mixed with deeper emotions, and I wondered how many disappointments it took to create that look.

"Well, I hope he's good to his word this time." With nothing left to say, I unlocked the door and pushed it open. Ethan's hand on my arm stopped me.

"I'm glad we're friends, Lexi. This trip would have been miserable without you."

I reveled for a moment in the feel of his warm, strong hand on my arm, then met his gaze. "For me, too."

He leaned in and laid a soft kiss on my cheek, lingering for a second and then pulling away. "See you tomorrow." He backed away, leaving me standing in my doorway, heart pounding like mad.

We exchanged another long look before each of us finally slipped into our rooms.

I tumbled onto my bed, grabbed the folded towel monkey on my pillow, and stared at the dopey grin on its face—certain that it matched mine perfectly.

Chapter 18

Palermo, Sicily, surpassed anything I could have imagined. A golden rim of mountains surrounded the medieval village like something out of a magazine or a storybook. Small sailboats speckled the coastline, and the busy port bustled with local tour guides and dockworkers. To my disappointment, we were shuffled onto a tour bus before I had a chance to explore. Maddie assured me we'd come back before the end of the day and "nose" around. As we rumbled our way through town, I noticed the generations of architectural styles featured throughout the business district and watched the port fade as we headed into the hills beyond.

Maddie sat behind Ethan and me, chatting with an elderly man with an apparent dead battery in his hearing aid, who kept asking her to repeat what the tour guide said. Our guide, Maximo, with his Italian features and romantic accent, continued to share about the many plant species that had been imported from locales as far away as Australia and America. I only caught half of what he said, so captivated by the exotic landscape I could barely click my phone camera fast enough through the window. We wound through hills along narrow roads, each turn as we climbed upward revealing new and even more interesting sights.

Staggered throughout the terraced hillside were houses of tan and cream adobe, the terra cotta roofs giving them a uniform appeal. Each house had many small square or rectangular windows and verandas overlooking the turquoise sea below. I tried to imagine what it would be like to live there—to wake to the amazing view of the Mediterranean every day.

The bus climbed to the top of Monta Pellegrino, a little village that was like an array of picture postcards. We visited Cathedral Square and had lunch at Il Café di Ruggiero, enjoying a lemon iced tea and the best Italian cookies I'd ever tasted. Lush plants hung from balconies, narrow cobbled walkways tunneled between buildings with shops and art galleries, and colorfully dressed people milled about the area, making me feel as if I'd stepped into a spy movie or one of those romance novels where the woman escapes to some foreign country and falls madly in love with a hot guy with a sexy accent.

Maddie stopped in every store, exiting with some souvenir, article of clothing, or trinket, assuring me it was simply her way of supporting the local artisans. She handed off her bags to Ethan—who had inadvertently become her valet—and tipped her hat down to block the late morning sun.

"The economy of these little villages is solely dependent on the tourist trade, and with everyone up in arms over the dangers of international travel, places like this won't be around much longer." She draped a silk scarf around her neck and pulled a compact out of the bottomless pit that was her purse. "Besides, it never hurts to make a good impression in a foreign land. We are representing our country, after all."

Ethan and I exchanged a grin. Maddie, primping as if she was about to meet the Pope, powdered her nose and then stuffed the compact in her bag. We fell in line behind the tour guide as he held up his little orange flag to rally our group. I hung back with Ethan.

"I've been watching that young couple over there at the edge of the square. I bet they have some primo weed," I whispered and pointed out a group of teens hovering around a young couple who were darting nervous glances across the square and covertly exchanging something small for a few Euros. It was the first opportunity I'd seen for any chance at scoring some weed. I couldn't be sure, but they looked like the type, and my radar was up.

Ethan studied the group and then took me by the hand. "We need to catch up to our tour. Besides, buying drugs in a foreign country is a really bad idea," he whispered. "Trust me. It's not worth getting caught."

I sighed and dismissed my plan, picking up my pace. Aside from my chronic state of irritability over the past week since I'd last been high, I missed the buzz—that foggy haze that made everything seem a little brighter and a fraction less bleak. The fact that Ethan hadn't brought up any more about my pot smoking or the trouble I'd gotten into back home gave me one more reason to be grateful for his friendship. It seemed he'd come to understand my need to dull the ever-present ache that resided in my heart. At least he didn't appear to hold it against me.

When we finally reached the church on the hill, Maddie had already entered. I tossed the requisite shawl over my shoulders and ducked inside, happy to escape the heat for a few minutes. The high domed ceiling and stone walls gave the place a cavernous feel. Giant, full-length stained glass windows depicting the "passion of Christ"—according to Maximo—echoed the sacred cross that adorned the front of the church. Tall, red candles stood on an altar along one wall.

I was surprised to see Maddie lighting a candle and then kneeling in a front pew. The polished, ancient wood, gleamed in the sun's rays that showed through the stained glass in a kaleidoscope of color. She looked serene as she gazed up at the cross, and I wondered what she could be thinking. Was she praying for Grandpa

Henry, my dad, Amanda…me? A familiar fragrant scent wafted through the air. My throat closed and suddenly I couldn't breathe.

"I need to get out of here." I turned to dart for the entryway.

Ethan was at my side when I reached the heavy wooden door. "What's wrong?"

I sucked in a deep breath as I burst out into the hot sun, the scent of Frankincense still strong in my nose. "Ever since…Amanda…I can't stand the smell of that incense. It makes me feel sick." I pushed through the crowd heading into the church, passing an ancient, weathered man who stood hunched and toothless, handing out scarves to the tourists who irreverently bared their shoulders. I flung off the shawl and balled it into my hand as I made my way to a nearby bench overlooking the village below.

Ethan dropped down beside me. "For me, it's the smell of hospitals. After spending so much time there when my mom was sick, I can't stand the smell of antiseptic."

"That could be a problem if you're planning to be a doctor," I said, allowing a fraction of a smile to surface and glad to take the focus off me.

"You think?" he said, a wiseass grin spreading across his face.

"Does your dad know you don't really want to go to medical school?" My tone grew serious.

"I haven't had more than a three sentence conversation with him to even talk about it."

"Don't you think you should tell him?"

He slipped his hand into mine. Our fingers laced together, my pinky sliding naturally between his last two fingers and settling into a comfortable fit that felt like it had always been there.

"That's the problem. I don't know. Being a doctor seems like a cool idea. Saving lives, helping people. I could see myself in family practice maybe. But my dad sets the bar pretty high. I don't think I could deal with all the pressures of being a surgeon. And I've seen how demanding it is. I don't want it to take over my whole life, you know?"

"You don't have to be a surgeon. You don't even have to be a doctor if you don't want to. You're eighteen. You get to decide for yourself what you want to do. You're lucky. At least you have a choice, now. I can't wait to turn eighteen so I can do whatever I want."

"I'm not sure it really works that way." Ethan cocked his head toward me, raising a dark brow. A sarcastic grin slid in place. "It's not like I turned eighteen and instantly had unlimited options. As long as I'm in school, my dad kind of holds all the cards." He rubbed his thumb across my knuckles, sending a curl of warmth to my insides. Then his expression changed to one of curiosity. "If you could do anything you wanted, what would you do?"

"I wish I knew." I looked down at our entwined fingers. "Mostly, I want to be able to make my own decisions. But everything gets so complicated. If I want my license, I have to pass my test, get a job, and pay for my own insurance. If I want a car, I'll have to pay for the gas and repairs. If I move out and don't go to college, I have to get a full time job that pays enough for me to live on. It all seems like…too much."

Ethan chuckled. "I hear you. Becoming an adult kind of sucks, right?"

"I'm just tired of people telling me what to do and how to feel." I leaned my head against his shoulder. Warmth seeped deep into my chest and I sighed, a measure of contentment mixing with the restlessness that was making my head spin.

"It won't be long before all that adult responsibility crap falls onto both of our shoulders," Ethan said with a hollow tone. "Maybe we shouldn't think about it anymore. Can't we just try to enjoy the cruise and have some fun?"

"That's what I was trying to do earlier when I wanted to buy some weed from those locals. I know you were looking out for me, but I'm not dumb. I could have scored us a joint for later on board the ship. That would have made my day."

A low chuckle escaped and Ethan squeezed my fingers. "You are trouble with a capital T, aren't you?"

"That's one of the most interesting things about me," I said smugly. I lifted my chin to see a wide, full-lipped grin that made my insides float.

He laughed. "I'd hate to see your less charming qualities."

"I think you already have," I replied. "I know I apologized about the other day, but I wanted to say it again. I'm really sorry for the attitude. My nerves have been on edge since this trip started. Not only did I not want to be here, I pretty much decided right from the start that Maddie was conspiring with my mom and stepdad to make my life miserable."

"It doesn't seem that way to me. Maddie is actually pretty cool for a grandparent. You could do worse. I never even knew any of my grandparents. They were all gone by the time I came around. My mom and dad had me later in life. I guess Dad wanted to wait until he finished medical school, and by the time they tried to start a family, it wasn't as easy as they thought. My mom had trouble carrying to full term. She had a bunch of miscarriages and then finally—me." Ethan stared out at the mountains overlooking the sea as if the weight of his words might bring them crashing down.

I leaned into him and nudged his shoulder, bringing his focus to my eyes. "I'm glad they kept trying." His lips curved up as I met his gaze. "The world would be a lesser place if you weren't in it. I can't imagine this trip without you," I added with a shy, downward glance. "I think you're one of the most amazing people I've ever met."

When I looked up to see his response, Ethan's smile lit his eyes. The green reflected the sea, and golden flecks danced with the sun's rays.

"That's the nicest thing anyone has ever said to me." He squeezed my fingers and laid a kiss on my forehead, then relaxed his shoulders and stared into the distance. "I wish my dad thought so."

Chapter 19

I was sad to say good-bye to Palermo but I was excited for the next day. Although seeing the Vatican Museum and St. Peter's Basilica would undoubtedly be amazing for its history, art, and architecture, I was more concerned about Ethan, who shifted anxiously from foot to foot beside me as we waited to pour out onto the dock to meet our tour guide. If all went well, Ethan's dad would be on shore waiting to join us.

A wall of heat rolled over me as we stepped into the bright sunlight, the day's temperature expected to climb into the ninety's and already a notable change from the cool breeze out at sea. I'd worn a pair of checked board shorts that went down to an inch or two above my knees, and a plain white tee with my requisite water bottle and sunblock stuffed in a small daypack slung over one shoulder. I'd found a sweet hat with a visor to keep the sun exposure to a minimum and was glad for my new shorter, cooler hairstyle. I slid my sunglasses in place.

Ethan pointed and called out, "There's my dad!" He waved to his father who stood on the other side of a fountain in the center of a large square, statues of Romanesque women circling the marble base. The man tucked his phone into his shirt pocket and waved us over, his smile only half lighting his face. An ominous twist hit my gut.

We made our way through the crowd heading for the buses, but veered off toward Ethan's dad, Maddie in tow, carrying a purse large enough to house a litter of puppies.

"Did you really need to carry that bag with you?" I asked, a little embarrassed as she rummaged through the oversized tote and drew out her sunglasses.

"You never know what you'll need on these excursions." Her arm delved into the bag up to her shoulder. "I hope my Mounds bars don't melt." She dug deeper, her whole face disappearing as Ethan's dad walked up. She popped her head up when he spoke.

"Maddie, right?" His grin widened for a moment at the sight of my grandmother. "Nice to see you again."

"Likewise," Maddie responded as she slid the bag up onto her shoulder, instantly charmed when he shook her hand. Then he turned his attention to Ethan and the charming smile faltered. I felt Ethan go still beside me and wondered if he had stopped breathing. "That was the hospital in Paris. My patient has been running a low grade fever all week. Unfortunately infection is a common problem after this type of surgery. He's a high level official at the French Embassy and...well...it's very important that nothing interferes with his recovery." He looked from Ethan to Maddie as if he was waiting for someone to acknowledge that he wasn't invisible. Everyone remained silent and I heard a low *humph* come from Maddie.

"Can't you even stay for the tour?" Ethan's voice sounded a little desperate and my heart stung for him. His father shook his head.

"I'm sorry, son...I..."

"Whatever." Ethan turned on his heels and beat a path back toward the ship.

"Wait..." his father called.

"Let him go. I'd like a few words with you," Maddie said, her tone steely. She shot me a glance and gestured for me to go after

Ethan. I left the two of them standing by the fountain, Doctor Kaswell's face a rigid mask of regret.

It took me a minute to catch up with him, only steps from stalking back up the gangway. "Ethan, wait." He stopped but kept his back to me. I reached out to rest a hand on his shoulder, but he flinched away.

"I don't need you feeling sorry for me. I'm fine."

"You don't seem fine," I said softly, letting my hand drop. "Why don't you come on the tour with me and Maddie? You don't want to miss out on your chance to see Rome just because your dad's being a jerk."

Ethan swung around. "He's not a jerk. He's a doctor. I know that his patients come first. It's just..." his voice shook and he closed his eyes as if searching for control. "I'm sick of it, that's all." By now his tone had dipped to barely a whisper and his fingers had flexed into fists. He peered, narrow-eyed at his father who was in an intense exchange with Maddie, her doing most of the talking I noticed with satisfaction.

"I wouldn't want to be him right now," I said, drawing a tiny smirk to the edge of Ethan's mouth. His shoulders relaxed a fraction, and he crossed his arms over his chest as his father headed our way with Maddie in the lead. Martin Kaswell's face held deep creases that suddenly made him appear much older. As soon as he reached the gangway, he focused on Ethan, his expression pleading.

"I know I've said this before, but I'm truly sorry about this, son. I'll make it up to you...I..." he stopped short of the word promise, knowing full well his word meant very little. Unexpectedly, he pulled Ethan into a tight hug. Ethan responded with a half-hearted embrace and then let his hands drop.

"So when do we meet up again…or shouldn't I ask?" Sarcasm laced Ethan's tone, his face stony, but his eyes were too sad to hide the emotion behind the comment.

A frown crossed the doctor's face. "I'll call you tomorrow and let you know. I don't want to promise a plan until I know I can make it work." He glanced at Maddie. Meanwhile, the tour guide waved insistently at us to join the group. "You go on the tour with Maddie and…"

"Lexi," Ethan said, clearly annoyed when his father hesitated.

"Yes, Lexi," he replied, smiling at me for the first time and meeting what I hoped was a premium grade scowl. "Of course. You two have fun on the rest of the cruise." He turned back to Ethan. "As soon as this patient is stable and I can get away, I'll fly to wherever you are. The French government has given me full use of their transport." He ran his hands through his hair, sweat beading on his forehead. "I'll see you soon."

When he disappeared into the crowd, Ethan let out a long breath—the one he'd been holding since his father's arrival.

"It looks like you're stuck with us for today," Maddie said. She held up a credit card with Doctor Kaswell's name on it. "Let's go blow some money in Rome. I think some retail therapy is in order."

Chapter 20

Maddie picked out a five hundred dollar suit coat and held up a tie for Ethan, who shook his head and made a face. She shrugged, a warm smile lighting her eyes. "Too business for your needs. How about this?" She picked up a slick brown leather jacket.

"It's kind of warm for leather," Ethan said, putting the tie back on the rack. "Honestly, I don't really need anything."

"Oh, this isn't about needing anything, my dear boy. It's about revenge. And about making a point," she added as Ethan and I shared a look of shock. "Your father needs to have the point driven home that nothing…and I mean nothing, is more important than you. There will soon come a day when you'll be so busy in your own life, you will have no use for him. When that day comes, he will be one sorry man that he neglected to show you how special you are to him." Maddie picked out a cashmere sweater vest. "Oh, this is nice."

"I'm not really a cashmere kind of guy." Ethan grabbed a pair of Italian leather boots off the shelf. "So you're saying that spending my dad's hard earned cash will get his attention?" Ethan kicked off his sneakers and jammed a foot into a boot. "I hate to break it to you, but I've tried that before. It hasn't worked." He tugged on the second boot, then checked out how they looked in the mirror.

"Nice," I said, my focus so *not* on the black leather boots. He caught me admiring the way his jeans hugged his hips. His ears turned red, but he gave me a grateful smile as he pulled the boots off and handed them to the saleswoman.

Maddie nodded her approval. "Well, something has to get his attention. It's not right that he makes all those promises and then lets you down time and again. It's not fair to you, and he is missing out on what a wonderful young man you are."

I grinned inwardly at Maddie's lioness stance on the issue and how adamantly she defended Ethan. Clearly, she was very fond of him. I could see it meant a lot to him, but his words still carried the weight of disappointment.

"I don't need his attention that badly," Ethan said. "I'm not a kid anymore. If he hasn't figured it out by now, I doubt he ever will." A dejected expression clouded Ethan's face, and I wanted nothing more than to hug him and to do whatever it took to erase his pain. The tour guide waved the orange flag and shoppers congregated outside the exit of the store, ready to move on to our next stop.

To avoid long lines and give Maddie a chance to rest before we hit the Vatican, we took the tour bus highlighting the main attractions in Rome. We crossed the snaking Tiber River, which bisected the city, and then we drove slowly past the Coliseum and the Forum. Our tour guide, a slender Italian woman with a thick ebony pony tail, spoke in heavily accented English.

"Completed in 80AD, the Coliseum once housed as many as fifty thousand spectators—all crowded in for entertainment as unarmed men engaged in a battle to the death against lions or against each other. Violence was a drug in a depraved society. Some might find a parallel in today's spectator sports like your American football, no?" She said it with a mischievous grin that had the tourists chuckling.

I tuned out the rest of her history lesson and focused on every cut stone and massive archway we passed. I was dying to get out and walk around inside the ancient ruins, but it would be impossible to see it all with the little time we had. In awe of the ingenuity and the feat of human strength it took to build a structure that could withstand two thousand years, I admired the ornate archways and incredible detail in the sculpted stone of the Coliseum and the massive carved amphitheater of the Forum. I'd always been fascinated with architecture, but this was…incredible.

We drove past the Piazza di Spagna, known as the Spanish Steps, a massive marble staircase where people congregated and took photos as if they were supermodels on location. Then it was past the Trevi Fountain and I wished I had time to get out and toss in a coin to ensure I would return, a romantic tradition Maddie said was made famous in movies, but one that made perfect sense to me. I craned my neck to catch every statue, every fountain, and every monument.

"Isn't this amazing?" I turned to Ethan, who sat quietly beside me.

"Yeah, great." He stared blankly past me out the window.

"Still bummed about your dad?"

"I was kind of looking forward to seeing Rome with him. We've talked about it for years. He and my mom came here on their honeymoon. He was supposed to show me all the places they went together. I thought…it doesn't matter what I thought." His expression darkened and he released another sigh.

I slipped my fingers through his and gave his hand a light squeeze. "Now you'll have memories of your own, right?" I tried to act happy but the sad look in his eyes made me instantly angry with his father. Doctor or not, he was a jerk for hurting someone I'd grown to care very much about. My heart ached for Ethan. Knowing that our time was limited and that in a matter of days, all we would have was memories of each other to take with us, I was filled with new determination to make the best of our time together. Attempting to draw a smile, I nudged his shoulder. "Wait 'til you see the Sistine Chapel. I hear it will make a grown man cry. Should we stop and get a box of tissues?"

He nudged me back and there it was—that wise-guy grin. "I think I'll make it through without bawling, thanks."

When we finally reached Vatican City, the two of us were laughing and joking, in no small part thanks to Maddie who had engaged us in a conversation about the attire of the ancient Romans and how their thigh high garments were likely a precursor to the miniskirts worn in her day. "Funny how fashion always seems to come back around," she remarked. "But my Lord, how clothing is getting skimpier with every generation." She nodded at a teenaged girl wearing a mini that barely covered her butt.

The line to get into the Vatican snaked on for what seemed like forever, and the hot sun filled the cloudless blue sky overhead. Maddie fanned herself with her hat and finished off her bottle of water before the main entrance came into view. I didn't mind the wait so much, as it gave me time to check out the Basilica's classic Renaissance and Baroque architecture. And to people watch. Across St. Peter's Square, past the massive obelisk made of marble, and in front of the Metro station, several shady-looking teens congregated, no doubt dealing or pick-pocketing unsuspecting tourists. Nearby stood a vendor advertising water and Italian ice.

"Ethan and I will go get some ice cream and a couple more bottles of water," I said, glancing at Ethan conspiratorially. "We'll be right back, Maddie." Before she had a chance to protest, I'd grabbed his hand and dragged him out of line and through the crowded square. My head spun as I took in the moment. Bernini's Colonnade, the monument erected in honor of the square's designer stood center stage. I soaked in the beauty surrounding me and felt more happy and excited than I had in a long while. I was free and in Rome—with a hot guy.

"Grab us some of those Italian ices. I'll be right back," I said, pulling away.

"Wait! You shouldn't…"

But I'd already disappeared around the corner and down the steps into the dark recesses of the Metro Station where I'd seen a couple of teenagers about my age duck out of site a few minutes earlier. As I suspected, they were off in the shadows, exchanging a few Euros, one speaking in broken English, the other, an American boy who was tucking a couple of rolled cigarettes into his pocket. They both stopped abruptly as I approached.

I looked around to make sure I wasn't drawing attention, and then smiled amiably at the two boys. "Can I get in on some of that action?"

The two regarded me warily and then the American darted off, leaving the local boy to shift nervously. It took a few misunderstood phrases between us for me to walk away with a grossly overpriced joint, but I'd gotten what I came for. Feeling smug that I hadn't been kidnapped, assaulted, or arrested, I returned to Ethan's side in front of the vendor's cart.

"What was that all about?" he asked, annoyed and obviously worried.

"Just a little exploring. I wanted to see what Rome's underbelly looked like."

"Well, don't do that again. There are pick-pockets and thieves around here. It isn't safe for tourists to go off alone—especially someone like you. Human traffickers could have…"

"But they didn't," I interjected. "And what's with the *someone like me* remark? Do you mean a stupid American girl?" I gave him my best unappreciative glare.

He handed me an ice cream. "NO. Actually I meant young and pretty." The annoyance faded from his eyes and sincere worry took over. "I don't know what I would do if anything bad happened to you."

"Oh—sorry." My cheeks burned and I gratefully took the ice cream, feeling once again as if I'd gone too far. "We'd better get back to Maddie," I said, not wanting to ponder the possibility that he was right. It had been stupid of me to risk everything—including my life—for a joint. My only defense was that I'd been caught up in the moment, and I'd seen an opportunity I couldn't resist. It wasn't the first time I'd acted without thinking—a truth about myself I wasn't sure I wanted to face.

It took another half hour before we finally entered the Vatican Museum, but by that time, Maddie was looking refreshed. In some respects, my grandmother seemed young and vibrant, like one of her bright hats or floral tops. At other times, she appeared old and wilted like a plant gone un-watered for too many days. For the moment, my concerns faded when Maddie squealed like a teenager over the exquisite artwork before us.

The museum's treasures were displayed in a series of galleries that would stretch four-and-a-half miles end-to-end. We followed Giuseppe, our guide, through each gallery, every one more amazing than the last. Ornate archways and carved marble moldings overhead were lined with giant sculptures of deities, saints, and angels. The rich, burgundy carpeting underfoot and the divinely inspired artwork on the vaulted ceilings made me feel as if I'd been transported to another time and place, lost in a maze of antiquity and beauty. We crossed mosaic stone and marble floors that came alive with color. Gold and burnished bronze statues gave the place a warm feel. At the same time, all the stone and marble, and the cavernous ceilings kept the space feeling cool and dry. Overwhelmed by the sheer volume of the history, I captured picture after picture, certain I'd never retain the full experience. A quick glance at Ethan, and I was happy to see he was as enthralled as me and Maddie—his father's betrayal momentarily forgotten.

When we came into the Sistine Chapel, I was awestruck. Words failed me as I craned my neck to see in all directions at once. The voices of the tour guides could be heard above the hushed whispers of the crowd, and a sense of reverence pervaded the scene in a way I'd never experienced before. Michelangelo's most inspiring frescos arched overhead. I felt dizzy as my head spun to capture the overwhelming beauty of it all. I imagined the painter, over fifteen hundred years ago, lying on his back on ancient scaffolding, measuring every minute detail and line that came off his brushstrokes. The magnitude of the job boggled my mind. The patience it had taken, the passion for his art, the amazing fortitude required to see the job finally completed.

"I can't believe one man did this whole thing in only four years," I whispered as I leaned into Ethan, who seemed to be in a daze as he took it all in.

"Makes you look at four years of college a little differently, doesn't it?" His head tipped further back as he turned in a slow circle.

I took what he said to mean that both of us could learn from the artist's dedication and discipline. Maybe it was time I stopped looking at college as some sort of exile or punishment—a place full of unknown dangers and overwhelming responsibilities—and start seeing it as the opportunity to create something amazing for my future.

Chapter 21

"Get whatever you like," Maddie said as she dozed in a chair waiting for me to decide on a new dress. The sales clerks brought out the works, including shoes, bangles, and bling, making me feel like a princess or a supermodel on a runway as I tried on one designer outfit after another. Maddie perked up occasionally and nodded or grinned in agreement about what she liked or didn't, and Ethan goaded me on to try one more. He was either the most tolerant boy I'd ever met, or he actually enjoyed our company. I was definitely enjoying his.

We shopped ourselves out until Maddie called it quits just in time to meet the tour bus and head back to the ship for dinner.

"Are you planning on spending the whole evening in the bathroom? My blood sugar is dropping as we speak." Maddie's voice sounded muffled through the door. I'd slipped one outfit into the pile without first modeling it. When I came out of the bathroom, she raised a brow. "Was it your aim to pass for my thirty year-old daughter instead of my granddaughter?"

I'd picked out a short leather skirt and a frilly, capped-sleeve, fitted blouse that barely covered my belly post. The scooped neckline showcased more cleavage than I'd known I had.

"This is what all the girls my age are wearing." I tugged the shirt down an inch.

Maddie let out a sigh and continued to fuss with her jacket in the mirror, finding a tiny piece of lint on the shoulder to pluck at.

With the red, open-toed pumps I bought to go with the outfit, I did look years older than my age—an effect I was sure wouldn't go unnoticed by Ethan, but a niggle of doubt crept in at Maddie's disapproval. Would Ethan think I was trying too hard? Would it make me seem desperate...or worse...slutty? I suddenly had the urge to change clothes, but before I could decide, Maddie pushed me out the door, citing what bad manners it would be to arrive late for dinner.

My fears fled when I saw the appreciative look on Ethan's face.

"Wow," escaped his lips as he approached our table and pulled out a chair. His green eyes shimmered in the ambient light, and his short hair was nicely gelled and spiked on top. He wore a blazer and collared shirt with nice fitting jeans, and had intentionally forgotten to shave the past few days, giving him a mysterious dark shadow over his upper lip and on his chin. I nearly giggled out loud but held it back, hoping to appear cooler than I felt.

"Right back at you," I said, smiling as he unraveled his fork and knife from his napkin and then laid the white linen across his lap.

"You both look quite metropolitan," Maddie said, grinning. She ordered herself a bottle of wine and we waited for the others who would be joining our table for dinner. Tonight's seating included Ben and David, who Maddie had become great friends with after the magic show and a few nights of ballroom dancing. Another couple settled in at our table, bringing Maddie to life with their introduction as Mary and Joe and their admission that yes, they were Jewish—apparently part of a *Jews for Jesus* convention on board. Conversation bounced back and forth and I tuned out the repetition of each person's life story, how many kids and grandkids they each had, and what they had all done before retirement. Even the delicious flavors of the gourmet foods couldn't take my attention away from what mattered most—the super cute and awesome smelling guy sitting next to me.

After dinner, Maddie excused herself, the wilted expression returning. "I don't know what's gotten into me," she said. I'll have to start taking some vitamins or something. I'm completely exhausted after that long day of sightseeing and shopping. I'm going to run off to bed. You two go and enjoy the show. There's a wonderful cabaret act in the Vista Lounge."

"Are you sure you don't want to come with us?" Ethan asked politely. I wanted to elbow him in the ribs. All I could think about was being alone with him again, and the smell of his manly scented soap made my mouth water.

"No, I'd rather hit the hay early. They have a tai chi class tomorrow morning I want to attend. You two have fun—but behave," she added sternly, eyeing me like she knew exactly what was on my mind. She turned to Ethan and threatened with a wag of her index finger. "I trust my granddaughter is safe in your care."

"Yes, ma'am," Ethan responded, a charming and dimpled grin covering his face as if he were the most trustworthy guy on the planet.

I ground my teeth and sighed. Maddie gave me an eye of warning one more time and turned toward the elevator leading up to deck four. I grabbed Ethan's hand and pulled him in the opposite direction.

"Follow me. I have a surprise for you."

Ethan checked over his shoulder to see Maddie disappear as the doors closed. "Should I be scared?"

"C'mon. We're on our own for the night. Let's have a little fun." I led him up the main staircase and up several more flights until we reached the top level of the ship. We burst out into the warm air, the breeze raising my hair and taking my breath away. I laughed as Ethan picked up his pace to stay with me. We rounded the pool and hot tub, which were empty by this time. A few crew members passed us by and headed for the stairs down, leaving us alone on the highest deck of the ship, looking out over the dark night sky and endless expanse of water. Lights shone far in the distance, outlining the coast of Italy. We would be at sea for a day before coming into our next port of call in Dubrovnik, Croatia.

"Hey…" Ethan stopped and caught me in his arms, ducking us into the shadows of the lifeboats. "Did I tell you how pretty you look tonight?" His eyes sparkled under the starlight and the angle of his jaw appeared sharper and more masculine than I'd noticed before. This close, with his warm breath on my skin and his arms encircling my waist, I saw a man before me and not the boy I'd met only days ago.

My cheeks heated and I bit my lower lip. "I think the 'wow' earlier was sufficient."

A grin spread. "That obvious, huh?"

It took all I had in me, but I pulled away, anxious to see if Ethan really accepted me for who I was and not only as a hot girl in an Italian leather mini on an exotic vacation—someone he was never going to see again after this trip. A crack edged its way into my heart. I shut out the painful sensation and focused instead on what seemed a plausible cure for my impending heartbreak. I checked to make sure we were alone and pulled out the joint.

Ethan's eyes grew big. "Are you crazy? If we get caught…"

"We won't. Don't worry. There's no one else around." Having confiscated matches from the smoker's lounge, I lit the joint and took a big hit, letting the burn in my chest expand and holding the smoke until it made me cough. I let it go slowly, handing the joint over to Ethan.

He eyed me warily, scoping out the area, on the lookout for other passengers and crew. "You are nuts," he whispered. After a moment's hesitation and a raised brow of challenge from me, he took his turn and inhaled deeply, bursting into a coughing fit.

"Take it easy there, killer," I said, chuckling softly. I took another hit and passed it back to him.

"I told you I don't smoke. It would kind of interfere with Lacrosse. I need all the lung capacity I can get," he said, choking as he held in another hit.

"I wish I was that committed to something," I replied with a shrug. Then changing the subject away from me, I asked, "Has your dad ever seen you play?" I regretted the question when I saw a hurt look darken Ethan's eyes.

"He used to come to games once in a while when I was younger. He hasn't been around much the past year or two."

"Sorry. I didn't mean to bring up a sore subject. Tonight is supposed to be about helping you forget about him." After another sharp lungful, I handed him the joint one more time. He took it, taking another deep inhale and letting it out slowly, his eyes narrowing against the burn of the smoke.

"Nothing for you to be sorry about. My dad's the one who let me down…again."

After a few more hits each, the two of us relaxed. "I wish I could do something to take the hurt away," I said.

Ethan rested his head on one of the lifeboats hanging down behind us. "I'm done," he said, waving off another hit. He closed his eyes as if contemplating the meaning of life or looking as if he was ready to drop into a deep sleep. I traced the outline of his jaw in the shadows and ran a finger over his ear, drawing a sliver of a smile to his lips. "I'm totally stoned," he said, sounding not at all like the put together guy I had come to know so well.

"Lightweight." I laughed, took one more hit, and snubbed out the joint. I slipped the remainder into a little baggie and dropped it and the matches into my clutch for another time.

Ethan popped to his feet and grabbed my hand, pulling me up from the deck.

"We'll see who's a lightweight."

Chapter 22

Just as I'd hoped, Ethan led me to his cabin stateroom, a match to the one Maddie and I were staying in, but slightly larger and nicer. We each sat on the edge of one of the neatly made double beds, facing each other. As happy as I was to be there, I suddenly felt like a fish out of water—too late to jump back in and hide under the nearest rock ledge.

"Mind if I fix myself a drink?" Ethan surprised me as he popped up off the bed and nervously went about rummaging through the mini bar. He grabbed several small bottles of vodka and brought out a bottle of tonic water. "What can I get you?"

"Ginger ale is fine if you have it." My stomach had taken a turn toward queasy as soon as he mentioned drinking. He handed me the soda, his fingers brushing mine and sending a tingle up my arm.

"Thanks." I smiled and focused my attention on how I was going to get Ethan to go back on his promise to Maddie and kiss me again. As much as I knew it was probably a bad idea, the thought of his lips on mine and his hands on my skin had every nerve in my body strung tight with longing and anticipation.

He finished mixing a drink for himself. "You sure this isn't a problem for you?"

"No big deal," I said relieved that he asked and hadn't tried to convince me to drink with him.

Looking as nervous as I felt, Ethan took a long swig, set his drink on the bedside table, and kicked off his shoes. He hopped onto the pillows, loosening his shirt from his pants and resting his hands behind his head.

"So what do you want to talk about—and it can't be anything depressing," he added, stuffing another pillow behind him.

I scooted back, dropped my chunky heels to the floor with a thud and fluffed my pillows so I could sit sideways and watch Ethan. I studied him for a moment, and suddenly envied him—so sure of himself and completely at ease in his skin, whereas I was a bundle of nerves—worrying that my skirt was too short, my hair too boyish, and wondering if my makeup was intact.

He closed his eyes and the hint of a smile curved his lips as if he was thinking of something pleasant. It was nice to see him relaxed. The hard edges of his features had softened, making my heart melt a fraction more. His biceps bulged and the sinewy muscles of his shoulders pressed through his shirt, the smooth skin of his chest peeking out from the now opened buttons. My mouth went dry.

"Um…we could talk about all of your wild guy adventures." I grinned across at him to the next bed. "You do have friends, don't you?"

He tossed a towel giraffe at me. "Yes—I have friends." He leaned over and took another sip off his drink and I followed with my ginger ale, glad to add cool moisture to my parched throat.

"Tell me about your best friend."

"I don't know if I have a *best* friend," he replied, his brows furrowing in concentration. "Kyle and Greg have been around since my first year of private school. We played Lacrosse together and hung out sometimes. Before I met them, it was a geeky kid with glasses named Doug who lived across the street. He got me hooked on video games and Cheetos. I still can't play Madden 25 unless I have a bag. Man, could I go for some Cheetos right now."

I laughed. "Munchies, huh?"

"Want to order room service?" Ethan rolled to the side and grabbed the menu, still restless and noticeably edgy underneath his calm. He ordered cheese pizza, a salad for me, and two chocolate shakes, and then demanded a bag of Cheetos, arguing with the service staff that he was certain they could find a bag somewhere on board a ship this size.

I giggled.

"How much will that be?" I heard him ask. "Add a bottle of your best champagne to that order, please. And charge it to the room." When he hung up the phone he slumped back onto the bed, slugged down the rest of his drink, and huffed out a breath. "Can't wait to see the old man's face when he sees the bar tab and the room service bill."

"You're really taking Maddie's advice to heart, then?"

"Oh, you mean about getting my dad's attention by hitting his wallet? Or maybe I should toss my "good guy" image and get into trouble to prove the point that teenagers need supervision?" He laughed, rolled off the bed, and fixed another drink. "It won't matter to him. I'll get a lecture about being responsible, and he'll sweep it all under the rug so he doesn't have to feel like a failure as a parent."

I shook my head when he offered me a bag of peanuts.

"It's your turn. Tell me about your friends," Ethan said as he slid back onto his bed. This time, he moved the pillows closer to the edge and closed the distance between us by two feet, making the hairs on my arms stand to attention. I took another sip of my soda, considering my answer.

"When I was little, it was all about me and Amanda. I followed her everywhere." I swallowed past what felt like a stone. "Nothing depressing, right?" Clearing my throat, I continued. "D.D. is my closest friend. Her parents are divorced and her life is always a mess, but she and I can talk about anything, you know? And who am I to talk about messed up, right? Sometimes I hang out with Sami, but she just graduated and has her own crew of friends. Mostly we hang out to jam together. She's an awesome drummer."

We traded a few more stories of childhood friendships and adventures of mayhem, every story ending with how we'd each fallen from grace with our parents in some way and adults in general. Our common denominator was that we were both sick of trying to make them all happy. By the time room service came, Ethan had already polished off his third drink. The waiter eyed him and me as he uncorked the champagne but said nothing about our under-age status. He left us alone, and a moment later, I reluctantly took the glass Ethan handed me.

"C'mon. It's only one," he coaxed. "It's summer vacation. What should we drink to? Oh, I know," Ethan said. "Let's drink to failure." He swayed slightly as he tipped his head back and guzzled. He sat down hard on the edge of the bed, bottle sloshing in one hand and the empty glass in the other. I took his glass and set my own on the table, the bubbles deceptively happy.

"It's been my experience that failure is the best teacher," I said, realizing how true that was. I took the bottle out of his hand, walked to the sink in the bathroom and poured it down the drain.

"What are you doing?" Ethan jumped from the bed and stumbled to the doorway.

"Keeping you from feeling like crap in the morning."

Ethan crossed his arms over his chest and scowled. "That was a hundred dollar bottle of champagne."

"Well, making yourself sick kind of defeats the purpose of punishing your father. You hanging your head in a toilet bowl— that'll show him." I drained the last drop and handed him the empty bottle as I tried to brush past him.

He grabbed my arm and spun me around, pulling me close. Eyes filled with emotion he stared down at me. "Haven't you ever just wanted to…forget?"

"Every day," I said softly. I touched my palm to his cheek and gave him a weak smile. "But hiding in a bottle or running away isn't the answer." I heard my words as if they were coming from someone else. They made sense, but sounded hypocritical and foreign pouring out of me—*the queen of running away,* Amanda's voice whispered.

Ethan's brows drew together in contemplation, then he grinned. "And yet, getting trashed right now seems like a perfect idea." He leaned heavily against the doorframe blocking my exit— or possibly holding himself steady. His eyes lost focus and he blinked several times.

"How's that working out for you?" I slapped his face gently but hard enough to get his attention, sobering him up slightly.

"I guess we'll see in the morning," he snorted.

"I hate seeing you like this." My voice was hoarse and I worried it might crack.

"What? Drunk, or pathetic and miserable?"

"Both." I ran fingers along his cheek and a grin appeared, softening the lines around his eyes.

"I knew you cared about me," he teased. He captured my hand in his and laid a soft kiss on my palm, tender and sweet, sending a shockwave of affection through my heart.

"Of course I care about you," I said. Our fingers wove together, the front of our bodies almost touching.

A flicker of appreciation overshadowed the sadness in his eyes and warmth radiated through me when he stroked a finger up my arm. I met his gaze squarely, which had a spark of fire in it I hadn't seen a moment before. My nerves ignited. A part of me knew

I should be afraid, being that Ethan wasn't likely in full control of his faculties, but I couldn't quite make myself fear being alone with him. Somehow I trusted him in a way I'd never trusted anyone before.

I had a heartbeat of apprehension before I draped my arms over his shoulders and wrapped my hands around his neck. The two of us together pushed off from the doorframe and danced to some unheard tune, our feet shuffling side to side into the bedroom. His eyes, glassy, but dark and wide, met mine.

"Can you stay with me?"

My teeth caught my bottom lip as if to stifle my totally insane response—and failed. "I'd like that," I whispered as our noses touched.

He closed his eyes and rested his forehead on mine. "I was hoping that's what you'd say."

Chapter 23

Ethan dipped his head and kissed me. He tasted fruity, like lime, and his breath was sweet from the champagne. When his mouth opened and his tongue met mine, my first instinct was to pull away. But as his hands brushed my lower back, my whole body sank into him, and all I wanted was…to be closer. Denying me, he drew back and gave me a satisfied but crooked grin, then proceeded to drive me even crazier. A jolt of sensation to the lower half of my body drew a groan from deep in my throat as his lips followed a trail along my jaw and down my neck.

I grabbed what I could of his hair and pulled him close, finding his lips once more and attaching myself firmly as we fumbled to maneuver our hands around clothing and over each other's flesh. We fell onto the bed in a tangle of arms and legs, fingers tugging at buttons and mouth's fused together. The dull taste of alcohol reminded me that I should be thinking of something other than tearing Ethan's clothes off, but my heart stampeded in my chest and every cell in my body screamed for connection. I'd never wanted to be part of someone else so badly. Thoughts crashed against the humming vibration in my body and the fuzzy barrier in my head. I couldn't think of a shred of a reason why I should resist the opportunity to go all the way with the coolest, sweetest, cutest guy I'd ever known. Drunk or not, he was hot. And he was the only boy who had ever made me feel this way…like I was beautiful…like I mattered…like I was wanted.

I unbuttoned the last button of his shirt and my hands raked across his bare chest, the smooth warmth of his body against my palms setting my insides on fire. I came up for air long enough to see from his expression that the feeling was mutual. The blazing intensity in his eyes only fanned the flame hotter. But as I climbed on top of him, I only had a moment to enjoy the exciting new sensation before his hands grabbed, vicelike onto my arms. He pushed me back—a look of disgust taking over his face. My heart plummeted and dark emotions dowsed the flame like ice water.

"We can't…" he said, breathless. "You…you have to go…right now." He rolled out from under me and leapt off his side of the bed, hands running through his hair to straighten himself out. His shirt hung open, his pants half unzipped. He looked down, zipped his fly, and fumbled with buttons, his chest still heaving. "I can't do this."

I pulled my skirt down over my thighs and slowly slid to the edge of the bed, my heart thundering, but feeling set adrift. "Maybe I misunderstood the meaning of *stay with me.* Did I do something wrong?" My voice sounded small, embarrassment creeping into my cheeks as I straightened my blouse and tugged my bra into place.

"No…God, no…you're…" Ethan punched his fist into the palm of his hand, groaned, and began pacing, clearly sobering with each step. "I'm an idiot. You…you, are perfect." He stopped pacing and stared at me from across the room. "I'm so sorry, Lex. I shouldn't have ordered that stupid bottle of champagne. And I shouldn't have been drinking. I wasn't thinking about you, what happened to your sister, or…that drunk driver who killed your dad. You must think I'm a total jerk." He resumed his pacing, still muttering self-recriminating curses under his breath.

I couldn't let him believe my dad was a saint or that I was some kind of victim, although being called perfect had a certain appeal. I stared at the wrinkled bedspread and cut off his tirade. "My dad *was* the drunk driver, Ethan. He killed a kid because he'd had too much to drink and then decided to drive home."

He skidded to a halt, his face shattering. "Oh, God. I am an idiot."

"Yeah, you mentioned that," I said, a smile sneaking across my lips. "I didn't tell you to make you feel worse. I just thought you should know the whole truth." I studied my fingernails, resisting a hangnail itching to be gnawed. "Maybe it'll help you understand why I don't drink, and why I think that no matter how messed up your relationship is with your dad, you should appreciate that he's someone you can be proud of."

A sad smile stretched across his face as his resistance faltered. "I'm beginning to wonder which one of us is really the black sheep around here. You're pretty special, Lexi."

"Glad you think so. I was beginning to have my doubts about how you felt." My cheeks burned, but my heart leapt with relief as his eyes filled with affection.

A look of recognition dawned as he realized how his rejection had stung. He lowered himself to the bed beside me and took my hand between his. "I like you way more than I should under the circumstances." He trailed fingers up my arm, across my collar bone and around the curve of my ear, his eyes focused hazily on my lips. "You have no idea how hard I'm trying not to throw you down on this bed and kiss the hell out of you right now. But..." his eyes avoided mine. "I'm totally unprepared for what that might lead to. And I shouldn't have let things get so out of control," he added sheepishly. "I don't even have any...protection." His ears turned crimson. "Besides, you're only sixteen and...I wouldn't want our first time to be because we—I—drank too much or smoked pot. Then there's the whole vacation hook-up cliché." He brushed my bangs out of my eyes and peered at me through a hooded expression. "I don't want you to think…I'm using you."

"I'm tired of admitting it," I said shaking my head. "But you're right again." I bit my lip, secretly grateful that at least one of us was thinking about the aftermath, but at the same time, totally wishing he wasn't such a Boy Scout, and embarrassed that he had more self-control drunk than I did after only a few hits off a joint.

"I can't even imagine what it would do to Maddie if she caught us like this," he said to drive the point home. Ethan's lips were as swollen as mine felt and if his spiky hair was any indication, we probably both looked a mess. Maddie was only a few doors down the hall.

"I'd better be going," I said.

I rose and pulled my hand out of his, smoothing my skirt down and squaring my shoulders. Regardless of all the good reasons Ethan had for stopping us, I couldn't help my disappointment. The ache of loss lingered in every square inch of my body. Even with his clothes rumpled, shirt buttoned askew and his hair standing up in all directions, I wanted him more than I'd ever wanted a boy before. But it didn't matter that my heart and my body were saying it would have been an amazing night. My head knew that Ethan's choice to stop before things got totally out of hand was likely the right one. Otherwise, I would never have known if he really wanted me or if it was the alcohol and pot at play.

He took my hand again and led me to the door. After he laid a soft kiss on my forehead, he closed his eyes and swayed, holding me tightly once more as if drawing strength to stand firm. Then he whispered against my hair, "I promised Maddie I would take good care of you, and that's what I'm going to do."

∞∞∞∞

Disoriented when I woke to bright sunlight the next morning, I pulled the covers over my head. The night before came back in a flood, and a muffled groan escaped. My fuzzy brain tried to make sense of it all, but my heart could only contain one image. Ethan beneath me, gazing up and wanting me in a way no one else ever had—his green eyes deep and dark with passion and sincerity. There was something about the way he looked at me, the expression on his face saying, *I want you to be mine.* The look that followed—the one that said I was off limits, had me wondering how long Ethan thought either of us could hold out. A year and a half until I was eighteen and out of high school seemed like a lifetime, especially since the memory of Ethan's lips locked to mine brought a searing spike of heat tingling to my toes.

I grinned, stretched, and yawned, letting the covers slip under my arms as a loud rumble rolled up from my stomach. Even the thought of Ethan being miles away and in college for the next eight years couldn't dampen the warmth that radiated from my heart out to every cell in my body. There was something between us I knew couldn't be contained—an attraction as strong as a moth to a flame.

Which of us was the moth and who was the flame remained to be seen—a thought that brought another wave of excitement and nervousness coursing through me. Whatever the risks, I was determined to take them.

Maddie walked out of the bathroom, her hair in a towel and cold cream caked on a half inch deep.

"What time is it?" I asked, still confused and worried I was late for something.

"It's almost nine o'clock. We're at sea for the day, so I thought I'd let you sleep in." She rubbed lotion into her hands. "You came in very late last night. I trust you and Ethan behaved yourselves?" The question came out in a reproving tone, twisting a shard of guilt deeper.

"Define behaved," I replied. I rolled to sitting and scrubbed my hands through my hair.

Maddie grew still and her expression turned instantly hard, making me wonder what the goo on her face was made of. "You didn't do anything you'll regret, I hope." Her blue eyes widened, stark against the white cream. A spark of fear shone through.

"We didn't have sex if that's what you're asking." I rubbed the sleep out of my eyes and yawned again. "Ethan was a perfect gentleman." A slight exaggeration, maybe. But it lead me to realize how hard it must have been for him to step up and stop us from going too far. Either he had the most self-control of any eighteen year-old guy on the planet, or he'd figured out that giving into the 'vacation hook-up cliché,' as he'd called it, would only lead to heartbreak and disaster for us both. Perhaps he'd decided that since long term was out of the question, it wasn't worth starting something we could never finish. The smile slipped from my face. "I'm not going to do anything stupid. Don't worry."

"This is a first for you, then."

Maddie's barb caught me and I flashed a frown at her. "Meaning?"

"Would I be considered too optimistic to think you're finally ready to take some responsibility for your actions and make smarter choices?" She wiped a wet cloth over one side of her face and then the other, leaving a swath of white cream across her forehead and a stripe down her nose while she paused, apparently waiting for my response to her rhetorical question.

I groaned. "Really? Do I need to answer that or can we both assume I'm not a total moron? Besides, we're on a seniors cruise.

How much trouble do you think we could find to get into?" I didn't want to think about the dozen or so ways our last night's activities could have landed me and Ethan in a heap of complicated.

Maddie lifted a brow and retreated to the bathroom to rinse her face. She continued from there. "You know exactly what I mean, young lady. You two clearly have the *hots* for each other, and I don't want some silly crush derailing your future." She turned away and faced the mirror, instant irritation taking over her voice. "If I hadn't been so tired last night, I would have kept a closer eye on you." She proceeded to add moisturizer and then spackle on her layers of makeup.

"I don't need a babysitter," I said, grabbing my swimsuit and a set of shorts to wear for the day. "Ethan and I…we both know the score, Maddie. We aren't stupid. And I'm not a little kid anymore. I'll be seventeen in six months, and I'll graduate high school next year. If everyone would stop pressuring me to grow up—like yesterday," I said, jamming my feet into my flip flops, "—maybe I could figure out where I'm going after that and start planning for a future."

Maddie removed the towel from her hair and shook it out, fluffing the red curls in a halo around her head. "That's the smartest thing I've heard you say since you came to stay with me. There might be hope for you yet, my dear girl."

But even as she said it, thoughts of a future without Amanda in it sent a cold chill through my insides. Moving forward seemed like a betrayal somehow. As if by living my life and being happy, I'd be slapping my sister in the face. The mere thought of going off to college, especially after what had happened to her, sent jagged edged glass to my insides. The only way I could see myself going on was to move past my fear, past my sadness, and past my guilt over being here—while she was…gone.

Add to that, my confusion over what to do about Ethan. It wasn't like I could expect him to wait around for a couple of years while I finished high school and figured out what I was doing with my life. College for him would undoubtedly include access to girls his own age and all that went with living away from home and making his own decisions finally. My chest tightened at the thought of him with anyone else and my jaw clenched, sending a shooting pain to my forehead. Whatever future lay ahead of us was full of unanswerable questions and more unknowns than I could bear.

Chapter 24

Our day at sea started with a light breakfast on the Lido deck and hanging by the pool until noon. Ethan had slept in and appeared slightly bleary eyed stepping off the elevator as I was coming out of the water. The hot sun beat down, warming my skin. Then a slight breeze sent a chill through me. His gaze cascaded over my body and then he glanced away, his ears turning bright pink. He made his way to the table and addressed Maddie.

"How are you today?" he asked, keeping his eyes diverted from me in my bikini.

Maddie lowered her sunglasses and peered up at him. "I suspect I'm better off than you. I must say, Ethan. You look positively green." She turned her attention to me. "And cover up young lady. You girls these days show off an obscene amount of flesh. You're going to embarrass this poor boy." Her attention shot back to Ethan and she narrowed her eyes. "You aren't suffering seasickness, are you?"

Ethan and I exchanged a glance as I dried off and wrapped the large towel around my body and under my arms. A low mumble came from his throat in response to her question. "No ma'am. It must have been something I ate." He stuffed his hands into the pockets of his shorts and shuffled his Teva-clad feet side to side. His white tee with the words *Life is Good* arcing over a skier in mid-jump seemed unconvincing compared to his pained expression.

"With your appetite it doesn't surprise me." Maddie chuckled as she pushed her sunglasses into place. "I think we should all have a chat."

My stomach twisted. I lowered into a seat and cast a glance at Ethan who followed, pulling a chair closer to the table and slowly taking his place across from my grandmother, who appeared to be prepping for either an interrogation or a world-class lecture. Sliding the plate of muffins and assorted pastries in front of Ethan, Maddie signaled the waiter, who proceeded to pour coffee and juice. Ethan nibbled a muffin and sipped the coffee, his eyes closed as he took in the scent of the aromatic blend.

"You two obviously have it bad for each other," Maddie started. "So what are we going to do about it?"

I sucked in a breath through my nose, followed by a frustrated sigh. Ethan stopped chewing, his Adam's apple jumping twice before he swallowed. Clearly, neither of us wanted to be part of this conversation.

But much to my mortification, Maddie continued, focusing her laser-like gaze on Ethan. "What are your intentions toward my granddaughter?"

Ethan straightened in his chair, slugged down half his juice, and took a slow breath. "I…well, I'd like to date your granddaughter." His eyes darted to mine. "I understand that our relationship will have some—restrictions." A pink tinge crept up his neck and down from his ears, turning his face a splotchy red. I wondered if he would pass out. He carefully chose his next words as he brought his full attention to meeting Maddie's cool gaze. "I know it might be challenging with Lexi having another year of school and me going to Columbia, but I'm hoping we can keep in touch and…see where things go from there."

The blush in my own cheeks flamed to the surface. At least he wasn't dismissing the idea altogether.

"You are wise beyond your years, young man." Maddie released her stiff posture and stern expression, lifting her coffee to her lips and leaving a bright red ring on the edge of the cup. "Then I don't want a repeat of last evening's…hmm…shall we call them *activities*." She raised her hand before Ethan or I could try to cover with a protest. "I don't want the details, and I don't want any silly excuses. I have eyes and ears everywhere on this ship, so don't think you can pull the wool over my eyes. The fact is, you two are faced with a difficult situation over these next few days. I'm not so old that I've forgotten the attraction of hormonal lust. When you add an exotic location and a romantic cruise with plenty of opportunities to be tempted, it's a recipe for trouble." She crossed her legs and adjusted her long skirt to cover the bony prominences of her knees. Then she pulled her wide brimmed hat lower and slid her sunglasses off again for emphasis. "Obviously I can't chaperone you every minute, so I'm counting on the two of you to be responsible. I know I'm asking a lot, but please respect my wishes and move slowly with your friendship. You have plenty of time ahead of you to let it unfold naturally. I don't understand why young people are in such a hurry." She reached for a second cheese Danish, leaving the conversation open for a response. My jaw clenched and words crept to the surface without a thought.

"Maybe because we know how short life can be," I said in a low voice, avoiding eye contact with Maddie. "Ethan and I both know there are no guarantees about tomorrow." I glanced at Ethan whose face turned serious, a look of comprehension passing over his features. "Maybe that's why it seems like now is all we have, and waiting feels like a stupid waste of time."

My voice sounded small and the heat returned to my face. Speaking aloud the revelation I had discovered not long after Amanda's death seemed too intimate to be sharing with anyone, but it had to be said. Maddie needed to know that there was more at play than simple teenage hormones, no matter how powerful those might be. Ever since Amanda had died, I felt a certain urgency to live life to the fullest, to experience everything I could, to try not to worry about the future and what tomorrow might bring. Maybe it made me impulsive and unfocused about planning ahead, but it also gave me a sense of control—however elusive and fleeting.

"I see." Maddie nodded. "It's true you've both suffered terrible losses in your young lives." She hesitated, shifting her gaze from Ethan to me. "But perhaps it's time to stop living in fear and start planning for a future. I'm not saying it's wrong to be in the moment and to enjoy each day. Live in the moment, but create your future through the choices you make in those moments." She must have noted my skeptical frown. "Don't discount that moving forward will bring you many more wonderful times in life—if you plan accordingly and make responsible choices."

I wanted so much to tell her that I was trying, but considering I'd spent the night before blowing my first two weeks of sobriety, I could hardly argue. Instead, I balled my hands into fists.

She turned her attention to Ethan, a sparkle in her eye. "Ethan has a fabulous future ahead of him, thanks to a solid upbringing—no doubt attributed to his mother's influence," she added dryly. "But success is about more than being afforded some privileges." Her face grew solemn as she addressed him directly. "Regardless of what you think, your father is very proud of you—as he should be."

Her expression turned cooler as she turned to me. "You, my darling, should take Ethan's good example to heart and stop this nonsense of smoking marijuana and getting into trouble. I know you miss Amanda, but you need to move on and smarten up. It's truly the best way you can honor your sister."

Anger crashed to the surface. The conversation had gone way beyond a little chat, and my insides felt raw—abraded by guilt and pummeled by accusation. Using Ethan to make me feel like a loser was bad enough, but using Amanda to make me feel guilty about my failures was over the top, even for Maddie.

I pushed my chair back and stood, letting the towel drop. "I've heard everything you've said, Maddie. And I don't mean to be disrespectful, but when and how I *move on* is up to me to decide." I jammed one foot and then the other into each leg of my shorts and tugged them up over my hips. "I'm sorry I can't get it together like everyone else, but this is who I am." I buttoned the shorts with harsh, jerky movements, my hands trembling. "If people can't accept me, that's their problem."

Tears stung my eyes as I grabbed my sunglasses off the table, turned, and stalked away. Where I was heading was anyone's guess.

∞∞∞∞

We sailed through the Straits of Messina along the coast of Italy, passing the tip of the boot. I stood on the top deck with dozens of other passengers as we cruised past Stromboli, an active volcano that jutted up out of the sea in the middle of nowhere, its crown shrouded in clouds. Tiny villages dotted the coastline and I wondered who in their right mind would build their lives on the edge of a precipice that was almost guaranteed to be wiped out in a boiling river of lava someday. Obviously people with no fear of consequences—people willing to take a chance on an unknown future.

Neither Maddie nor Ethan came looking for me and I was glad. I needed some alone time to process what Maddie had said. Deep down, I knew she had my best interest at heart. She was only trying to warn me about going too far, too fast with Ethan, and hoping to send me a message about being more responsible than I had been. Although her methods were dirty, and she'd mostly succeeded in making me feel like crap, I couldn't argue with her advice. At least Ethan had made it known that he wanted more than a vacation hook up and the thought cheered me more than I wanted to admit. How we would ever be able to make a relationship work was another question entirely.

I wandered into the Crow's Nest where Tommy was setting up for his afternoon show and *Name that tune* game. We'd had several conversations since I'd helped myself to his guitar. He looked up and grinned when he saw me. "Hey, Lexi. I haven't seen you around much. How's the song writing business going?"

Glad to shift my focus to something else, I settled onto the edge of the piano bench beside him as he slid over to make room. "I've got a couple songs in the works," I admitted. It seemed my music was the one place I could truly be me.

"I figured as much. Why don't you sing something for me?"

My insides squirmed. "I don't know. I don't like singing in front of people."

"Pretend you're all alone singing in the shower." He nudged me with an elbow and grinned.

"You really want to hear it?" My heart pounded and my palms felt sweaty at the thought of singing and playing in front of even an audience of one.

"Sure. C'mon. It's just you and me here. Show me what you've got."

I tugged my small music journal out of my back pocket and opened to a song I'd been working on. I wrote a few notes on the page, grabbed the guitar off the stand, and strummed the chords, my fingers itching to play again. Tommy caught the tune and jumped in on the Baby Grand, bringing the music to life in a way that sent a thrill through my veins. The added volume and perfect harmony gave the tune a richer quality and the words floated above the notes as I sang them out, low and strong. When I came to the end minutes later, Tommy let a toothy grin spread across his face.

"I like it! What do you call it?"

My lips curved upward slightly. "As of right now, it's called, *Ethan's Song.*"

Chapter 25

The next morning we arrived in the picturesque port of Dubrovnik, Croatia. When I stepped out onto the balcony I was met with a sweet little fishing village speckled with docks and boats. My mind could barely grasp the beauty of the breathtaking view, terracotta rooftops climbing the rugged hillside like step stones. I readied myself in record time and was at the tender waiting with Maddie when Ethan joined us, his chestnut hair perfectly in place and his deep green eyes full of sparkle. When our gazes met, my insides did a quick flip. As much as I needed my time alone the day before, I'd missed him at dinner and wondered if he was rethinking the whole 'dating' scenario, having had enough of the Hartman women.

"It seems you've fully recovered from your *food poisoning*," Maddie said, eyeing Ethan with amusement.

"I'm much better today, thanks," Ethan replied sheepishly. "I've been looking forward to seeing the Old Town area of Dubrovnik. I did a report not long ago on the war for independence back in the nineties. The city was devastated when over two thousand bombs were dropped by the Serbs in their effort to maintain control of the coast. I've heard the Croatian people have done a fantastic restoration job."

Impressed with Ethan's knowledge and our shared passion for architecture, I couldn't wait to visit Old Town myself. A short boat ride to shore and a quick bus trip along a coastal roadway brought us to Pile gate, the main entrance to the city. A stone wall, eight feet high and twenty feet thick surrounded Dubrovnik and an impressive set of turrets stood on each corner. I imagined medieval guards manning the walls, armed with bows and arrows to protect the villagers from land invaders. Several smaller towers lined the sea side, defending the shore from seafaring marauders, and the massive wall of mountains behind us guarded the inland approach from foreign invasion and harsh weather.

As we entered through the gates, it was as if we'd stepped into a magical realm where old and new collided to create the perfect balance of antiquity and technology. Amid the ancient walls, gothic style buildings, and stone monuments, an internet café was nestled nearby, overlooking the central Onofrios Fountain that had supplied water to the village since the fifteenth century. The sixteen-sided fountain had carved heads that spouted arcing cascades of water from their mouths as if spitting at the tourists passing by. People lined up to fill their containers with fresh spring water. Modernly dressed, many of the locals blended with the tourists from all over the world, the wide promenade a mecca for artists, craftsman, and writers.

Following our tour guide, Dinka, a young Croatian woman with a square jaw and expressive eyes that matched her golden hair, we toured St. Blaise Church. Located opposite the Town Hall, the 1700's replica of the original church was a stunning example of the baroque architecture I'd seen in the books I'd found in the ship's library. The light shining through the upper windows showcased its dramatic intensity and ornate moldings.

Dinka shared her rich history and that of the church's namesake, who according to legend, had saved Dubrovnik from Venetian attack in the tenth century. Stories of King Richard the Lion Heart having sought refuge during a deadly storm when he returned from the crusades in 1192, sent chills through me, despite the heat of midmorning sun crashing down on us. It was as if we walked with ghosts through the city, exploring Sponza Palace, Dubrovnik's oldest building, which dated back to 1520. I couldn't help admiring the beautifully crafted newer buildings, efforts to keep true to the original styles, obvious.

My head spun with the details of wars, historical facts and the million and one sights I wanted to commit to memory. The whole time, Ethan stayed beside me, whispering interesting side notes into my ear and keeping me focused on the best part of the experience—seeing it all with him. I took dozens of pictures, enthralled with the bright colors, festive mood, and the amazing culture that hit me at every turn. Ethan had hooked me on taking pictures of doors—each one unique and inviting me to imagine what secrets lay beyond. We strolled through the open-air market, a sea of red and white umbrellas offering protection from the sun. Maddie purchased several items, including a Dalmatian lace table runner and a jar of candied figs, which she loudly and embarrassingly pointed out might help with her "irregularity."

An hour later we were leaving the city and headed for the gondola that would take us to the mountaintop lookout above. Ethan continued sharing additional details about the history and economic evolution of the country. I was happy to hear the people had rebuilt and recovered after surviving war with the Serbs and earning their independence. Thanks to an active tourist trade and a healthy democratic leadership, the city—and the country in general—were prospering, a rare occurrence in the current European climate, I was informed by Maddie.

After a slow ascent to the top of the mountain, we stepped out of the gondola onto a massive cement platform and walked through a building, coming out onto a hillside with a gigantic cross standing guard over the walled village below. As Maddie slipped away to visit the sacred monument, Ethan and I went to the lookout point.

Small villas peeked through trees on the sharp mountain descent and the walls of Old Town below appeared as a miniature walkway around the outskirts of the fortified stronghold. The limestone streets and buildings gave the whole city a pale, uniform appearance, which stood out in contrast to the cobalt blue of the sea stretching away from the coastline.

Ethan took my hand and settled me onto a bench. "Beautiful."

"You can say that again." I inhaled deeply, closing my eyes and letting the fresh mountain air fill my lungs fuller than they'd felt in a long time. Warmth from the sun beat down on my shoulders, and I sensed Ethan's eyes on me.

"The view is nice too," he said with a shy grin as I turned to face him.

Heat blossomed across my skin. Since we were momentarily alone, I took the opportunity to bring up yesterday's conversation with Maddie. "Did you mean what you said when you told Maddie you wanted to…date me when we get back home?"

His lips curved into a smile. "I don't usually say things I don't mean."

"So how do you see this working?" I asked, my stomach flopping when his dimples deepened and his eyes bore holes through mine.

"We'll be about a three hour ride away from each other. During the week we can call and text, and maybe on the weekends, I can come visit you. Or you could come see me. You'll be getting your license soon, right?"

I didn't want to cement my loser status with Ethan by showing my doubt, so I simply shrugged and shifted the conversation. "I could always take the train into New York and we could meet there."

He nodded, his smile faltering slightly. "It's only for a year or so. It'll give us a chance to get to know each other better."

Warmth spread through my chest at the thought. I leaned my head onto his shoulder and looked out over the sparkling waters far below. A warm breeze blowing up the mountainside brought the smell of the sea. "I'm not looking forward to going back…home, I mean." My voice trailed off on the wind. "As worried as I am about my mom, the thought of having to face my life there gives me hives."

Ethan chuckled. "That bad, huh? Have you heard from her?"

I had explained my mother's fragile mental state and Ethan was more than understanding. I was certain he would wonder if the apple hadn't fallen far from the tree and that I might be infected with mental instability by association, but he'd been cool about the whole thing and seemed concerned only for how it affected me.

"Nope. Maddie said Mom would call when the doctor said it was okay. As hard as things have been between us lately, I have to admit I miss her. I need to know she's all right." I raised my head, and Ethan wrapped a strong arm around my shoulder as he studied my expression.

"She'll be okay. She just needs some time. I bet she misses you, too."

His warm smile infused me with a rush of contentment and a sense that whatever he said must be right. I wanted more than anything to believe him, to trust in someone else's judgment of the situation—my own being totally impacted by my guilt.

"I'm not sure my going home is going to be all that much help to her. I seem to be making things worse."

"Maybe if you try not breaking *every* rule," he said, releasing me and taking my hand again, a small smirk pulling his lips.

I punched him in the arm. "Not you, too?"

He rubbed his arm, a mock look of pain on his face. "No judgment here." His free hand came up in a gesture of surrender. "I'm only trying to help. If you want things to be better at home, you might need to think about making a few changes. That's all I'm saying."

"Like finding new friends, focusing on school, and being more responsible?" I mimicked Mitch's deep throated voice, raising another chuckle from Ethan.

"Something like that."

"Everyone is pressuring me to be someone I'm not. I'll never be Valedictorian or a cheerleader. I'm not smart like…Amanda was," I said, my voice growing soft. The afternoon sun had passed its peak and dipped toward the sea, its reflection arcing across the water and setting the surface on fire.

"I don't think anyone wants you to be like your sister. Obviously, she wasn't so perfect, right?"

"Maybe so," I conceded for the first time. Ethan rubbed my knuckles in slow strokes with his thumb, making my brain feel fuzzy and light.

"As weird as it sounds, I think parents mostly want us to be the best version of ourselves we can be." He laughed lightly. "I've heard it's their job to turn us into useful members of society and make sure we don't turn out to be serial killers. It might reflect badly on them."

"You mean my juvenile delinquent status is a reflection of my parents' failure? We can't have *that* now, can we?" I lifted my head, giving him an amused grin.

Ethan pressed his lips to the back of my hand, sending another flutter to my heart. When he looked up, his eyes, deep green as the sea, shone bright in the sunlight. "If it were up to me, I would say don't change a thing. But I think life has a lot less drama if you don't try to swim against the tide all the time."

"Why do you even like me," I asked, my voice dropping to just above a whisper.

"I don't know." Seeing my eyes grow wide, he rushed to continue. "It's not just one thing…you're smarter, prettier, and way more talented than you think. I could see it the first time we met…well…maybe the second time," he grinned. You try to hide behind that edgy front you put on, but I see past it. Underneath all that unpredictability and fiery emotion, there's someone who wants to do the right thing and just be happy."

I drew a deep breath and sighed it out, wondering if maybe he really did know me better than I knew myself. Pushing aside the fear of disappointing him, I focused instead on the warm rush of emotion that filled my chest, knowing that he believed in me with such certainty.

One thing was clearer than ever. If I wanted a future that included Ethan I would apparently have to work for it—literally. Finding a job that would pay me enough to save what I needed to get a car, and taking my driving test again was first on my agenda when I returned home. Hopefully, my brush with the law and completing the mandatory drug classes I had to endure for twelve weeks wouldn't derail my plan. Then again, finding someone to hire me under the circumstances wouldn't be an easy task. I definitely had my work cut out for me. Another long sigh escaped me.

Ethan's fingers snuggled tightly between mine and the heat of his body leaning against my shoulder seeped into my bones—as if we were melting into one. A new sensation of connection eased the ache in my heart and I had a moment to consider—whatever it took, the chance at a future with Ethan was totally worth it.

Chapter 26

The next few days were a whirlwind of activity and adventure as we explored the Greek Islands. Our first stop was Corfu, also called Kerkira, Greece. Our guide was Mika, a pretty young woman with long black hair and dark eyes, five months pregnant and radiant. She took us to a monastery with breathtaking views of the Ionian Sea.

Grapevines hanging on trellises created shade as we followed the granite pathways—polished by age—down to the lower level monk's quarters. Here, men gave their lives for the sole purpose of transcribing ancient texts, a pursuit I found fascinating and horrifying all at once. The thought of spending an entire lifetime translating and writing someone else's story in perfect brush strokes with no erasers seemed like torture, but I was completely in awe of their dedication and skill. The walkways were lined with gardens of basil—known as the royal herb, according to Mika—and jasmine— the combination fragrant and slightly medicinal. The smell of the ancient parchment took over once we entered the museum filled with centuries-old books. The atmosphere gave the sense we'd been transported back in time.

Later, as we traveled by bus through the historic town, Venetian style buildings marked the Italian influence of year's past, with airy balconies, wrought iron railings, and especially ornate window grilles. We stopped to visit the city square where the wide granite streets, smoothed from hundreds of years of wear, provided an open air feel to the village, and narrow limestone side streets were lined with boutiques and restaurants. Maddie insisted we stop in and spread some more cash to help the local economy.

Lunch of Spanakopita, hummus, and falafel clarified that we were indeed in Greece and made me commit to finding authentic Greek restaurants back in Connecticut. Nutty, earthy herbs, and tangy sauces infused the food. As I vowed to introduce Mom and Mitch to my newfound taste for Greek cuisine, I thought of all I'd left behind. The ache of homesickness sank a little deeper.

I had anticipated missing my friends, but the sense of helplessness I felt when I thought of Mom struck me as foreign. I'd only been away for two weeks, but knowing she was in a hospital, all messed up about Amanda and thinking I was a lost cause, made my insides hurt. I had been so self-absorbed in my own grief—unable to face the depth of anyone else's pain—that I had missed how close to the edge she'd been. I'd screwed up big time, made things worse for her, and I had no idea how to fix it—or even if I could.

∞∞∞∞

The next day we landed at Katacolon, home of ancient Olympia and origin of the Olympic Games. Massive ruins melted one into another and the full day of walking, listening to our guide, and taking more pictures than we could possibly ever look at, took its toll on Maddie. She sat on a bench in the shade of an olive tree while Ethan and I ran the length of the Olympic field. Dust rose up around us, and I imagined the buzz of cicadas resembled the cheering crowd that once observed from the stone bleachers forming a stadium around us. Ethan gave in and finished a few feet behind me, the two of us breathless and laughing as we rejoined Maddie.

"I wish I still had your energy," she said, smiling. She fanned her face with her hat, her cheeks rosy. "We'd better get back to the bus."

Other tourists lingered and I saw Marcos, our guide for the day, still talking to our group not far off. Apparently we had plenty of time, but I didn't argue. With each passing day, I'd noticed Maddie grew more apprehensive about being separated from the tour guides and left behind, an insecurity which seemed out of character for the usually self-assured steam-roller of a woman I'd come to know and respect.

By the third day in the Greek Islands, Maddie decided to stay behind to rest up for the upcoming tour of Ephesus, which would require a long walk up the hill to the house of the apostle John, who supposedly kept Jesus' mother Mary protected from persecution in the final years of her life—a 'must see' according to Maddie's plan for my education in European history.

Maddie encouraged Ethan and me to join the tour of the island of Thira, called Santorini, on our own. Glad to be free of my grandmother's eagle eye of surveillance, and her disapproving tone every time Ethan and I got too close, a new lightness rested on my heart.

Ethan took my hand as we exited the tour bus in the little village of Oia. Pronounced *EE ya*, according to Nikko, our guide for the day. With eyes blue-green like the sea, light hair against olive skin, and muscles pressing against a tight white button-down shirt, Nikko drew everyone's attention. Through a thick accent and a wide grin, he addressed the group. "Here, you are free for the day. You may wander the streets of Oia and take in the shops and museum. If you would like to see our lovely beaches and harbor, you may take the cable car, ride a donkey, or walk the three hundred steps down to the beach. Enjoy yourself in one of our many outdoor cafés."

He dismissed the group with an agreed upon time to meet later in the day and then there we were—Ethan and I alone and on our own for an entire day on a beautiful Greek Island. It seemed surreal...and romantic. I squeezed Ethan's hand and walked by his side through the idyllic little town, feeling more excited than I had in far too long.

We made our way up the main street past jewelry shops, art galleries, and clothing boutiques, and soon found ourselves in a small connecting alleyway with smooth white steps leading between the buildings. Ethan led the way.

"C'mon. You've got to check out this view." He tugged me along, smiling and laughing at my resistance.

"Where are you taking me?" I giggled.

"You're going to love it. Trust me."

We came out of the maze of square white buildings, and my breath caught in my throat. It was like every picture I'd ever seen of Greece. The cerulean blue sea stretched out before us, a small group of islands not far off. Water taxis ferried passengers in between. Blue domes on box shaped foundations marked the Cycladic architecture the region was known for. I'd read up on it in the magazine I'd snagged from the plane I'd first arrived on—and read again a dozen times on the long flight to Europe—which now seemed a lifetime ago.

"This is fantastic!" I drew in a deep breath as the warm breeze off the sea tossed my hair around my face. "I've never seen anything so pretty."

"Awesome, isn't it?" said Ethan, his voice soft.

I turned to see him staring at me and my heart jumped as heat rose to my cheeks under the hot sun and Ethan's equally fiery gaze. His fingers wove between mine and he pulled me closer.

"I can't imagine sharing this with anyone else," I admitted. Our noses touched as we slipped into an easy embrace. Before I could say more, Ethan dipped and captured my parted lips. I melted into the kiss—no hesitation, and no thought for anyone seeing us. We probably looked like any other young couple, caught up in the magic of the place, unable to resist falling in love.

The word filled me. It exploded as if on a loudspeaker in my head, drowning out any voice of reason that said it wasn't possible to feel so helplessly connected to someone in such a short amount of time. My heart beat against my ribs, reaching out to match Ethan's, whose own heart was pounding at a furious rate against my palm.

I slowly broke away, and the words slipped out before I could take them back. "I think I'm falling in love with you," I whispered loud enough to be heard above the wind and sea.

Ethan's eyes widened, his dark lashes standing at attention. He opened his mouth as if to respond, but nothing came out. He looked as if he was drowning, his mouth opening and closing and no air getting in or out. Pulse pounding in my ears, I had two choices. Die in the silence between us, or rescue us both.

I pulled him into a kiss, parted his lips with my tongue, and dove in as if attempting to give him a life-saving breath or cut off any further messages to his brain. As for me…it was too late. I was already lost, and there was no turning back.

Chapter 27

After a heart-pounding and much too short make-out session and a few last minutes enjoying the view, no more was said about my declaration or Ethan's glaring silence. Doubt crept into my head, but I refused to pout or let it ruin my day. I'd said what I said, and now it was out there. What Ethan did next was up to him.

The hike down to the beach was long and crowded, with no chance for a heavy conversation—much to my relief. Traveling down a mountain on a smelly donkey hadn't sounded at all entertaining to me, but the line for the cable car stretched around the corner. Far too much time to try to make small talk. Besides, after watching the cable car plummet down the shear stone cliff, swaying in the brisk wind all the way, I decided it looked like a ride which had disaster written all over it. By the time we reached the bottom of the stairs and the blackened beach, we'd moved on to safer topics.

"Your knowledge of architecture is kind of impressive. Is it something you've studied in school?" Ethan shouldered up next to me on the boardwalk that connected the beaches and the small bars, cafés and boutiques. Beside us ran a long stretch of dark sandy beach, created by the volcanic ash that settled on the island at its formation. We'd fallen into a crowded party central, tribes of teens and college students playing Frisbee on the beach while topless sunbathers slathered on oil. I diverted my gaze and Ethan followed suit, his ears a bright shade of pink. A group at a nearby table clinked glasses of wine and called out the Greek cheer, OPA! Followed by drinking and raucous laughter.

I settled into a chair at the small bistro, ravenous for lunch. "They don't have any design classes at the high school, but I like to read architecture books and magazines," I continued, picking up the conversation. My insides shifted when Ethan reached across the table and took my hand, his eyes crinkling at the edges.

"Well, you're obviously interested. Have you thought about studying architecture after high school?"

I slipped my hand out from between his. "What's with everyone trying to plan my future for me?"

His brows dipped together in a frown. "I was only asking if you'd thought about it, that's all."

The hurt in his eyes stopped my next snide remark. My heart sank. Taking out my frustration on Ethan wasn't the answer to evading the pressure I was under to make some kind of decision about my future.

"Sorry." I slipped my hand back beneath his. "It's just that everyone seems to think they know what's best for me. Mom thinks I should go to community college, and Mitch says I'll be lucky to graduate high school. Maddie already put in her two cents and wants me to do a year of studies abroad. Honestly, I'm not sure I want to be so far from home while my mom is so…messed up. Although she'd probably be better off without me," I added in a whisper, my throat tightening around the words.

"You know that isn't true," Ethan argued, giving my fingers a gentle squeeze. "She probably needs you now more than ever. But you have to do what's right for you."

"I wish I knew what that was," I sighed. "Maybe a year away from home is a good idea," I said, eyeing a glass of ice water being set on the table by a stunningly cute waiter. He took our order, focusing a perfect set of white teeth my way.

"I think being on your own in Europe is a bad idea," Ethan said as he glared at the waiter, who nodded and turned away. Then he cleared his throat and his lips curved up slightly. "I mean…it would definitely kill our idea to see each other on the weekends." He turned his glass around in his free hand, causing the condensation to drip down the outside. "Look, Lexi. I don't ever want to be the kind of friend who doesn't support your decisions, or the guy who tries to tell his girlfriend what to do." Pink splotches rose up his neck as he focused on the ring of water seeping into his napkin. "You need to be your own person. I only want to see you happy…and it doesn't seem like you are."

Tears pinched behind my eyes. "I think I have a few reasons to be miserable, don't you?" I pulled my hand away, and Ethan sat back, tugging at the edge of the checkered tablecloth.

"Believe me, I get it. But I can see you're dying to break free of whatever is holding you back." He leaned in again, capturing my gaze. "Sometimes people can get stuck in their grief. They call it survival guilt."

"Oh really? Have you decided that your medical specialty is going to be psychiatry now?" I couldn't help the sarcasm that slipped out. I hated that Ethan was one more person who thought he knew me better than I knew myself.

He dared to take my fingers once more and studied our hands intently. "When my mom was dying, she made me promise to try to be happy and to have a good life. It took some time, but knowing that's what she wanted for me helped me move on after she was gone. It's what keeps me trying to be my best—to live life—in a way that would make her proud." His voice sounded rough, as if he was breathing through gravel. "Don't you want to have the best life you can for your sister's sake? I'm sure it's what she would want for you, right?"

A lump formed and I blinked away tears. "I guess I hadn't thought about it that way before." I sipped my water, relieved when the young waiter came back with my Greek salad and slid a Mediterranean wrap in front of Ethan. I used the moment to take a breath and change the subject before the conversation went any further. I wasn't about to start crying, and admitting he had a point didn't seem much better of an option.

"If you're so smart, how is it a guy who gets into medical school at Columbia on scholarship is hanging out with a messed up stoner like me?"

Ethan stopped chewing and swallowed. His gaze met mine, his expression solemn. "I don't think of you like that. And you shouldn't either. Smoking pot is what you do. It isn't who you are. You have a choice about who you're going to be, you know."

I laughed, sipping the sweet tea the waiter had brought. "Mitch and my mom would beg to differ. They act as if I'm an out of control drug addict or something."

"They don't know you like I do. You're a strong person, Lexi. You've just been going through a rough time. You'll get past this." He averted his gaze and focused on his food again.

"You've only known me for like two weeks," I countered, both amused and grateful as I dug into my salad. "How can you be so sure?"

"I have a sense about people." His eyes lit with warmth. "Besides, it feels like it's been a lot longer than two weeks."

"I was thinking the same thing." A smile tugged at the corner of my mouth as I wiped salad dressing off with a napkin.

We were still in the middle of our meal when the waiter offered to take our picture. Ethan came around to my side of the table and wrapped an arm around my shoulders, the two of us cheek to cheek and smiling, a memory of our time together that I would likely have plastered as wallpaper on every electronic device I owned. My chest filled with sadness again. In only a few days, Ethan and I would have to say good-bye—maybe for weeks or even months—maybe forever if we couldn't make a go of a long-distance relationship.

The waiter handed me my phone and I noticed the message count. There were two from D.D.—probably crying about her latest breakup with Kevin—and a text from Sami about an upcoming gig she wanted me to play in. I sighed. Still nothing from Mom or Mitch. I tucked my phone away, unwilling to worry any more about why my mother wasn't calling. I needed to stop thinking about all the things in my life I couldn't fix and start thinking about what I could.

"Is everything okay?" Ethan asked when he noticed me watching him. He ate the remainder of his wrap and wiped his mouth as he finished chewing.

"Funny how time can either fly by or seem like it drags."

"No word from home, huh?"

I shrugged as if it didn't matter. "It's not like it's really been that long. I'm sure my mom will call me when she can."

Apparently unconvinced, Ethan lamely attempted to distract me with a philosophical discussion. "Time is irrelevant if you believe in eternity," he said as if it were fact.

"That's deep."

"A while after my mom died—when we were both really missing her—my dad said that time was relative to which side of heaven's gate you were standing on. Meaning," he said, as I stared at him blankly, "this life is just a drop in the bucket of time." I must have looked clueless to him since he frowned and leaned toward me.

As if maybe I wasn't hearing him. "Haven't you ever thought about fate, destiny—eternity?"

"Only when I'm stoned." I stuffed another olive in my mouth, grinning.

He tossed his napkin on the table and kicked back, shaking his head as he crossed his arms. "You're impossible. I'm serious here."

"I get what you're saying. I do. But personally, I think we're all part of some big video game. Better yet, one of those old pin-ball machine games. God puts in his quarter, shoots us out of a gate, and off we go, bouncing chaotically as we crash from one minute to the next until one wrong move and…bam—sucked into some abyss, all for His amusement." I chuckled, tearing off a piece of bread and dipping it into the dressing at the bottom of my bowl.

"That would mean we're only here for an undetermined amount of time and then we're done…or we get shot out of the gate again for another round.

"That would explain re-incarnation." I laughed.

"For argument's sake," Ethan countered, smiling, "if we only get one chance to make a difference, then shouldn't we try to do something amazing with our lives?"

"Like being a doctor?" I raised a brow in challenge.

He nodded, his expression turning serious. "Do you want to know my worst fear about becoming a doctor?" Ethan leaned forward again, his voice low and his hands folded around the empty plate in front of him.

"Tell me." I gave him my full attention, genuinely curious about why someone like him—who seemed to have life all figured out—would be afraid of anything.

"I don't think I'd be able to handle losing a patient. If someone died on my watch—or worse—if I made a mistake, I couldn't live with myself."

I reached across the table and laced my fingers through his, wanting the connection more than ever.

"It's a lot of responsibility. That's for sure. But nobody is perfect, Ethan. I think you need to focus on all the people you would help, and lives you would save. I know you would make a fantastic doctor." I smiled across at him, hopeful he'd see my sincerity. "If it's what you want to do, don't let fear stop you."

After a silent moment, his eyes came up to meet mine, sharp and intense. "I could say the same to you."

My pulse quickened and I met his gaze. "What do you mean?"

"It seems like you're afraid of a lot of things. Playing your music in front of people, facing your mom…forgetting your sister if you decide to move on with your life. You need to get over it, Lex. Or maybe you think you owe it to her to be miserable forever."

My mouth opened but no words came out. A lump froze in my throat and tears instantly burned behind my eyes.

"You don't have to answer." Seeing the hurt, Ethan's tone softened. "I'm not trying to be mean, but we both know it's true. I felt that way for a long time after my mom died. I felt really lost for a while. I was afraid it would be an insult to her memory for me to be happy—for me to go on living a real life without her. Eventually, I understood it was what she would have wanted and that I could never forget her. She'll always be a part of me. Just as Amanda will always be a part of you. You need to stop using your sister as a reason for standing still in life. She wouldn't want you blaming yourself, and she sure as hell wouldn't want you to give up on your future."

Tears cascaded over and ran hot down my cheeks, dripping onto my arm. I sniffled in a breath. "I know you're right...but...I can't stop thinking about her. It's like she's living inside of me—haunting me. Every time I try to move on, she's right there, pulling me back and reminding me that I...owe her."

"Owe her what?" Ethan asked, his indignant tone making me grit my teeth. "She was obviously troubled. She drank herself to death. How is that your fault?"

"Stop it." I tugged my hand away from his and swiped at the tears on my cheeks, drawing attention from the next table.

Ethan laid money on top of the bill as soon as the waiter brought it, and stood. "Let's walk."

I didn't argue, glad to be out of the bistro and out of the uncomfortable conversation. But Ethan wouldn't let it rest. After a brief discussion about not taking the three hundred steps back to the top of the town in the afternoon heat, I conceded to taking the gondola, which would carry us up to Oia's town square where we would meet the bus. Ethan wrapped an arm around my shoulder.

"I'm sorry. I didn't mean to upset you. But I don't understand why you feel so responsible for Amanda's death. It was an accident. A stupid one, but an accident, right?"

"I wish I had told someone sooner about her drinking. I didn't think it was a big deal. It wasn't like she was doing crack."

"Like smoking pot is no big deal as long as you're not drinking or doing hard drugs?" He let me go when I pulled away, turning on him as we stood in the long line at the bottom of the mountain, waiting to take the swaying cable car to the top.

"I thought you understood."

"I do...but drugs are drugs, and obviously it's causing problems in your life. Maybe it's time to quit."

"Now you sound like Mitch," I snapped.

"I'm not judging you—"

"The hell you're not. Just because you're Mr. Perfect, it doesn't give you the right…whatever." If I continued my thought, it was likely I would say something I'd regret—something I couldn't take back. I turned away, my face hot. "So much for you knowing the real me," I grumbled. I craned my neck to look up the giant hillside, etched with what looked like a thousand stone steps beside the cables drawing a line straight up the mountain. "You can stay here. I'll take the stairs."

Chapter 28

I awoke the next day to the subtle movement of the ship plowing through the open sea. Maddie thought I was imagining it. "You can't feel the movement of a ship this big. That's ridiculous." She yanked open the curtains and peered outside. "Oh…well…we are pretty far from the coast. We'll be in Turkey tomorrow. I've never been. It was one of the destinations Henry and I never made it to. We always talked about seeing the house of the Virgin Mary outside of Ephesus. That was Henry's wish anyway. He turned quite religious in his older years…" her voice faded as I tuned out yet another long drawn out story about her life with Grandpa Henry.

I dragged the pillow over my face, determined to sleep in. I'd stayed late at the piano bar with Maddie, listening to old American standards and Maddie's tales of her days on Broadway, most of which she'd already told me. I tried to enjoy myself, but thoughts of my conversation with Ethan and how our perfect day had ended on such a crappy note kept me distracted and edgy.

I wanted to stay mad. And I wanted him to be wrong. But by the time I'd reached the top of the long stairway and arrived back at the bus, my anger had fizzled and I could see where he was coming from. He was working hard to make a life and a future for himself. Whereas I was…pretty much going nowhere. When I got on the bus, Ethan had already taken a seat next to old Mr. Feinstein, the two discussing the merits of the infield fly rule in baseball for way longer than was necessary. He ignored me all the way back to the ship, and I did nothing to remedy the situation, sulking against the bus window and sitting as far away as possible once we were on the tender.

It seemed everyone but me was in agreement that I was heading down a wrong path and Ethan was the last person I wanted lecturing me. It wasn't like I was an addict. Most of my friends smoked pot. Hell, most everyone I knew did. It was hard to imagine weed not being a part of my every day high school experience. Who would I hang out with? The thought of having to give up my friendships or being on the outside of the small crew I considered family made the emptiness I already felt look like another deep pit from which I wanted to steer clear.

Ethan was nowhere to be found after we returned to the ship and left Greece behind. Again, I'd been a jerk to him when I knew he was only trying to help. I could take the judgment from Mitch—and even Mom and Maddie. But from Ethan, the betrayal stung. Just when I thought someone finally understood me, it was obvious I was on my own. I pulled the pillow tighter over my head.

"Why don't you get up and come to sunrise Tai Chi with me?" Maddie encouraged, pinching my toes that stuck out from under the covers at the foot of the bed.

"You're kidding, right?" I peeked an eye out from behind the pillow and checked the clock, 7:30 a.m. "I'm all set, thanks." I grumbled and rolled over, my back to her and the deadly rays of dawn. "I'll see you at lunch." The words came out in a mumble from beneath the pillow.

Maddie sighed. "Well don't sleep this beautiful day away." Her cheerful tone grated.

"Yes, maaaam," I yawned, tugging the covers up to my ears and closing my eyes again. A moment later the door clicked softly and I was alone, drifting on a sea of imagination, Ethan at center stage.

A single bright spotlight illuminates a small square stage. Ethan glides out from the shadows. As he steps into the light, his deep green eyes glisten with warmth, hitting me like a crashing wave. Dressed like a spy in a black tux, he moves with grace and ease toward me. I see myself from above as if watching a movie and I hardly recognize me. I'm wearing a rose colored dress that hugs every line and curve like a satiny second skin, and my shoulders are bare. My hair is styled short and wild and dark eyeliner accentuates smoky lashes. Deep red lipstick shimmers on the mouth of the girl in the dream. With shoes that perfectly match my dress and appear horribly uncomfortable, I'm apprehensive. I know I'm dreaming and that this isn't really me, but Ethan closes the distance, takes me in his arms, and spins me around to the music, and I never want to wake up. I'm suddenly floating. And I'm laughing, a burst of joy bubbling to the surface so powerful it makes me dizzy.

Then a piano is playing and we're dancing. Slow circles around and around, our bodies molded to one another, touching in all the right places and setting my skin on fire. Our gazes connect. My heart races as I'm falling into his eyes, my every cell wanting to dive deeper. Our lips draw close and press together, a soft crushing of moist skin on skin as if we can share all that's inside of us in this one simple act of kissing. Warmth envelops me, wrapping around me like a fleecy blanket. I'm happy...safe...in love, and for the first time in my life, completely unafraid.

Ethan's hands press into the curve of my back and he pulls me to him as his kiss becomes more urgent. I think I'll drown...but

I don't care. I don't want to stop him. It all feels so good...so right. Me and Ethan together. As he brushes my cheek with the tips of his fingers and spreads kisses along my jaw, I melt into him. His lips follow a trail along my neck to my ear. The lobe disappears between his teeth and a jolt of electricity roars from my ear to my toes, warm fuzzy sparks dispersing to every part in between. Sensations cascade through me in a torrent of mindless bliss, every cell ignited by pleasure. Heat grows low in my body and when Ethan slides a hand along my ribcage and brushes his thumb across another part of me that is taut and tingling, I shatter.

I bolted upright in bed, disoriented and half expecting to see Ethan beside me. I shook off the residual buzz humming along my nerves. My hands flew to my face as a wave of embarrassment washed over me. Crashing back onto my pillow, I blew out a sigh, waiting for the heat that flooded my body to subside.

I lay still for a long time, staring at the ceiling and contemplating the dream until my heart rate slowed. Since reliving the steamy encounter would produce no positive result toward starting my day, and I wasn't at all ready to face Ethan or Maddie, I decided to shower, dress, and go to breakfast alone. I needed some time to think about how to make up to Ethan for snapping his head off and see if we couldn't come to some kind of agreement about him not siding with all the pushy adults in my life. It wasn't like I hadn't thought about quitting smoking pot. It was just that I needed to do it on my own terms. I'd always thought it was something I'd grow out of eventually. A habit that would stop making sense once...I was in college...or maybe afterward.

Thoughts of my sister disrupted whatever bliss remained from my dream state. Amanda hadn't stopped at pot. She was willing to try anything once she started drinking, a fact I'd learned when I went to visit her at school one weekend and saw firsthand how out of control she was. Even then, the sister code prevented me from ratting her out to Mom. I dragged my hands through my hair, grabbing on tight enough to feel the sting of tears. My head pounded as the morning sun assaulted me with light. Irritation setting in, I took a deep breath and forced it back out.

Maybe I'd quit smoking weed when it didn't hurt so much to think about Amanda. Numbing the pain sounded like a decent plan…if only effective in the short term. I didn't want to forget her. I only wanted to erase the feelings of guilt and loss that came with every memory of her. Was Ethan right about me using her as an excuse to be afraid of life?

I sighed again and rolled out of bed, knowing there was no easy answer and determined to start my day and make the best of it, whatever lay ahead. A dopey grin curved my lips as I stepped into the hot shower, flashes of my dream with Ethan replaying in my head—new thoughts and feelings I had no desire to erase.

∞∞∞∞

I wandered the ship after a hearty breakfast, anxious to rid my head of the chaotic thoughts crashing in from all sides. I found myself once again at the Crow's Nest. Maybe Tommy would let me practice with his guitar if no one was around. And maybe by lunchtime, I'd feel a little more like a human being and a little less like a savage. My jaw clenched as I considered how badly I'd messed things up with Ethan—again. As much as I wanted to blame him for taking the side of the enemy, I couldn't say he was totally wrong. Not as supportive as I thought he should be, but not wrong either. But where did it leave us? Was my being a stoner a deal breaker for him? My heart plummeted into an abyss when I realized for the first time that more than not wanting to quit, I wasn't sure I could—no matter who wanted me to and how many times I'd told myself I could quit anytime.

I pushed through the smoky glass doors of the lounge and saw Tommy in deep discussion with a gray haired man with a sharp nose and cool eyes, his white suit pressed and starched to match his expression. I waited until the two parted and Tommy was left standing beside his piano, his face pale.

"What's up?" I asked, almost afraid to hear the answer.

Tommy croaked out, "I've got laryngitis." He lowered onto the piano bench. "I was just explaining to my boss, Mr. Owens, I'd be able to play tonight, but I can't sing."

"You look like you should be in bed."

Glassy, fatigued brown eyes stared back at me. "The show must go on," he said with a weak smile. Then his face lit up. "I have an idea."

I knew from his expression I wasn't going to like what was coming.

"You could sing for me. You know all my songs by now. I've seen you singing to them in the crowd."

"No way…I can't…I just can't," I said with finality before he could go on trying to persuade me. Sweat broke out on my neck.

"Sure you can, kid." Tommy rasped.

I winced in sympathy. "No. I can't." I folded my arms across my chest.

He patted the seat beside him. Reluctantly, I settled onto the bench. He lowered his voice to barely above a whisper. "I used to be like you. I thought people would laugh at me when I performed. Worse, I thought they would either hate my music or ignore me. Or…they might see inside the place where my deepest thoughts and feelings are held." He patted a hand over his heart and eyed me as if reading my mind and knowing he'd hit the nail on the head.

"I guess maybe I'm a little afraid of all of those things."

"Much worse has happened to me at one time or another. Don't make me tell you about the rotten tomatoes." His voice cracked and he coughed as he laughed. "But you know what?" He winked as I gave him a sideways glance. "It doesn't matter what anyone thinks. I play because I love to play. Music comes from the heart and soul of a person and it's meant to be shared. It's how some of us connect to the world. Think about how empty life would be if no one sang or played music because they were afraid of being seen." He faced me and laid a hand on my shoulder. "You have real talent, Lexi. You sing like a songbird." His brilliantly white grin widened.

My cheeks warmed and I considered his argument for a minute. "So how did you get over it?"

He rubbed a hand along his dark, well-groomed beard. "If I look out at the crowd and see one person smiling and enjoying themselves, that's the person I'm playing for."

Still unconvinced, I shook my head and let out a long sigh.

In fatherly fashion, he wrapped an arm around my shoulder. "Do one song. C'mon, it won't kill you. I promise."

"It could. I'll probably die from embarrassment when the crowd hisses and boos." My stomach turned sour even as my palms grew clammy.

"You would be a first." He laughed and then rubbed his throat, a pained expression taking over. "Now don't make me argue with you about this. Meet me here at four and we can practice a few songs before the show tonight."

I took a deep breath and nodded, still terrified, but willing to give it a shot. If I bombed on my first song, I'd walk away, hide in my room for the next four days until the end of the cruise, and never have to see these people again. Thoughts of Ethan slammed into my mind. I had four nights and three days to make things right with him and decide if we had any kind of future together. Even the idea of a future seemed fragile. As if tomorrow might not come, and if it did, it could bring catastrophe. Maddie's words echoed in my ear. *Live in the moment, but create your future through the choices you make in those moments.*

I needed to find Ethan.

Chapter 29

While checking all of Ethan's usual hotspots, beginning with the dining hall, I came across the wall of photos that changed daily and had the latest pictures of passengers as they disembarked in port the morning before. I searched the wall until my gaze fell on a picture of Ethan and me at the start of our day in Santorini. His arm hung loosely around my neck, and I had mine tucked behind his waist, my head resting on his shoulder. The happy couple grinned back at me, and a shard of regret and longing pierced my heart.

Glimpses of happiness seemed to come at a price—always accompanied by a pound or two of guilt. I ran a finger over Ethan's lips in the picture, wishing he were here in front of me to kiss away the doubt and fear that flooded my mind. Thoughts of Amanda and my new found desire to let go of the past collided in a whirlwind of mixed emotion. Being with Ethan had the insanity-inducing effect of making me happier than I'd ever been, and yet terrified that if I let myself be happy, it would all be taken away.

I shook off the weight of my confusion, determined to face my demons. I headed to the dining hall, which I found wasn't open for lunch for another hour. My next stop was the sports bar, which housed only a few elderly men enjoying a hand of poker while their wives undoubtedly lounged by the pool or browsed the jewelry store on mid-deck. Finally I reached the Loft and there he was, stretched out on one of the stuffed chairs, his muscular legs bent so his arms could rest on his knees. His thumbs flicked over the joystick toggles with mad speed, and his eyes had the glazed-over look of a zombie.

I cleared my throat, drawing his attention. I heard an explosion on the screen as he turned his full attention to me.

"Hey," Ethan mumbled. His eyes lingered on me for a few seconds, and then drifted back to the mayhem of the game.

"I've been looking all over for you."

"I've been here." He didn't look up a second time. Instead, he proceeded to annihilate the aliens in front of him.

My face grew hot. "I probably need to apologize…again."

"Probably."

"You're not going to make this easy, are you?"

"Nope."

I released a frustrated sigh. "What did you expect yesterday when you came down on me like an overprotective parent? I don't need another one of those." I folded my arms across my front and tapped my restless foot. "Look, I'm sorry if I overreacted, but I…thought you were…different." I chewed the ragged edge of a cuticle.

Ethan focused on the game, a look of satisfaction flashing across his face as bombs flew and alien ships exploded at an alarming rate. Then he lowered the controller and our eyes met. "I'm not interested in telling you what to do, or even changing you. I like who you are." He climbed to his feet and faced me, his gaze locking onto mine. "I was only trying to help."

"I don't need that kind of help, Ethan. But I have to ask…is me smoking weed going to be a problem for you?" As much as I feared his answer, I needed to know.

Ethan stood close enough that I could smell the fresh scent of his shampoo, a blend of coconut and almond that somehow soothed my raw nerves and yet set them on fire. "We'll have to wait and see," he said finally. With no hint of lightening up he added, "I can tell you I don't really like it that you're doing it. If you keep going the way you are, it's bound to get you deeper into trouble. With Mitch being a cop and your mom struggling to hold it together, I would think the last thing you'd want to do is complicate things."

I turned away, the weight of his judgment stabbing like a sword through my chest. Anger bubbled up again. I spun to face him. "So you're saying that I'm a complication for my family? Because I can't be perfect like you and tow the parent line, I'm an inconsiderate jerk?"

"I didn't say that." Ethan stood his ground, his face full of sharp angles. "But it might be nice of you to consider someone else's feelings besides your own." His tone was as sharp as the cool look in his eyes.

"So now I'm selfish?" My jaw ached from clenching.

He didn't flinch.

I turned away again, this time with every intention of sparing him the tears about to follow. "I came to apologize, but now I think I'd better go."

Ethan grabbed my arm.

"Stop running away, Lexi." He spun me around to face him again.

"My name isn't even Lexi. I'm Ali! My stupid grandmother started calling me Lexi just so I'd grow up overnight and become this smart, brave girl who wants to live her life on the straight and narrow for a change. I can't be what you all want me to be…" By now tears were brimming over the edge and dripping down my cheeks. I wanted to pull away and run, but my feet wouldn't move and the warmth of his hand on my arm kept me glued in place. He stepped in closer, his breath warm on my face.

"Lexi or Ali. It doesn't matter." His gentle tone resonated through me. "You don't get it, do you? No one is trying to change who you are or make you feel bad about yourself. And no one is perfect." A small smile lifted one corner of his lips and his eyes softened. "Not even me." He let go of my arm and his hand came to my cheek, wiping away a tear. "I'm saying these things because I care about you, and I want you to be happy." He captured my chin as I tried to pull my gaze away. "I would bet your mom wants the same thing."

I swallowed the lump in my throat. "I hear what you're saying, Ethan. Maybe the problem is…that I'm…lost right now. I don't know what I want, where I'm going, or how I'm even going to make it through another day. But what I do know is that I need some time to figure it out…and I have to do it on my own." I wanted him to argue, kiss me, and tell me I didn't have to be alone, but I knew that wouldn't solve the problem.

Apparently…as usual…the problem was me.

Chapter 30

I met Maddie for the buffet lunch on the Lido deck and helped myself to a humongous portion of bread pudding, added a scoop of vanilla ice cream, and topped it off with whipped cream. No sense in spoiling dessert by having lunch first. No doubt I'd pay for my lack of restraint when my jeans wouldn't button upon my return home. My heart ached at the thought of being home. Wondering what was happening with Mom and imagining the worst was eating me up inside. I plunked into a chair across from Maddie and shoveled a spoonful of ice cream into my mouth.

"Is that what you're having for lunch?" She shook her head and sighed when I flashed her a venomous eye and took another big bite. "What's wrong now? Are you and Ethan fighting again? I swear, you teenagers live for drama. What happened?" She slipped her sunglasses down her nose and pinned me with a cool glare over the rims.

I savored the sweet, cinnamon covered, gooey pudding, and then swallowed, uncertain of how much to confide. Despite her quirkiness and her old-fashioned ideas, she'd proven to have some useful advice when it came to life and relationships. I wouldn't mention the fact that Ethan was on her and everyone else's side about my recreational drug use.

"I don't know," I started, leaning back in my chair and swirling my spoon in the melting ice cream, mixing the flavors. "We can't seem to agree about whether this relationship is going to happen or not. It's complicated, you know?"

"Relationships always are." She sipped her lemonade. "Maybe you need to stop trying so hard to make things happen. If it's meant to be, it will all work out. You and Ethan have your whole lives ahead of you. Try not to put so much pressure on yourself to figure it all out today. Have a little patience, Alexis. It will be worth it in the end." She grinned broadly and finished her drink, picking up a newspaper and sliding her glasses back in place.

I spooned another glob of soupy sweetness into my mouth and thought about what she'd said. It was clear that if I didn't decide to stop smoking weed, Ethan probably wouldn't be interested in being my boyfriend for long. But if I quit because he wanted me to, I'd resent him for taking away the one thing that seemed to be helping me deal with all the tragedy in my life. The Medusa Lady called it self-medicating. *Whatever.* I'd seen how badly the meds Mom was taking messed with her mind and her moods. Pot seemed like the far lesser of two evils in my book. Either way, the decision was mine to make. I dropped the spoon in my dish and faced Maddie with a long sigh.

"If you could do one thing over in life, what would it be?" I asked out of the blue.

Maddie lowered the paper and eyed me over her glasses once more. She took only a moment to consider her answer, and a nostalgic smile lit her face. "I would have quit show business sooner and stayed home to enjoy my family. I missed so much of your father's young life. I would have liked to have had more children as well, I think." Her expression clouded and she lifted the paper again. "But there are no do-overs, my dear. We each have to live with the choices we make. Too bad we can't all learn that lesson before we have to live with regrets."

I bit down on my tongue, causing my eyes to tear. I knew I'd brought it up, but if I had to hear one more comment about consequences, choices, and regrets, I would scream and jump overboard. Shark infested waters seemed infinitely more appealing than hearing about what a screw up I was. A puddle of melted ice cream with chunks of bread pudding sat in the bottom of my bowl. The rest settled into my stomach like a ball of raw dough.

∞∞∞∞

After my non-lunch and the serious talk with Maddie, I was glad to disappear into a quiet corner on the promenade deck. Lying on a lounge chair with my ear buds pounding out some Katy Perry and the cloudless blue sky above, I imagined myself alone on a deserted island surrounded by blue-green sea, palm trees, and the smell of salt air. No one to tell me what to do, how to feel, or who I should be. I stared out over the sun-dazzled water, a hazy strip of land touching the horizon far in the distance.

We would be in Turkey by morning and on a trek to see the Virgin Mary's house. Memories of Catechism from when I was little played back in my mind. Amanda and I would put up a fight about going, but we always had fun once we were there. Playing games, learning prayers, and sitting together during story time were some of the best memories I had with my sister. We'd stopped going to church after Dad died, and I realized I missed the sense of community and belonging I'd felt there—one of the few places our family shared that felt sacred and unscarred by life's tragedies. I couldn't say exactly why, but I'd stopped praying somewhere along the line, too. After Dad's accident and all that had happened with Mom and Amanda since, I had my doubts as to whether God was listening.

Just then, a dolphin breached the water alongside the ship and leapt high into the air. I sprang out of my chair and ran to the railing to catch a glimpse as it disappeared beneath the water. Another dolphin shot up and dove back down beside the first, keeping pace with the ship. My heart pounded as they danced in and out of the water side by side.

An overwhelming sense of gratitude filled me. As if God had answered some unspoken prayer and sent the dolphins to remind me Amanda was close by. My throat tightened and tears spilled over in a rush, as usual, catching me off guard. This time, though, I didn't fight them. I allowed the tears to fall, asking God to somehow use them to wash away the crushing sadness and finally help me to let go of my sister. For the first time in years, I had hope that He was listening, and I had the distinct feeling that my future depended on me believing it.

I fiddled with the charm bracelet on my wrist as the dolphins followed the ship. Lost in the moment, I imagined me and Amanda, still together, side by side—happy, and free.

∞∞∞∞

Wrung out and totally not ready to face yet another of my *issues*, I made my way up to the Crow's Nest late in the afternoon to practice with Tommy. Lighter after my meltdown, the glimpse I'd gotten of possibly living without guilt weighing me down like an anchor seemed fragile at best. Guilt was one thing, but fear was an entirely different monster to tackle. Whether or not I chickened out about actually performing in front of people, I was drawn to the notion of playing the guitar and losing myself in my music.

A grin spread across Tommy's lips when I walked in. "So you decided to come rescue me," he croaked, his voice even more gravelly than it had been that morning.

"I won't promise anything," I responded warily. "But it won't hurt to play a few songs with you before the crowd comes in for dinner."

Tommy slid onto the piano bench, leaving the stool in front of the mic open. The guitar rested in its stand as if waiting for me. I spent the next few minutes tuning the strings and strumming lightly on the chords until I was satisfied the instrument was ready and the sound was right.

Tommy led me in acoustic renditions of some old James Taylor and Beatles tunes, all of which I was familiar with from growing up with Mom and Dad's music of choice. I'd graduated to listening to classic rock and folk music, thanks to an old music teacher who had grown up in the seventies. Tommy slammed out a Billy Joel tune—Piano Man—and I strummed the chords beneath the notes, catching his melody and matching it perfectly. He grinned and encouraged me as I sang out the lyric, sweeter and stronger with every line as I followed the sheet music in front of me. My heart floated on the vibration that rang through my chest, filled my lungs, and even numbed the top of my head. It was the closest thing I knew to getting high, and I didn't want the feeling to end.

A few people wandered in to listen as I began another song. My pulse pounded in my ears as I strummed the chords and focused my attention on the music stand before me. The words to a Carol King ballad echoed through the silent room as passengers flowed in and sat down, obviously captivated by the sound Tommy and I were creating.

With each note, my voice and my confidence grew, and I found the nerve to glance out at the growing crowd to catch a glimpse of smiling faces. My heart swelled and a sense of pride rose up. I couldn't have imagined it possible that I would actually have fun playing in front of an audience. Tommy nodded and grinned broadly, approving my choice of the next song, an Elton John tune I'd always thought was cool.

As I played Crocodile Rock, memories of dancing around the living room flashed in my mind—me, Amanda, and Mom, laughing—and Dad cheering us on. I was so small then...so innocent...so happy. The memories poured out in the lyrics, opening my heart, my mind, and my soul. Emotions came in full force. Feelings I thought maybe I'd never have again. Instead of tears, joy erupted as I cranked out the notes and swayed with the music. One foot perched solidly on the rung of the stool while the other tapped the stage to the beat. The happy memory clung to the front of my mind, acting as a barricade against any sadness that might try to tag along. I refused to let it in to spoil the moment and instead, let the music carry me away.

Ethan and Maddie walked in and sat down in time to hear the rest of the performance. The look admiration on their faces flooded my chest with warmth. When the song ended, the room erupted in applause. I bowed my head and swept my hand toward Tommy, hoping to take the attention away from me. As I lifted my gaze, a massive little-boy-like grin crept over Ethan's face. He whistled and clapped louder than everyone else, making my face heat with what was probably a brilliant pink glow.

Whatever doubts and questions I'd had about what came next for me, I was certain of one thing. I wanted music in my life—and I wanted Ethan there to share it with me. We would figure it all out as we went, but I resolved to do whatever it took to make him mine. Moving past our differences wouldn't be easy. Compromise was inevitable. But seeing the look of affection and warmth in his eyes as he supported me with his cheers and whistles told me it would be well worth whatever I had to do.

Chapter 31

Exhausted from the excitement and emotion of the night before, morning came all too soon. We had to disembark with our tour by nine o'clock, and Maddie was taking extra time in the bathroom perfecting her makeup. I didn't have the heart to tell her it would all melt off by noon in the desert sun of Ephesus, with temperatures expected to reach a hundred by lunchtime. When Maddie and I arrived in the auditorium, Ethan was looking frantic.

"You made it!" Relief mixed with a happy grin, and he quickly led us to our assigned group. We hadn't talked last night about the way we'd left our painful conversation, and both of us seemed fine with letting the disagreement go for the time being. Determined to make the best of the day for Maddie's sake, we kept the mood light while we shuffled our way down the gangplank with a herd of other passengers headed for shore.

The brilliant blue waters of the Aegean Sea stretched across the coastline, and the beachfront spread the length of the broad harbor, its white sand and pristine waters like something out of a dream. West of the port gate, a small island with a Pirate's Castle, one we were told was used *against* pirates and not *by* them, dominated the tiny islet, linked to the mainland by a long walkway. We found our guide holding up a tall sign. His name was Izzet.

Izzet, a short, good humored man with dark brown eyes, black hair, and a well-fed belly, waved us all in, already spouting facts about Turkey's history and the people of Kusadasi, the town we were about to tour. We followed along ancient stone streets through a metropolitan area overrun with tourists, coming and going from shops along the main street. Some vendors were dressed in traditional garb and long robes, while others were outfitted in attire as modern as the tourists. Shops with beautiful jewelry, amazing leather crafts, and every pattern of silk imaginable lined the wide streets.

Our tour brought us to a carpet factory where we watched a demonstration by a pretty young Turkish woman hand weaving an amazing multicolored carpet. We sat on benches around a central room where the owner served us tea and wine, both local favorites. The tea, infused with cardamom and other spices, settled my stomach, which was a bundle of nerves with the bustling energy of the place and the crowded market buzzing around us. Several young men rolled out carpet after carpet for display, each one more beautiful and intricate than the last.

Ethan sat beside me, not touching me, not holding my hand or even looking my way. I wondered whether it was out of respect for Maddie, or if he had simply decided that staying friends for now was his only option. After all, having a "dope-fiend" for a girlfriend was probably not on his list of to-do's in life. I cringed at the embarrassing rush of heat that crawled up my neck. For the first time, the idea of someone I cared about being ashamed of knowing me sent a worm of doubt niggling its way through my armor.

A heated haggling session between Maddie and the salesman caught my attention, so I left Ethan watching the next demonstration on his own. Maddie was completely captivated by a medium sized throw rug that would set the average person back half a year's pay. Facing off with the man, she stood her ground on the price.

I tugged at her arm and gave her my best practical look. "Do you really need a rug?"

"I can't take it all with me, dear." She winked. "Are you worried I'm spending your inheritance?"

"Of course not." I scowled, offended. "I just figured that if you don't already have everything you need, this carpet probably isn't going to do it for you."

"Oh, you're probably right." Turning to the bewildered man, she nodded politely. "I'm no longer interested, thank you." She crooked her elbow through mine and led me out into the bright sunlight. "I only wanted the fun of haggling with a Turk," she whispered as Ethan caught up and fell in alongside us.

We left the carpet district and followed the tour guide through the outdoor markets where Maddie picked up some Turkish coffee and some bath salts made with Aegean Sea salt and local herbs, guaranteed to keep her "young and vibrant." By the time we reached a local hotel for lunch, we were all starving. Ethan's eyes widened when a dozen waiters surrounded us with trays. They laid out every kind of Turkish food imaginable and before one plate was empty, they brought something new to try. Decorative dishes stacked with stuffed grape leaves, bowls with steamed vegetables, and cups of fruit, yogurt and dipping sauces lined the table. I passed on the meat kebabs and stuck with the ample selection of fruits and vegetables, savoring the sweetness of a particularly juicy melon.

"Oh…my…God. I could live on this food," Ethan groaned as he grabbed another meaty skewer.

Before I could comment about his barbarism, the sound of music and tambourines filled the air and a parade of a dozen dancers filed into an open square alongside the tented dining area. The men were dressed in long red and black robes while the women were covered in white from head to toe, only their exotically made-up eyes showing. The troupe moved in sync with the music, their bodies as supple and graceful as swans. My heart tapped out the percussive rhythm as the dancers flew through the air, showcasing amazing feats of athletic ability followed by fluid and intricate steps that rivaled anything you'd see on an American stage.

The show went on for some time, and I was glad to be sitting in the shade of the large tent with the warm sea breeze blowing in from behind. With the dry heat and temps soaring, I was even relieved when the dancers removed their robe-like layers.

Dark skinned, the women had a gypsy look about them, with scarves covering their faces, slipper like shoes, red puffy pants, and sequin encrusted bikini tops. With lean, strong bodies, the young men wore the same puffy pants and shoes as the women, only theirs were in white. Red vests revealed their bare chests and each wore a white turban atop his head. How they kept them on while jumping and flipping through the air as they did was nothing short of a miracle.

"I'm stuffed like one of those grape leaves," said Maddie as we walked back to the bus after lunch.

I patted my stomach in agreement.

Ethan waved Maddie and me ahead of him as we climbed onto the bus. "The food, the show, the city…that was awesome," he said as he settled in next to me, allowing me the window seat.

Maddie sat behind us with Mrs. Fitzgibbons, the two of them having hit it off at the bridge table back on the ship. They busied themselves with talk of the carpets each of them liked the best, Maddie expressing her regret at not buying one when she had the chance.

I grinned at Ethan and shook my head. "This whole trip has been…unreal. With visits to so many incredible places in such a short amount of time, it makes me a little dizzy thinking about it," I said. Staring out the window at the ancient buildings passing as we climbed out of the city and traveled toward Ephesus, my mind spun with new appreciation. "I didn't realize how lucky I was until today. I shouldn't have been such an idiot about Maddie making me come on this trip with her." Warmth and affection shown in Ethan's eyes and another pang of deep appreciation washed over me as our gazes met.

"I'm glad you did. I kind of can't imagine my life without you now." He slipped his fingers through mine, and his dimples deepened as his lips curved into the sweet smile I'd come to love.

I bit the inside of my cheek, hopelessly relieved. "Me too," was all I could think to say. Regardless of what the future held for us, being on this trip with Maddie and meeting Ethan had been an unexpected gift I would cherish forever. "Have you talked to your dad?" I asked, anxious to escape the uncomfortable silence growing between us.

Ethan rubbed my knuckles with his thumb and stared past me out the window, checking out the herd of sheep a local shepherd corralled alongside the road. "I spoke to him last night. He said he's wrapping things up in Paris, and he'll meet me in Athens tomorrow." He shrugged. "We'll see if he shows, right?"

An ache seeped into my chest as a world of emotion settled behind Ethan's eyes, ending with resignation. "I'll keep my fingers crossed." I squeezed his hand and grinned, determined to look on the bright side—a new and terrifying prospect for me.

After a long and bumpy twenty mile ride up into the mountains and away from civilization, we reached a level parking area with all the modern conveniences, including rest rooms and a snack vendor selling ice cold drinks and memorobilia. Maddie picked up bottles of water for the short hike up to the Basilica of St. John, home and tomb of the beloved apostle, who Jesus named to care for Mary after the crucifixion. Maddie was excited to see the place, but I was more interested in checking out the next stop, which would be the ruins of the temple of Diana, one of the Seven Wonders of the ancient world.

We followed the silent crowd up the dirt road in the heat of the afternoon sun. My feet ached, and I wished I'd worn my sneakers instead of my stupid flip-flops like Maddie had suggested. I hated it when she was right. Ethan teased Maddie about she and I teaming up for tonight's karaoke competition, which lightened my mood and distracted me from complaining.

Between breathless pants and wiping the trickling sweat off her brow beneath her floppy hat, Maddie insisted we stop and take in the view. Ethan snapped pictures of me and the grandmother I'd hardly remembered before a few weeks ago, and who now meant so much to me. She gave my shoulders a quick squeeze and kissed my cheek, her papery skin brushing mine before she pulled back, her eyes glistening.

"We must savor this pilgrimage. Seeing the home where Mary lived out her final days is a privilege we may never have again. It's not likely either of us will return here, so take it all in, Alexis."

Gazing out over the vast openness of Turkey, with its cities far below and mountainous terrain stretched across green scrubby hills and arid desert passes, I soaked in the magic of the moment and realized Maddie was right. I might never have another chance to travel to such an exotic place again and I wanted to hold the moment close to my heart.

"If only Amanda were here to share it with us."

Maddie patted my hand. "She's here in spirit."

Shedding the sadness that threatened to intrude, I held onto the thought.

When we finally reached the top, Maddie took a deep breath and released a long sigh. "I'm going to have to hit the treadmill when I get home. Either that, or curb my appetite." She laughed, patting her stomach. "I should know better than to hike after all that food I ate."

Ethan and I, only slightly winded by the walk, led Maddie to where the tour guide was already speaking beside the tomb of St. John, whose remains had been buried there in the fourth century A.D. We passed a fountain with several ancient spigots sticking out in a row. Tourists lined up to drink from the sacred waters or fill small glass jars to take home and bury with a loved one—a local tradition that had spread far and wide.

The actual House of Mary turned out to be a slightly underwhelming and simple stone structure, having been reconstructed several times since the original was built high in the mountains as a hiding place centuries before. Made of stone blocks with a domed roof and few windows, the small two room building housed not much more than an altar and a table, tourists being shuttled through five or ten at a time. We entered through an arched wooden doorway, and would have made our way out the other side in only a few seconds, but Maddie stopped at the altar and crossed herself—something I'd only seen her do once many years before. It had been at Grandpa Henry's funeral, and I had a sudden image of my grandmother, kneeling at an open casket, sobbing and crossing herself over and over and begging God not to take her Henry away.

An eerie sense of doom washed over me. As I was about to fall into line with the other tourists to leave the dank, shadowy interior, Maddie clutched her shoulder and turned wide eyes on me. Her mouth opened but no words came out. The sound of my shriek echoed off the stone walls as I watched her collapse to the hard cold floor.

Chapter 32

Within seconds Ethan was crouched beside Maddie and a crowd had formed. Shouts reverberated inside the stone building. I fought my way through and dropped to my knees, my muscles uncooperative, and my breath caught in my throat. As he lifted his head from checking for signs of life, I met Ethan's intense gaze with a stark look of my own. He faltered and I froze, afraid to ask if she was breathing. Chaos erupted when he began CPR. My mind reeled, panic setting in until my voice finally found purchase.

"Someone call an ambulance!" I shouted.

A hand rested on my shoulder. I looked up to find Izzet, our tour guide, trying to pull me from the scene to make room for medical personnel. I resisted and pushed his hand away. Barely aware that the crowd behind me was clearing and the room was filling with emergency workers, I let the numbness take over my body and gave in to being dragged off. Ethan continued CPR until someone forced him aside.

He joined me and wrapped a reassuring arm around my shoulder. "She'll be okay. They know what to do." But even as he said it, I heard another worker in a thick accent commenting on how it might take an hour before an ambulance made its way up the mountain. I looked to Ethan, feeling helpless and heartbroken. Tears streamed and dripped from my chin. Ethan pulled me tightly into his arms. "I'll be right back," he whispered against my hair.

He left me standing there—confused, terrified, and empty—my arms wrapped around my middle and my limbs shaking. I stared at the scene, shock giving way to grief. How fitting that this should all happen now in this place—this sacred house that Maddie had so wanted to see—a pilgrimage she'd made to honor her dead husband. The irony kicked me hard and woke me to the gravity of the situation, and I wondered with horror if she'd known her life would end here. A shudder passed through me, and I looked to the altar above the place where the motionless body of my grandmother lay and a prayer I'd learned in childhood rose to my lips. *Hail Mary, full of grace, the Lord is with thee...*I whispered the prayer over and over again, my face wet with tears and a burning lump in my throat making it impossible to swallow or breathe.

"I have a pulse," someone called out. A wave of relief slammed into me, and I held onto the small thread of hope. Ethan returned, his face solemn. I crumbled into his arms as the tour guides and medics worked on Maddie. A man with a commanding voice and solid shoulders tucked a rolled up towel beneath her head and laid a blanket over her, his English better than most. "We've done all we can. Now we wait for the ambulance. It may take some time...the nearest hospital is far from here."

Ethan interrupted. "I made a call to my father. He's going to see if he can get a helicopter transport to come up here."

The man kneeling beside Maddie shook his head. "It's unlikely that will happen. I'm afraid it's too dangerous to land a helicopter in these mountains."

"If my father said he can make it happen, he will," Ethan snapped. But we both knew his father's word. My doubt must have shown on my face because Ethan met my gaze squarely. "He'll come through this time…he has to. I told him if he doesn't…I'm done."

"Done with what?" My voice shook through my sniffles.

"Done being his son," Ethan answered, his tone final. "He'll send someone. Trust me."

The next thirty minutes ticked by in excruciatingly slow increments. Maddie lost her pulse twice more, sending my own heart into overdrive and forcing me into hysterics while the medics worked on her. Thankfully, they'd had a defibrillator on one of the buses and both times were able to bring her back. Ethan half carried me out of the small stone house that now seemed like nothing more than a tomb. Just when I was about to meltdown completely, the sound of a helicopter in the distance caught our attention. Ethan and I ran down the hill to the parking area, the only flat space available for a landing site. The buses had been moved and people were backing away as the wind from the blades scattered sand and dust in every direction.

It took only minutes for the medics to climb the hill, strap Maddie to a stretcher, and load her onto the helicopter. A large red cross was painted on the side and bottom of the chopper—which was on loan I'd been told, from the metropolis of Izmir over fifty miles away. Barely conscious as they slid the stretcher aboard, Maddie reached out to me, her eyes filled with fear and regret. She mouthed my name, but I couldn't hear her with my heart pounding in my ears and the thunderous thwacking of the helicopter blades.

"Do you want to ride with her to the hospital?" One of the medics yelled over the noise.

My mouth went instantly dry, the thought of flying bringing on a rolling wave of nausea. Ethan must have seen the expression on my face. Before he could decline on my behalf, I grabbed his hand and pulled him into the helicopter. I sucked in a breath and said one more prayer to Mary as we lifted off the ground and my stomach lurched.

Chapter 33

By the time the chopper set down on the roof of the hospital in Izmir, my nerves were frayed. My legs wobbled as Ethan helped me climb down and pulled me away from the thunder and wind created by the whirling blades. Despite wanting desperately to drop and kiss the rooftop, I took up a spot alongside the stretcher and followed Maddie inside the building and onto the elevator. Her face was pale beneath the oxygen mask. Only her blue eyes, filled with fear and edged with pain, stared out, looking for something—someone—to hold onto.

"I'm right here, Maddie. You're going to be fine." I clutched her hand in mine, trying to pour life into her frail body. The words sounded hollow in my ears, as if someone else were speaking. The voice was sure and strong—two qualities far from me at that moment. Maddie nodded and closed her eyes. The medic pushed me aside. Forced to release her hand, I drifted into the corner of the elevator to make room for them to work. Ethan ducked in beside me.

When the elevator doors opened, the medics handed the gurney off to a bustling group of doctors and nurses, all dressed in green scrubs and speaking a foreign language, which cut me out of the conversation completely. Ethan grabbed my arm as I tried to follow them down the hall.

"We need to let them work." He looked over his shoulder. "There's a waiting area over there." His head tipped toward a spot down the hall in the opposite direction. Chairs lined the walls and magazines lay fanned out on a coffee table next to a vending machine. I looked back toward the giant double doors that had just swallowed Maddie. The knot in my chest tightened.

"What if…what if she doesn't make it?" I couldn't bring myself to say the word that flooded my mind.

Ethan slipped his hand into mine and stepped in close, forcing me to meet his gaze. "Maddie's a tough lady. She's going to pull through this. I think we got her here in time." In spite of his words of reassurance, his face held deep concern.

Tears erupted and all the tension from the past hour rushed out in a flood. Her collapse, Ethan jumping in to perform CPR, waiting for help to arrive, and the dips and twists of the forever-seeming helicopter ride. Remembering the sensations of the flight over the mountains and across the foreign landscape, a queasiness rolled through my insides. My legs threatened to buckle but Ethan wrapped his arm around my waist, leading me to the waiting area to sit down before I collapsed.

"I don't know what I'll do if she…" A sob escaped my lips even as the word stuck in my throat. Ethan lowered me to a chair and settled into a seat beside me. Despite the warm hands surrounding my icy fingers, a cold numbness seeped into my bones. "I can't lose her," I whispered. "I just found her…"

"Don't even think like that." Ethan rubbed my hands between his as if trying to warm them and shake me out of the shock I was in. Every nerve inside me crackled like burning embers waiting to ignite the next piece of fuel that came my way. I stared down the hall at the doors, willing someone to come through them to tell me Maddie was going to be all right. My knee bounced furiously until I popped up off the chair.

"I can't sit here and do nothing," I cried, tears burning to the surface again as I wrung my hands together.

"Try to stay calm, Lexi. Maddie wouldn't want you to be all upset like this. It won't do her any good for you to fall apart. You need to stay strong."

"I don't know if I can." My face fell into my hands as my shoulders shook. I turned away to hide my pitiful display of weakness. He was right. Maddie needed me to be strong. Mom and Mitch were continents away and I was on my own to make whatever decisions had to be made for Maddie's care. She needed me to be tough and there I was, crying like a baby and thinking about myself and how much I would be hurt if she…died. Reining in my emotions, anger rode to the surface and the realization hit me. I hadn't told her I loved her. I'd waited too long—just as I had with Amanda. "I can't go through this again," I said, dropping fisted hands to my sides and clamping down on my tears. I wiped my cheeks with the backs of my hands as I stared out the window at nothing.

In the next second, Ethan was behind me, his arms wrapped around my waist in a tight embrace that instantly shored up my quivering limbs. "You aren't alone in this, Lex." He turned me around and pulled me to his chest, where I gladly buried my face and let him stroke my hair, drawing strength from the steady beat of his heart against my ear. Whatever happened up to now was beyond my control. But what I did have control over was how I handled what came next. I clung to Ethan for a long minute and then reluctantly pushed away with a sigh.

"Thanks for the pep talk. I needed it." I held his hand and mustered a small smile. "I mean it. I don't know what I would have done if you hadn't been there today. You were really amazing. If anyone is responsible for saving Maddie's life it's you. The way you jumped in and started CPR, contacted your dad and got that helicopter—that was really something."

A slight pink tinge crept up Ethan's neck. "I just reacted—that's all. I figured it was as good a time as any to call my dad out on what he owed me. I told him if he did this for me, we'd be square." He looked at a clock on the wall. "I only hope he comes through. He said he would come as soon as he could get on the Embassy jet. He probably needed all kinds of clearances to fly into Turkey. No telling how long it will be before he's here." Seeing the look of panic that rose on my face, he added, "I'm sure Maddie's in good hands."

I hoped he was right. The corridor was now quiet and empty, and the hospital, though clean and smelling of antiseptic, seemed small and not at all what I was used to seeing in the States. Before I had a chance to voice my opinion, a tall, round faced man in a white lab coat pushed through the double doors and headed our way. It took all my strength not to rush him, but Ethan's hand in mine held me in place.

"I am Doctor Rossoff," said the man as he tugged off his surgical cap, revealing a short curly mop of black hair. His long craggy nose and deep set, dark eyes, identified him as Turkish as much as his thick accent and broken English. "The patient is your grandmother, no?"

I nodded, my mouth dry and my palms clammy.

"Mrs. Hartman is stable and has been moved to our cardiac care unit. We will monitor her closely. She is a very lucky woman. If treatment was not started so quickly, she would not have made it."

I flashed a sincere look of gratitude at Ethan and then addressed the doctor. "When can I see her?"

"Mrs. Hartman is not out of danger yet. We need to do further testing, but I believe she will need bypass surgery. She says this was not her first heart attack, and I suspect we will find blockage of her arteries. I'll have more information for you after we complete our tests."

A nurse came up behind the doctor and handed me a clipboard. Dr. Rossoff smiled reassuringly. "The best you can do for your grandmother is to be patient and wait, fill out the required forms, and perhaps get something to eat in our café down on the first floor." Speaking Turkish, the doctor instructed the nurse and then turned to me and Ethan again. "Our nursing staff will assist you with any questions. Most speak some amount of English. Please be patient with the language barrier." He turned to leave.

Ethan called after him. "Doctor, did my father, Martin Kaswell, contact you about consulting on the case?"

The doctor turned halfway and remained in mid-stance. "I did receive a call asking to grant Doctor Kaswell hospital access, but I'm sure you understand how unusual a request that is on such short notice. His participation needs to be approved by our administrators. It seems the French Embassy is working to expedite the process, but none of that will matter if Mrs. Hartman takes a turn for the worse and we need to move forward with surgery before Doctor Kaswell arrives. We will do everything possible to include him in our plan of care, but rest assured, we are quite capable of caring adequately for our patients."

A strong sense of pride rolled off the doctor, and he was obviously insulted by the prospect of a foreigner moving in on his turf. Before Ethan and I could respond, he added, "Why don't we take things one step at a time? I'll keep you updated on your grandmother's progress." He nodded formally, turned away, and walked briskly down the hall. He disappeared behind the double doors again, leaving me holding a clipboard with paperwork written in what I assumed was Turkish, the pages covered in artful swirls, dots, and slashes. I sighed and lowered myself into a stiff, hard backed chair.

"What if your father doesn't make it in time?"

Ethan stared after the doctor as the door swung shut, his brows pulled together in a frown. "He'd better make it—and soon. If anything happens to Maddie, he'll have more to deal with than me never speaking to him again."

Chapter 34

"This waiting is killing me," I groaned, slumping into a chair in the large but stuffy cafeteria. Tables crowded with workers and visitors filled the room. Everyone spoke in Turkish, as chaotic a spoken language as it was in written form. Ethan placed a cup of aromatic tea in front of me, the tea bag floating in the darkening water. I mindlessly played with the string, watching the bag bob up and down.

Ethan's phone chirped out a tune. We both froze. Gingerly, as if handling a detonation device, he answered. His face remained stern for several seconds as the person on the other end spoke. Then his shoulders relaxed and a small smile appeared. "Great. We'll see you in an hour. And Dad…thanks." Hanging up, he tucked the phone back in his pants pocket. "He has to go through customs but should be here in a little while."

I let out a slow breath. "Thank God. I'm sure Doctor Rossoff is good, but Maddie deserves the best." This bit of good news bolstered my mood better than anything could—other than seeing Maddie. My heart squeezed when I thought of her on her own in a room with all those doctors and nurses poking and prodding at her and running all kinds of tests. "Maddie must be freaking out," I said, my smile dimming.

"We'll get you in to see her as soon as possible, okay? Look, here comes the doctor now."

I turned to see Doctor Rossoff approaching. The expression on his face sent my stomach plummeting.

"Miss Hartman, we need to talk." His words crawled along my skin and lifted the hairs at the base of my neck. As he pulled up a chair, my worry meter shot through the roof. "Your grandmother does have significant arterial blockage. She needs bypass surgery immediately. Although there are always risks with any kind of surgical procedure, I assure you, I have done this many times before with good success." He slipped the paperwork in front of me. "I need your permission as her nearest relative to proceed with surgery."

My mouth went dry and sweat broke out on my forehead. "I can't make this decision," I said, my hand too shaky to reach for the pen. "I'm not even eighteen." I looked to Ethan.

"Can't the surgery wait an hour? My father is on his way."

"I'm afraid that waiting any longer will put Mrs. Hartman at risk for further damage to her heart or may even possibly cause a stroke. She isn't getting enough blood flow and oxygen to her brain and other organs. Left untreated, her organs may begin to shut down or she could sustain permanent damage." Seeing my expression turn to panic he rushed to add, "Since your grandmother is from outside our country, the circumstances are complicated, but out of respect for your wishes as her closest relative, we will wait. I am simply giving you an update on her current condition. For the moment, it is still up to you whether I proceed."

The only other life and death decision I'd ever had to make was when I knew my sister was in too deep and I decided to keep my mouth shut. I'd made the wrong choice then. What made anyone think I was capable of making the right choice now? I shook my head.

"I need to call my mom."

The doctor looked as if he wanted to argue, but instead, simply nodded and walked away, leaving me again with the clipboard—and the weight of the world on my shoulders.

∞∞∞∞

It took over fifteen minutes to get through to Mitch and have him get me in touch with Mom—at my hysterical insistence and against his better judgment. When I finally heard my mother's voice, I broke down all over again. Through intermittent hiccups, I choked out the details leading up to the current crisis. "I don't know what to do." The uncontrollable trembling in my body carried into my words.

"Try to stay calm, Ali. Is anyone there with you?" Even though I knew my mother was in a hospital recovering from a nervous breakdown and that I shouldn't be depending on her for stability and support, the sound of her familiar voice gave me an instantaneous burst of strength. I pulled myself together enough for a conversation.

"Ethan Kaswell is here with me." Briefly explaining who Ethan was, I looked over to see him standing by a window watching me intently. Hollow eyes showed not only how worried he was for Maddie, but how much he cared for me. In only a few short weeks, it seemed he had become part of our family. My heart swelled as he nodded reassuringly and a small smile curved his lips. I relayed my dilemma regarding Ethan's father and the decision I was faced with.

"Is this Doctor Kaswell really the best?" Mom sounded unsure, making me falter in my resolve.

"Ethan seems to think so…and I trust *him.*" What I didn't say was that Doctor Kaswell's track record for being a man of his word was more than a little shoddy. If I decided to wait for him and he didn't show up, it could cost Maddie her life. My heart tripped into overdrive and I took a shuddering breath. "Please, Mom, tell me what to do."

"I never thought I'd hear you say those words."

An involuntary laugh escaped my lips. "Me either."

"I'm sorry I'm not there to help, but I can't tell you what to do. You have to trust your instincts. I know you'll make the right decision," she added. Her voice faltered. "You were right. After what happened to…Amanda, I overreacted. I've been suffocating you and I have to start trusting you."

"Now you want to trust me?" I wanted to revel in hearing those words but disappointment and frustration seeped in. "I don't know if I can do this."

"Yes, you can," she argued, her voice strained. "It sounds like it's out of your hands anyway. If this Doctor Kaswell doesn't get there soon, the doctor in charge will have to do what he thinks is best."

"I suppose you're right," I sighed.

"Wow, another first," she said with a weak laugh. A moment of silence later, she added, "I've missed you, kiddo."

"I…I've missed you too," I said, my throat tightening as I held back another round of tears and tried to sound strong. "How are you feeling, anyway? Will you be able to go home soon?"

"I think so. I'm hoping to be there when you get back. Mitch really misses you, too."

"I bet," I snorted. My old snarkiness came through and I immediately regretted it. "I'm…sorry, Mom. I didn't mean that. I know I've been a pain in the butt this past year, and you and Mitch have only been trying to help."

A long silence had me wondering if we'd been disconnected, but before I could ask if she'd heard me, she responded, "I'm glad to hear you say that, sweetie. I hope you know how much we love you." Her voice broke and I could tell she was crying. "It's been so hard—without your sister—"

"I know, Mom. Please don't cry. I'm going to do better when I get home—I promise. I'll go to those stupid rehab classes and I'll work harder in school. It'll be okay." By now I was crying right along with her.

Ethan crossed the cafeteria in three strides and took the phone from my hand. After a few words of consolation to my mother, he hung up. "Are you okay?"

I nodded and sniffled, wiping my nose with a crumpled tissue that was in need of replacement. He wrapped an arm around my shoulder and walked me back to the waiting room. It wasn't long before Doctor Rossoff found us.

"Your grandmother is stable for the moment."

"Can I see her?" Despite my mother's leaving the decision to me, I wanted Maddie's opinion if it was at all possible. It really should be left up to her and not a sixteen year-old who couldn't even make sensible choices about what shoes to wear. Peering down at my flip-flops, I suddenly felt young and wanted nothing more than to be at home in my room, even if it meant I was grounded for life or forced to attend meetings for the next six months. All of the problems I had been dealing with for the past year seemed distant and less important than they had even a few days ago.

"Mrs. Hartman is sedated, but I can let you in to see her for a few minutes." He nodded to Ethan. "I'm sorry, but only family members are allowed."

I released Ethan's hand and sent him a reassuring smile, then I followed the doctor back down the long hall and through the big double doors—once again trying to imagine what lay beyond them. My heart raced as I looked back and watched my tether to sanity grow further away. The doors swung shut behind me, and Ethan disappeared.

Shocked by the brightness of the light and the sterile conditions, I immediately noticed the white walls, the spotless floors, and the staff members all dressed in green scrubs scurrying along, focused on their various tasks. It all made me a fraction less fearful of putting Maddie's life in their hands.

A nurse stood over the hospital bed, blocking my view as I entered the room behind the doctor. He took a medical chart from her hands and they exchanged a brief conversation in Turkish. The sound of their voices faded to the buzzing of insects, and my focus honed in on the beeping monitor beside Maddie's bed. When she came into full view, I sucked in a breath. Her shiny red hair was now matted, her face a sickening shade of gray. Tubes came out of everywhere. A hard lump formed in my throat and I swallowed past it. Scooting around the bed to a chair on the other side, I lowered myself down on shaking legs and slowly reached for Maddie's hand.

The doctor turned his attention to me. "You can stay for a few minutes. It's fine if you talk to her, but I can't guarantee she will hear or understand you." His compassionate expression turned to one of stern determination. "When I come back, I'll need you to sign those papers."

My insides tightened as he exited the room. I looked into Maddie's face, the crooked oxygen tube in her nose drawing my attention. I reached up and tentatively adjusted it, hoping she would open her eyes, but she remained still.

"You hate all of this, don't you?" I asked into the silence. Burning behind my eyes signaled tears were about to follow. Seeing her at the mercy of machines—so vulnerable, so frail, so *not* her usual feisty self—made my heart ache. She was always so put together...but now...she looked small and helpless—a state she would clearly despise. Up until that moment, I'd never considered how fragile human dignity was. Tears spilled over and I squeezed her icy fingers. "Of all the times to not offer advice, you picked a fine one." I pulled a smile out of nowhere despite the fact she couldn't see it, and I tried to sound strong. "I'm not sure what to do here. I know you would only want the best doctor working on you—someone you trust—but I don't think we should wait for Ethan's dad." She didn't respond. Instead she lay there, motionless and looking nothing like the grandmother I had grown to love and respect more than I thought myself capable of. I continued talking, trying to keep my voice steady and ignore the fear that burrowed into my chest and the tears that wet my cheeks. "I talked to Mom. She's doing better."

Maddie lay still, machines registering a steady heartbeat at her side. "I don't know how long it will take for Doctor Kaswell to arrive, or even if he can get permission to do surgery here, but I don't want to wait until…" I stopped before the words *it's too late* escaped my lips.

I let out a long sigh and swiped at my jaw where tears were poised, ready to drip onto her hand. Maddie didn't need me laying this on her, whether she could hear me or not. She needed me to be strong—to take charge—to be a grown up about this and make a decision.

"Don't worry about it, okay?" I said, rising and standing over her inert body. "You just worry about getting better. You and I have lots more to talk about. I know there must be stories you haven't told me about Dad and Grandpa Henry. I want to hear them all, so you have to get better…you have to." My voice was barely above a whisper. I rested a hand on Maddie's forehead, aware that her skin was cool and smooth, pulled tight over her skeleton as if gravity was drawing her to the earth—either holding her there to keep her from floating heavenward, or forcing her back to the ground from which she'd come. I pushed a fine strand of auburn hair away from her face and laid a soft kiss on her cheek. "I love you, Grandma." As I stood upright to leave, ready to make the decision she so needed me to make for her, I felt a flicker in her grasp.

Her lips moved and her eyes fluttered open and then closed again. Bending close, I strained to hear. A grin crept over my face as the words became clearer.

"Don't call me Grandma," she rasped.

Chapter 35

"Don't try to talk. Save your energy. You're going to be fine." I said all the words Maddie needed to hear. I kept my tears in check and gave her the steadiest tone I could muster. "You're in a hospital in Turkey. You had a heart attack, but they're going to fix you right up."

She squeezed my fingers again and the hint of a smile found her lips. She nodded and tried to speak but no words came out. I leaned in close again to hear the one word she managed to say. *"Wait."*

I pulled back. "You heard me?"

A slight nod of her head acknowledged that she'd gotten the gist of what I'd said and that she wanted to wait for Ethan's father. "Are you sure that's a good idea? The doctor says he needs to operate now. I don't mean to be negative, but you know how Ethan's dad has been. I'm not sure we can trust him?"

She croaked out another word and I read her lips clearly. *"Trust."* I didn't know how, after all Ethan's dad had done, and after all the sadness and disappointments she'd suffered in life, that Maddie could utter the word trust with such certainty.

"But what if he doesn't come in time?" I had no time to be delicate and I needed her to be sure she knew what she was asking of me.

Her once sharp blue eyes, now dim and gray, stared up at me and she uttered one more word. *"Faith."* She sucked in a labored breath and the lines on the heart monitor spiked, sending my own heartbeat racing.

Doctor Rossoff's re-entry drew my attention. "You should let her re now. She will need all of her strength."

I looked back to Maddie who had closed her eyes again. Reluctantly, I followed the doctor out of the room and back to the nurse's station where Ethan waited. The nurse slid the consent form toward me and handed me a pen, a patient, tight-lipped smile plastered on her face. Studying the form, which she had kindly translated for me, I took the pen. I glanced from the nurse to Ethan, and then to Doctor Rossoff.

After a long few seconds I put the pen down again and took a deep breath. "I'm sorry, but I can't sign this. Maddie wants to wait for Doctor Kaswell, and I think it's best if we give him another fifteen minutes. If he isn't here by then, I'll sign the papers."

The doctor stared at me and shook his head in frustration. "You are taking a great risk with your grandmother's life…I won't be held responsible if…" He huffed out another breath. "I will respect your wishes." He turned to the nurse and barked out an order. Even though it was in Turkish, I assumed he was telling her to inform him when Doctor Kaswell arrived. I heaved a sigh as he stalked off, muttering something derogatory about Americans, still speaking a foreign language.

"Are you sure about this?" Ethan asked, his face filled with doubt. "You know my dad. He means well when he makes promises, but I never know if he's going to deliver. I don't want you making this decision out of some kind of loyalty to me."

"I'm not. It's what Maddie wants and I'm trusting she knows what's best. She told me to have faith and that's what I'm doing." Before I could say another word, the object of Ethan's doubt and

Maddie's faith stepped off the nearby elevator. Without hesitation, I ran up to greet him and threw my arms around his neck.

He stiffened upon my assault, and then wrapped his arms around me in a warm embrace. "I can't remember the last time anyone was so happy to see me," he said over the top of my head.

I released the man and apologized. "I've never been so happy to see a doctor in all my life. Thank you for coming."

"My son made it clear how important this was to him." His gaze honed in on Ethan. The two shook hands a little too formally and Martin Kaswell seemed at a loss for words when Ethan pulled him into a hug.

"Thanks, Dad. I knew you'd come."

Doctor Kaswell stepped back, his eyes misty and his brow raised. "You didn't give me much choice."

"I'm just glad you made it…for a lot of reasons." Ethan grinned. "We can talk later. Right now, you have a patient to see."

∞∞∞∞

After wading through a pile of paperwork and obtaining permission from the hospital board to do the surgery, Ethan's father assured me he would do his best and left Ethan and me to pace the halls for the next several hours. When I was finally so exhausted I couldn't remain standing, I sank onto a waiting room couch. I woke a while later with my head in Ethan's lap, his father's commanding voice catching my ear. I bolted upright and jumped to my feet.

Doctor Kaswell's expression held relief and genuine affection as he laid a large hand on my shoulder. "Maddie should be up and ready to take on the world in no time. She had several obstructed arteries, but the bypass was successful. She's not totally out of the woods, but she'll probably have a lot more energy and feel better now than she has in years."

"I don't know how I can ever thank you," I said, hugging him and letting the tears fall.

"No need." He patted my back and when he pulled away, he looked to Ethan. "You, on the other hand, son, can thank me by making sure this young lady gets back on board that ship safely and makes her flight home on Sunday. I'll have you two flown to Athens where the ship will be in port tomorrow morning. I can stay here until Maddie is ready for discharge in a few days, and then I'll arrange transport for her back to the states. Barring any complications, there's no reason why she can't recover at a hospital closer to home. I'll know better in a day or two, but I'm sure she would want you to continue on as planned."

"No way. I can't leave her," I argued. I looked to Ethan desperately. "Why can't I stay here?"

"I think we should listen to my dad," Ethan said, glancing from his father to me.

Doctor Kaswell smiled appreciatively, a look of pride flashing in his eyes. "Since I'll be here at the hospital round the clock for the next few days, I need to know you two are taken care of. Putting you in a Turkish hotel where neither of you speaks the language makes much less sense than having you back on board the cruise ship where I know you'll be looked after. Can I count on you to stay out of trouble and be responsible?" He shifted his gaze from one to the other of us, wearing the same expression Mitch often did—the one where he asked a serious question and expected me to say exactly what he wanted to hear.

"Of course—" Ethan started.

I cut him off. "I'm not going anywhere until I see Maddie and make sure she's okay."

Ethan's father nodded approval. "I understand. And from the few conversations I've had with your grandmother, I'm sure she would have my hide if I sent you away without allowing you to see her. She'll be out of recovery in a few hours. In the meantime, I'll take care of the flight arrangements. If you'll excuse me." He turned and strode down the hallway.

"You're dad's a man of few words," I said, watching as he pushed through a door without ever looking up from Maddie's chart.

"Tell me about it." Ethan's gaze followed along, a mixed look of confusion and admiration clouding his features. Stepping closer, he faced me and took my hands in his, an expression of affection softening the tiny creases around his eyes. "Well, I have a lot to say."

"Not right now, you don't." I looped my arms around his neck, took a deep breath, and drew him into a kiss. His arms tightened around me and his heart thumped against my chest. When our lips finally parted, a catlike grin spread across his face.

"How can I complain about a girl who thinks talking is overrated?"

Then he kissed me back and my toes curled in my flip-flops.

Chapter 36

When I walked into Maddie's room a few hours later, she was awake and already arguing with a nurse. This time, although there were still machines with tubes hooked like tentacles coming from her nose and arms, the color in her face had turned from blue-gray to a pasty white, a slight tinge of pink in her cheeks. The nurse took my coming as a reprieve, handed me a cold wet washcloth, and with brief instructions, left the room.

"Are you seriously going to give these people a hard time? They pretty much just saved your life. You might try being a little grateful." I leaned over to wet her lips with the cloth filled with ice chips as the nurse had tried to do before she'd made her escape.

Maddie's expression changed and she let me hold the cloth, obviously appreciating the cool moisture as she sucked some of the chips into her mouth. She closed her eyes and her chest rose and fell with a deep breath. When she opened them again, a sparkle there made my heart leap.

"Well look at you, doling out advice," she whispered, and then broke into a coughing fit.

I jumped to my feet. "Are you okay? Do you need me to go for help?"

She waved me off and settled back onto the pillow, clearly drained. "They cut my damn chest open. Of course I'm not okay." She lifted the blanket covering her and rubbed a weak hand over a thick bandage. "It feels like someone tore my heart out and then stapled me back up. I'll have a few words with my doctor, believe me," she whispered hoarsely. She started peeling the tape back but I grabbed her hand to stop her. She didn't fight me. Instead she let her hand drop into mine and squeezed my fingers as she winced. "I'm going to have an ugly scar."

I held her hand and smiled. "Look on the bright side. You'll have to go out and buy a whole new wardrobe."

"Well there is that, I suppose." A feeble grin curved her lips upward.

"And Doctor Kaswell says you'll be feeling better than you've felt in a long time. No more dizzy spells, no more chest pains, and no more shortness of breath."

"All this positivity from you—forgive me for saying—is uncharacteristic, and frankly a little unnerving." She signaled for another serving of ice chips, paused, and drew in a relieved breath as the cool moisture hit her throat. "Am I mistaken or has something in you changed?"

Her raspy voice tugged at something deep inside me and my chest tightened. "I guess you scared me. I thought...I thought I was going to lose you." Carefully rubbing the back of her hand, I smoothed a curl of tape peeling up from the IV. Deep bruises were already forming around the site. My gaze rose up to meet hers. "I was afraid I wouldn't get a chance to tell you...I love you." Tears welled but I blinked them back, determined to say what needed to be said and unwilling to let the opportunity pass again.

"I see." Maddie's expression softened, the blue of her eyes turning to misty gray. "I love you too, Alexis." She shook her head, clearing away the emotions rising to the surface. "Sometimes it takes a heart attack to wake us up." Her voice faded as fatigue or the pain meds kicked in. "Family—that's what's important," she whispered.

"We've already lost too much. I won't lose you too." I pressed my bottom lip between my teeth, willing myself not to cry.

"You are so much like your father in so many ways. He never saw how strong he was inside." Tears filled her eyes. "He would have been very proud of you today."

I held her hand gently and the two of us shared a moment of quiet. Despite the nail-biting drama of it all, we were, and would always be, connected by our experience—and by my father. I shared Martin Kaswell's plan to send Ethan and me to pick up the cruise in Athens. We would board in the morning and be on our own for the final three days before reaching Civitavecchia, Italy, for the flight home.

"Go see Athens for me. Take lots of pictures. You can tell me all about it when I get home."

"I don't want to leave you here alone."

"I won't be alone. Now," she said firmly, despite the strain in her voice. "I'm collecting on our bet. I won at Bingo, so you have to do what I tell you. You get back on the ship and finish this journey." She squeezed my hand and her *I mean business* expression took over her face. Incongruent with the stern look was the frailty in her voice and the presence of the oxygen lead that reminded me how close I'd come to losing her. Her next words held the weight she'd intended. "I'm trusting you and Ethan to be responsible. Remember, you always have a choice, and you can't lose by doing the right thing."

She had to know how hard it would be for me and Ethan to keep our distance, especially without her eagle eye on us. She also had to know that choosing to do the *right thing* was not my strong suit. I considered Maddie's carefully chosen words about my dad being proud of me today. She'd suggested that my father might not have been pleased with me during my epic drama days the past year, but that maybe, just maybe, I was becoming the kind of daughter he could be proud of. Now was my chance to prove it.

For the first time since my father's death, it mattered. I had been so angry with him for drinking and driving, for killing that boy and ruining our family, for not being here to keep me and Amanda from turning into screw-ups, and—for dying. For so many years I hadn't cared one bit about how he would have seen me. Whether he would have been proud of me or thought me a coward for not standing up to my sister and telling someone about her alcohol consumption and drug use. Whether he would have been disappointed in me for smoking pot and getting busted. None of that mattered since I'd seen him as a failure and a coward himself. Nothing I could have done would be as bad as what he had done…as what Amanda had done. But in that moment, it did matter. For the first time in as long as I could remember, I wanted to be someone that others could be proud of—someone I could be proud of.

"I'll behave. I promise."

∞∞∞∞

I hated leaving Maddie, but Doctor Kaswell assured me she was in good hands, recovering like a Marine, and that he would see her safely back to the States in a few days. He had arranged for a car to take us to a small airport an hour away where the French Embassy's private jet waited to shuttle us to the Greek port of Piraeus to meet the ship at dawn. The way the attendant catered to us, she must have thought we were royalty. But in spite of the cushy décor and comfy seats, it was still an airplane and my frazzled nerves took one more leap. As we lifted off, I clung to the armrests.

"You really don't like flying, do you?" Ethan said, stating the obvious.

"What gave me away?" I gritted my teeth and glared at him.

A sympathetic grin flashed before my eyes. I closed them again, sensing the front end of the jet tipping upwards and climbing. "If you squeeze the arm rests any tighter, you might break something. And I don't think I've ever seen your face quite that shade of green before."

"If I throw up, it will be all your fault and I'm sending it your way," I sniped, trying to keep the contents of my stomach in place.

"It wouldn't be the first time," Ethan said with a chuckle. He reached over and laid his hand on mine. "The rough part is almost over. Once we level out, it should be smooth sailing."

"Please, don't mention sailing." I covered my mouth and swallowed.

The attendant showed up with a cool wet cloth, a glass of ginger ale, some saltines, and a small paper bag in case all of her efforts failed. I gave her a grateful grimace and nibbled a cracker.

Ethan picked up the conversation—clearly an attempt to distract me. "We should get back to the ship in time to catch our tour of Athens—if you want to. Or we could stay on board for the day. I know you haven't slept much."

"I don't know if I can relax and have fun knowing Maddie is in the hospital."

"She would want you to enjoy the rest of the trip. We only have Athens, one day at sea, and then Messina before we reach port in Civitavecchia."

"At this point, I wish I could just go home." Exhaustion had set in and tears welled behind my eyes.

Ethan wove his fingers through mine, squeezing gently to keep my attention focused on him and not the ear-popping change in cabin pressure as we climbed. "A lot has happened the past couple of days, huh?"

"So much has changed," I whispered, peering out the window into an inky sky, lights below disappearing as we ventured out over the Aegean Sea.

"Like what?"

I sipped the ginger ale, noticing that the plane had leveled off and the ride had smoothed out. "I guess I've learned to appreciate the people in my life who care about me. I used to think my mom and Mitch resented me for still being alive while Amanda—wasn't."

"Why would you think that?" A look of confusion clouded his face.

"Amanda was everything to my mother. It always seemed like she could do no wrong in Mom's eyes—while I only reminded her of my dad—the way I disappeared into my music and fought her all the time." My father's image filled my mind. Once a source of pain, the image now brought a confusing mix of sadness and a comforting reminder of our special connection. Ethan's voice drew me back.

"I seriously doubt your mother loved your sister more than you. And I'm sure she doesn't blame you for Amanda's death."

"I knew what Amanda was doing. She had been binge drinking for a long time. I should have told my mother, but I didn't. I felt some stupid sense of loyalty, like I had to keep my sister's secret and protect my mom from the disappointment of knowing neither of her daughters was perfect. It cost my sister her life—it cost my family everything."

Ethan squared off with me, his eyes the color of the sea. "You have to stop blaming yourself. Your mother has to know it wasn't your fault. It was your sister's choice to do what she did. It had nothing to do with you."

"I realize I can't control what other people think or do," I said with a sigh, the truth finally seeping in. "I can only be responsible for myself, right?"

"Wow, what a novel concept. Does this mean you'll stop bugging me about eating meat?" Ethan laughed.

I nudged him with an elbow. "You wish."

"Seriously, Lexi. I'm glad you finally realize what happened to your sister wasn't your fault."

"Amanda was all messed up from what happened to our dad. She was older—remembered more. I'm not sure why, but I think she blamed herself."

"I guess kids do that…blame themselves for how unhappy their parents are."

I got the impression we weren't only talking about me and Amanda anymore. Ethan's drive to be the perfect son was probably a selfless attempt to make up for Martin Kaswell having lost the love of his life. But instead of focusing on how it affected Ethan, the man hid from his grief by burying himself in his work and leaving his son out in the cold. Ethan could have hated his father, but I could tell he didn't. Suddenly, I had a new appreciation for Ethan's capacity for love. I gave his fingers a gentle squeeze.

"I know I haven't made things easy for my mom and Mitch. But that stops now." I reclined my seat and closed my eyes, hoping the motion sickness meds I'd taken would kick in and knock me out for the rest of the flight.

"You've learned your lesson, and you're going to walk the straight and narrow, huh?"

"That's me—totally reformed," I said, opening one eye.

Ethan chuckled. "I'll believe it when I see it."

Chapter 37

We met the ship early the next morning. The two of us had fallen asleep on the plane and again in the car on the way to the port in Piraeus, Greece. By the time we boarded, each got cleaned up, and met for breakfast on the Lido deck, we decided taking the later tour would be sufficient. Neither of us was in any mood to shop in Piraeus, or in shape to go to the monastery in Dafni, but by noon, after answering a barrage of questions from the Captain and all the passengers who had come to know Maddie, I was ready to board the bus for an afternoon tour of Greece. Touring the Acropolis, Hadrian's Arch, and the Temple of Zeus, was sure to be a highlight of the trip.

We found our seats and listened as the guide filled us in on Greece's long and colorful history. From the classical period in 2000 BC to the Hellenistic period, through the Roman and Byzantine occupation, and finally through its years of Independence in the past two centuries, Greece had seen many changes.

We passed the Temple of Olympian Zeus, the Corinthian columns standing out impressively in the middle of the 21st century city of Athens. But as we drove through the modern jumble of poorly planned high-rise condos we noticed the poverty and desperation in the faces of the people.

"Unemployment has risen to an all-time high this year," reported the tour guide as we passed boarded up buildings and children begging in the streets. Traffic was sparse and parts of the city resembled a post-apocalyptic scene from a movie. "The economy here has suffered greatly the past ten years and a steady decline of tourism and industry has left many without jobs." Costas, our guide, who was a young man with curly dark hair and dark skin, smiled despite his sad eyes, obviously feeling fortunate to be among the employed.

When we reached the outer city and disembarked at the renovated Acropolis, I took in a deep breath. Hot, dry air filled my lungs, and I pulled my hat lower to hide from the bright sun. Without Maddie to remind me, I'd forgotten to wear sunblock. Ethan took my hand as we climbed the stone steps upward. When we reached the top, we passed through the Propylea, a colossal entry gate leading to the upper terrace. We studied the temple of Athena, also known as Nike. The long columns and massive head stone towered above us. Built in the fourth century BC in honor of the Athenian victory over Persia—a slanted V that looked like a check mark along with other Greek lettering stood out on the temple's header. It dawned on me where the familiar logo had come from—Nike being the goddess of victory.

"I'll never look at a pair of sneakers the same," I said as I gazed up in awe at the massive stone columns.

Even more amazing was the Parthenon that stood before us down the main way, greater than all the other ruins. As we drew closer, Ethan pointed at a perfect location to get our picture, the backdrop looking much like the post cards small children were selling to the tourists as they passed. Ethan posed us in front of a mammoth Doric column, and I held out my hand as if mimicking a tour guide as he snapped a selfie. I checked the pic and gave him the thumbs up and a satisfied grin before moving on and sharing my perspective on the ruins.

"The Parthenon is considered by many to be one of man's greatest structural achievements." I pointed out the flawless proportions, which featured a gentle upward slope, so the form appeared to be a perfect rectangle. "If you look closely," I pointed out, "the columns are slightly widened on one end to create a linear illusion."

"So cool. How did you know that?" Ethan snapped another shot of me with the Theater of Dionysus at the foot of the hill in the distance.

"I told you before, I like architecture. It blows me away to think how they accomplished such amazing feats of engineering over two thousand years ago without any modern equipment. They had to do everything with animals and slaves."

"I can only imagine what it must have been like," Ethan said, looking out over the ruins of the once majestic city, his brows furrowed in contemplation.

"In this heat? It must have sucked." I sat down on a large piece of limestone and wiped my brow, adjusting my hat so the visor sat back and I could see Ethan clearly. His skin glistened—golden in the sun—and in the afternoon light, streaks of red and bronze ran through his hair. My heart thumped harder as it always did when I took a moment to realize how cute he was. The idea that Ethan Kaswell could really be mine sent waves of warmth to my chest and filled me with a new contentment I wanted to trust and breathe in.

There was a part of me that knew how fleeting and fragile life could be, and I wanted to hold every minute tight to my heart. It was either that or choose not to love at all. I smiled as Ethan offered to take a picture of a young couple in front of one of the Corinthian pillars. The fullness in my heart told me whatever happened, Ethan was now a part of me—a part of the history that would make up the rest of my life and shape the person I would become. A new realization hit me and came with an instantaneous sense of freedom. I now knew that loving someone didn't mean holding onto them. It meant accepting the pain of letting them go and choosing to love them anyway, knowing they would always be part of who I was.

∞∞∞∞

By the time we got back to the ship, my skin felt tight with a slight sunburn, and I was starving and exhausted. Ethan and I agreed to change and meet for dinner for the last formal night of the cruise. I still had one dress Maddie had insisted on buying for me for the occasion. When I stood in front of the mirror, I had to admit she'd made an awesome choice.

The clingy, navy blue dress hugged my body and landed several inches above my knees. With a V neck, lace bodice, and wide shoulder straps, the dress looked both chic and elegant. Despite the sunburn, my skin looked more a deep gold than red and it had a healthy glow. I paired my outfit with strappy sandals, and donned the beautiful abalone Paua dolphin jewelry Maddie had given me, adjusting Amanda's heavy charm bracelet on my other wrist.

Another inkling of worry settled in when I thought about Maddie in a hospital room without me nearby. Ethan reassured me his dad would call if there were any problems, but I still felt badly about leaving her in the care of strangers. Her voice echoed in my ear. When I'd asked her before leaving the hospital if she regretted taking the cruise, she'd said, no, she wouldn't change a thing.

Life, death, near-death; it's all part of the journey, she'd said. I considered her words, determined to enjoy my last night on board. A sigh escaped as I fluffed my short hair—prompting it to curl—and swiped on pink lip gloss.

On the way to dinner, I knocked on Ethan's door. He swung it open and his eyes grew wide. "Holy—wow! You look amazing."

A blush flooded my cheeks. "So do you," I replied.

His hair was neatly gelled, the short spikes in order and sideburns trimmed to perfection. I leaned in and kissed his cheek, drawn to see if his clean-shaven face felt as soft as it looked. I was rewarded not only with the smooth warmth of his skin against my cheek, but an intoxicating spicy scent that made my knees weak. I drew back and met the happy grin that took over and the sparkle of warmth in his eyes. He wore a collared light blue dress shirt with a thin striped tie, a black blazer, and a pair of nicely fitted navy pants. He reached out, and I offered him my hand as we headed for the forward elevators. Happiness filled my heart and spilled over, bringing a genuine smile to my lips.

Dinner was outstanding and more than I could eat. As usual, a veritable feast. Both of us anxious to enjoy our time alone and avoid the onslaught of questions about Maddie and our experience in Ephesus, we sat at a table for two rather than joining the crowd we usually sat with. I admired the ice sculpture of a swan, and we talked instead about our day in Athens, reflecting on all we'd seen and how as spectacular as it was, it wasn't the same without Maddie.

The meal began with an appetizer of double-baked cheese soufflé, followed by apple, pear, and cucumber salad. By the time my main course of oven-baked eggplant parm was placed in front of me, I was slowing down.

"We have to get dessert," Ethan said, eyeing the menu. The overhead chandeliers glowed dimly and the moon shining on the sea outside the window made me feel as if I was Cinderella at the ball, waiting for the stroke of midnight to come and turn the ship into a pumpkin and me back into the girl I was when I first stepped on board only a few weeks before. My head spun, still trying to process all that had happened.

We ended up sharing a dessert of Belgian chocolate mousse with raspberry liqueur, and whether it was the sleepless night and anxiety of the day before, the sun, or the small amount of alcohol saturating our dessert, I felt a little buzzed.

"Do you want to take in a show? They have some famous opera singer tonight. Or we could go catch a movie," Ethan suggested.

"I'm pretty done in. I think what I need is a few laps around the deck to walk off that meal before I head off to bed," I said as we strolled through the doors and out onto the deck. The moonlight cast a beacon across the sea, lighting the night and turning the sky a pale blue against the dark waters below. I shivered in the breeze that rolled in from the coast in the distance. Tiny lights let me know we were far from shore and headed out to sea. Ethan took off his jacket and wrapped it around my shoulders, leaving his arm in place around me and pulling me close. We walked hip to hip in silence for some time until I stopped and turned toward him.

"I know we promised to stay out of trouble and to be responsible, but do you think—maybe—could you stay with me tonight?"

Ethan's brows drew together. "In your room?"

"Um—no. Out on one of these deck chairs," I teased. "Of course, in my room. It's not like we have to take our clothes off." I chewed the inside of my cheek, hoping not to die of embarrassment if he said no.

"Do pajamas count?" he clarified. A small grin edged his lips and caused his super cute dimples to appear.

My stomach pitched. "Technically, we'd still be dressed. C'mon, we can both behave, can't we?" The truth was, I wasn't sure that lying snuggled together in one bed all night was the wisest decision I could make, but I knew I didn't want to be all alone in my room. I would undoubtedly lie awake thinking about Maddie all night without something to distract me. Ethan, clad in boxers and no shirt would definitely prove distraction enough, but the thought of him holding me through the night chased every bad thought from my head in a way I knew nothing else could. I laid my hands on his chest and played with his tie. "Please?" My lower lip slid under my top teeth, and I held my breath waiting for his answer.

Ethan forced out a slow breath and pulled me into a hug, laying a soft kiss on my forehead. "Is it always going to be this impossible to say no to you?"

Chapter 38

When I came out of the bathroom dressed in gym shorts and a tee shirt adorned with a picture of Avril Lavigne with her dark eye makeup and messy blonde locks, Ethan's lips curved into a smile. He was lying on top of the covers, his dress pants had changed to UCONN basketball shorts, and he was indeed, shirtless. I swallowed through a dry throat.

"Avril Lavigne? Really?"

"Her last concert was awesome."

Ethan held the covers up for me, his cheeks flushing red as he studied me from the wispy mop on my head to my pink toenails. I slid under the covers on my side of the bed, flopped onto my back, and tried to pretend my heart wasn't beating like a bass drum in my chest. Keeping the conversation casual, I said, "She puts on an excellent show. And I like her music. The style of her voice—the way she plays guitar. She even writes her own music."

Ethan rolled toward me and propped onto his elbow, leaning his head into his hand and tucking pillows between us. "I bet you can play as well as she can."

I laughed. "Yeah, right. In my dreams. It doesn't matter, anyway. There's no point in pursuing music as a career. Most musicians never make it big, and I wouldn't really want that kind of life anyway. Making music is fun, but I don't think performing is for me."

"You were awesome the other night." Ethan wrapped his arm around the pillow and rested his hand on my shoulder, the warmth sending an instant flutter to my insides. "You have a beautiful voice. And I could tell you were holding back with your playing. You should go for it. If you love it, pursue it. Go to music school. Maddie would be telling you right now to 'follow your dream—but make sure you get an education too.'" He pretended to be Maddie, tipping his head back and dramatically bringing the back of his hand to his forehead.

I giggled. "Nice."

We cracked each other up for the next ten minutes, the two of us out-doing the other with silly impersonations of movie actors and famous people. Ethan did an outstanding impression of George Clooney and I gave him my best Angelina Jolie, puckering my lips up and trying to look exotic. Our teasing turned to pillow fights and tickling, Ethan allowing me the upper hand. He laughed out loud— a wonderful sound that filled my heart and brought rolling laughter of my own to the surface—a sound I hadn't made in eons.

The realization stopped me and I sat back on my heels, waiting for my breath to return. I brushed my bangs out of my eyes and leveled a gaze at Ethan. "Thank you," I said.

Ethan's laugh slowed and a curious expression came over his face. "For what?"

"I owe you so much. I hardly know where to begin. You have been amazing on this trip. You've helped me see so many things in such a short amount of time. I hardly feel like the same person I was three weeks ago." I pursed my lips. "What did you even see in me?"

"I knew you were special from the start," Ethan said softly. He sat up and leaned toward me, studying my face. Then he pushed a strand of hair off my cheek. "I could see that underneath all that tough girl exterior, there was someone sad and lonely just waiting to come to life. Someone who'd been hurt and needed healing. Kind of like a bird with a broken wing—trying to figure out a way through the cage doors so she could fly free, but too afraid of falling to try." His gaze roamed over my features and my heart soared. "What's important now is that you're taking control of your life and trying to be the best you can be."

A warm rush of emotion and heat scorched through my body. It was as if he were looking into my soul, and what he saw there was the me I wanted to be. Tears rose and the words I wanted to say next stuck in my throat. Ethan laid a hand on my cheek. I leaned into his hand, unable to resist melting toward his touch. Then I closed my eyes.

"I don't know if I can be the person you want me to be, Ethan."

And that was the awful truth. I was so afraid of letting down the people I loved, I'd either made sure I set the bar low, or I tried not to care at all. Now, I finally understood that I couldn't live my life in the shadow of other people's expectations, and I didn't have to be defined by the actions or character flaws of my family. I needed to choose my own path, and for the first time, I could see where a new path might lead.

"You're the person I want to be with," he said pulling my attention back to his voice. "And it doesn't matter to me whether you're Lexi or Ali, or even if you want me to call you Avril." His grin added tiny creases to the corners of his eyes. "Don't you get it? Did you think I would have put up with all your crap if I hadn't fallen in love with you the minute I saw you?"

I knew I should be insulted, but instead my head floated for a moment with the meaning behind the words. My jaw dropped and nothing came out. Then his mouth was on mine. Hesitation fled and I melted my body into him, diving deeper into the kiss, not caring if I ever took another breath. His hands threaded gently through my hair as he rose up on his knees and brought me towards him. My hands went to his waist and then wrapped around the hot bare skin of his torso. Struck by the contours of the smooth, taut muscles of his lower back, I dug my nails into the flesh, drawing a groan from deep in Ethan's throat that vibrated through me like a freight train. We pressed our bodies together, sinking completely into a long, slow kiss that had my heart pounding and my head flying with ideas about what came next—about what I wanted.

But warning signals wormed their way in. I tried to ignore them, to pretend Maddie's voice wasn't in my head, making me promise to be responsible, telling me not to make the same mistake my parents made. With all the strength I had, I pulled away from the kiss and flashed an embarrassed smile at Ethan as I heaved in a breath. "Maybe we should try to get some sleep."

"Right," Ethan huffed out as he dropped back on his heels and put a foot of unwanted distance between us. Tugging the covers up in front of him, he stuttered. "Definitely. Absolutely…" the words fell out on each labored breath he took, as if he was trying to convince himself that sleep was an option.

We settled into our respective positions, him lying on top of the covers with an extra blanket over him, and me snuggled beneath them, the decision clearly made that nothing else would happen between us no matter how much we both wanted it to. Ethan tucked a single pillow between us and then wrapped an arm across my waist.

"Is this okay?" he asked.

"Definitely…absolutely." I giggled, teasing him with his own words. I heard a low rumble of laughter and reveled in the feel of his warm, minty breath at my neck. I sank into his arms, the covers and pillow between us just enough of a buffer to keep him honest and me from squirming any closer.

Ethan gently stroked my arm until sleep took over.

I dreamed of dolphins taking turns leaping out of the sea—of being safe and happy—and feeling lucky to be alive.

Chapter 39

The next day was a day at sea. Ethan and I slept in, both of us exhausted from the previous few days' events. I woke first so I slipped out of bed and sat on the deck outside our room, enjoying the sunshine and warm breeze while I worked out the last of the song I'd been composing the past week. Through the open slider, I watched Ethan sleep. The morning sun shone on his golden tanned skin, and his long dark lashes framed his eyes in perfect half-moons. He looked so relaxed, peaceful—almost innocent. And so handsome, I could hardly breathe. I wondered what D.D. and Sami would say.

Grinning like I'd won the lottery, I put the finishing touches on my song, woke Ethan with a soft kiss on the cheek, and headed for the shower, leaving him smiling sleepily at me as I closed the door.

When I came out, he was gone. A note, written in neat left-handed scrawl, lay on the pillow.

Best night ever! Thanks for letting me stay. Meet you at breakfast.

Ethan

Xoxoxo

∞∞∞∞

After a hardy breakfast, Ethan made a call to his father, who let me talk to Maddie. She sounded tired but good, and another wave of relief and gratitude rolled through me. She would fly home the same day as me, and I would meet her at the hospital in L.A. when she arrived. Ethan's dad would make arrangements for a driver to pick me up at the airport. It seemed everything was covered.

I had already determined I would stay with Maddie for a few more weeks to help take care of her once she was well enough to go home. Mom and Mitch deserved a chance to spend some time alone when she got out of the hospital—which she'd said would be soon when I called her to update her on Maddie's condition. I looked forward to getting to know my father through Maddie's eyes and seeing pictures of him growing up.

Relieved of the burden of worrying about all the details of our immediate future, Ethan and I enjoyed our day. We hung out by the pool, played a couple of vicious games of Ping-Pong, and spent a ridiculous amount of time playing Minecraft. I felt lighter—and completely relaxed with Ethan at my side. With new hope for my future, it seemed the cloud I'd been under had lifted.

Later that night, after another amazing dinner, we ended up in the Crow's Nest. The room was already crowded. Mr. and Mrs. Feinbaum waved us over and asked how Maddie was doing. Having fielded the question several times throughout the day, Ethan jumped in to give them the rundown. It seemed his heroic deed of saving Maddie's life had spread among the ship's passengers and Ethan was somewhat of a celebrity. He handled it humbly, but I could tell it made him feel good to know his quick reaction had made a difference in saving a life.

Tommy—apparently recovered from his bout of laryngitis—caught my attention. I excused myself.

PJ Sharon

"You had such a great reception here the other night. Do you want to play a set with me?"

I glanced at Ethan, proud to have him as my date and thinking this might be the perfect opportunity to show him how much I appreciated him. I pulled my song out of my pocket and unfolded the paper.

"You think we can play this one?" I gave Tommy a few instructions on chord structure and key changes while I checked the tuning on his guitar and he looked over the music. Ethan looked up and smiled, then made his way over to a seat near the window, the dark night and moon-drenched sea behind him. Anticipation lit his eyes and the room grew quiet.

Tommy played the intro and I strummed in, shifting my gaze over the audience, the tables all full and people standing in the entryway. I let out a long slow breath and spoke softly into the mic, barely aware of my own voice over the pounding of my pulse in my ears.

"This is called, *Because of You*." I glanced at Ethan and a shy smile took my lips. I drew in a deep breath and let my heart sing.

When I look into your eyes
I see the window to my soul
You show me who I am
And suddenly I'm whole

And I want you to know
You see the me I never saw
You see the me no one knew
You see the me I am today
Because of you

259

You showed me how to smile
You made me laugh again
Through the tears we shed together
I know I've found a friend

You gave me courage to look back
Courage to face the ugly truth
That love can't save us from ourselves
My life before is surely proof

And I want you to know
You see the me I never saw
You see the me no one knew
You see the me I am today
Because of you

When this day is finally over
And our journey finds its end
We'll both go on to bigger things
But I'll always be your friend

'Cause love knows no distance
And love knows no bounds
All you have to do is call on me
And I'll always be around

And I want you to know
You see the me I never saw
You see the me no one knew
You see the me I am today
Because of you

Chapter 40

Messina Italy and Mount Etna, our final port of call, couldn't have been any more interesting, even if we were both missing Maddie's quirky wit. We saw sites like the graceful Orion Fountain dating from 1547, the ancient cathedrals, and the Orologio Astronomico, an astronomical clock in the bell tower that fascinated Ethan. Our time together was especially bittersweet—it being our last day before taking off on separate flights to opposite sides of the U.S. It was unlikely we'd see each other again for at least a month. The thought of being apart for so long tore at my heart.

In spite of my melancholy, I tried to enjoy the day. Our tour bus ambled and bumped through the countryside. Fertile landscape dwindled into a stark lunar-like surface as we ascended up Mount Etna. Overlooking the craters and more than 250 vents in the active volcanic mountainside, Ethan and I took picture after picture, neither of us wanting the journey to end.

I snuck a peek at Ethan as he helped Mrs. Goldfarb negotiate the hillside down to the parking area. A smile curved my lips and I sighed as he followed me onto the bus and settled in the seat beside me, taking my hand.

"You're such a Boy Scout," I said, teasing.

"Mrs. Goldfarb says I'm earning my Jesus points." Ethan laughed and the sound of it made my heart swell—a sound I imagined I would never get enough of.

When we reached Taormina in the afternoon, the sun was high and the sea below the cliff-top perch of Monte Tauro shone like blue diamonds, sparkling and alive. Lined with arches, columns, cupolas, and dark red cliff faces, the road up to the center of the village seemed to bring us back in time. Ethan and I had our picture taken in front of the Palazzo Corvaia, an interesting 15th century building, reflecting the typical black and white Taormina architecture. The Church of Santa Catarina stood behind us in the shot, its huge wooden doors harboring centuries of secrets. I immediately texted it to Maddie, knowing she wouldn't have her phone until she got settled into the hospital in California. The thought of her seeing it as soon as she opened her messages brought another smile to my face—an occurrence which was happening with much more frequency.

"What are you thinking about that has you looking so happy?" Ethan said as we settled into wrought iron chairs at a local café on the bustling main street to get something to eat and drink.

"I was thinking about how much Maddie would have enjoyed today's tour." The rich, romantic Italian language surrounding us sounded like musical notes to my ear, and I determined Italy was a place I could easily call home one day.

"Maybe she'll be able to come back again when she's recovered."

"Only because of you," I replied, gratefully.

Ethan shrugged off the praise as a young waitress approached our table. With a thick, braided bun that resembled a coiled snake atop her head, and dark lined eyes, she looked far too exotic to be waiting tables. She gave us a friendly smile as I ordered a lemonade and a salad. Ethan ordered a pizza with everything and made me promise to help him eat it.

"You could use a more well-rounded diet," he grinned.

"And you could eat a few more vegetables, Mr. Carnivore." I sipped the lemonade that the waitress, her nametag reading Carlita, set down in front of me.

Ethan laughed and shook his head. "Okay, truce. I promise not to try to corrupt you, and you promise to not call me out on my meat-eating habits."

"Only if it means you won't expect me to change my bad habits." Our eyes met and an uncomfortable silence settled between us. I hadn't meant to bring it up, and I definitely didn't want a confrontation again about my use of weed, but I had opened the door and Ethan wasn't one to shy away from speaking his mind—which I loved about him but found infuriating at the same time.

"I thought you quit." He glanced around to see that no one was listening.

I shifted in my seat, unsure of how to respond. "I said I would go to the classes."

His brows dipped together. "What happened to the "straight and narrow" speech you gave me the other night?"

"Don't get all preachy again," I grumbled, tearing my napkin into pieces and piling them up on the table in front of me. I still had half a joint in my room, and knowing I couldn't take it on the plane, I'd thought about smoking it on our last night. Obviously, Ethan wasn't interested. "I can only promise I'll try."

He didn't look entirely satisfied with my declaration but he didn't push. His head tilted and a smile flickered as he reached over to capture my hand. "I don't want anything coming between us. It's going to be hard enough being apart while I'm at school and you're in Somerville. I'm afraid once you get home, you'll get sucked back into hanging out with the same friends as before and get into trouble again."

I drew my hand away. "Can't you just trust me?"

"I do trust you, Lexi. But if you really want to quit, you're going to have to make some tough choices."

"Like my friends?" I hadn't thought about it before, but he was right. It would be hard being around my friends who smoked and not join them. But what kind of friend would I be if I walked away from them because they smoked. It seemed pretty hypocritical to me. Besides, hadn't I lost enough? I couldn't imagine trying to make new friends in senior year, or for that matter, giving up my old ones. A sinking feeling hit my stomach and I leveled a gaze at Ethan.

"I'm not making any promises. You and I will just have to respect each other's individuality. It's the only way a relationship can work, right?"

"Listen to you, all mature and grown up."

"I don't have much choice anymore," I said, the reality of the past several weeks finally sinking in. "There are people who are counting on me to step up and take responsibility. I don't want to be a screw up anymore." I rearranged the knife and fork on the table, lining them up with the edge of my place mat. "I don't want to hurt anyone, Ethan. I just want to be happy." Even as I said the words, the thought of never getting high again brought me down. I sighed, suddenly afraid that my lofty goal of living on the straight and narrow might be harder than I thought.

∞∞∞

Ethan and I returned to the ship and hurried to catch dinner. The kitchen and wait staff shuffled out in single file, singing and dancing their way around the room. After another fantastic meal, we walked the promenade deck, enjoying our last night at sea and watching the moon rise above the water, casting its bright light in a beam across the small waves. A school of dolphins joined us. They leapt two at a time into the air and dove seamlessly back into the sea.

"Aren't they awesome?" asked Ethan as he came to stand by my side at the railing.

"Amazing," I agreed. Ethan's arm wrapped around me, and I rested my head on his shoulder as we watched the dolphins in silence until they pulled away from the ship and disappeared into the inky waters. I rubbed the dolphin pendant between my thumb and fingers, thinking back to the last time I'd seen them and how I'd felt Amanda's presence so strongly. This time, there was nothing but the sea and the boy holding me close. The charm bracelet on my wrist jangled as I wrapped my arms tighter around Ethan.

"I don't ever want to forget," I whispered.

"The dolphins or the whole cruise?" he asked, amusement and wistfulness in his voice.

"Any of it. This has been the most amazing trip ever." I looked up into his eyes, and he brushed a tear away that had slid down my cheek.

"What's wrong?"

"Nothing. I just miss Amanda. Every day, she seems to grow further away, and it's harder to remember all the little things she said and did."

"I know what you mean. I feel that way about my mom sometimes. But whenever I think I'm forgetting her, I look at her picture or remember how she used to make chocolate chip cookies for me after school. Or how she danced around with me, my feet resting on top of hers. It's all right there, Lex." He gently placed a hand over my heart. "Amanda would want you to let her go."

"I know."

I fingered the charm bracelet I'd given her, feeling the weight of all the grief I'd been holding inside. Her voice no longer whispered in my mind, and suddenly, I had a clear sense of what she would want me to do.

The clasp resisted as I fumbled with the bracelet on my wrist. I removed the lute charm Ethan had given me when we were in France, and tucked it in my pocket. Later, I would add it to the dolphin necklace Maddie had bought me. I turned toward the sea, bracelet in hand. Tears rolled down my cheeks as I pressed my lips to the cool metal, the charms heavy as they clinked together. My words faded into the breeze.

"I need to let you go, Amanda. I need to move on." My jaw ached and my throat felt as if I'd swallowed a stone, but I forced the words past the pain. "I'll never forget you, and I'll never stop loving you."

I took in a sharp breath and tossed the charm bracelet into the sea.

∞∞∞∞

After Ethan dropped me off at my room, my head swimming with dark thoughts, I tossed and turned, unable to sleep. As much as I hated the idea of sleeping alone our last night together, I didn't think either of us would be able to stand one more sleepless night of *not* fooling around. Caught up in more than a few serious make-out sessions, we'd both reached our limit of frustration. Hands had strayed and our self-control was slipping. Although Ethan's ability to shut down when things got too hot both impressed and frustrated me, I wasn't so calm and cool.

Restlessness took over and I slipped out of bed. Donning my bikini and shorts, I stepped into my flip-flops and grabbed a towel. I found my way to the uppermost deck where the hot tub beside the pool was sure to be vacant at such a late hour. Other than a few crew members, who flashed weary glances as I passed, no one seemed interested in where I was going or what I was doing wandering the ship at midnight.

Finding the hot tub empty, I flipped the timer on for the bubbles, tossed my towel onto a lounge chair, and dipped in a toe, pleased that it was hot enough to sting. Maybe a good soak would do the trick. Slowly, I submerged into the steamy pool, hoping it would relax me and wash away the tension that had my body strung tight. Returning home came with bittersweet thoughts and more questions than I had answers to.

Would my mother be okay? Or would she fall apart again if I stepped the least bit out of line? I could see myself walking on eggshells, waiting for her to implode, terrified of disappointing her. Still uncertain if I had it in me to fight the urge to smoke pot again and quit permanently, I shuddered at the thought. And how was I going to explain the new and improved me to my friends—the only people who had really stood by me through everything? I closed my eyes and breathed a sigh, letting the heat of the water and the steady pressure of the jet at my back, melt away my worries. No sense in obsessing over the unknown.

From behind me came the sound of a familiar voice clearing his throat. I spun to see Ethan standing there, a wary grin edging his lips and his eyes sparkling blue-green in the reflection of the dim lights emanating from the pool.

"Great minds think alike, right?" He tossed his towel onto a chair and approached, sending shivers along my skin. I sank back down under the bubbling water, immediately aware of how little my bikini actually covered. "Mind if I join you?" he said, not waiting for my answer.

I nodded as he stepped into the hot tub, his board shorts hanging low and the dusting of dark hair drawing a line downward from his belly button capturing my full attention. He dipped down into the water across from me and hissed as the steaming water covered him from waist to chin.

"You couldn't sleep either?"

"I always have trouble sleeping the night before I travel."

"Nervous about the flight, or about going back home and preparing for dorm life?" The thought of him going off to college scared me far more than it likely did him.

"When passengers aren't throwing up on me, I actually enjoy flying," he chuckled. "And as for dorm life it won't be any different than boarding school…except for the beer and the wet tee shirt contests."

I rolled my eyes, unwilling to engage in his teasing or show signs I was jealous.

He grinned and leaned his arms up over the edge of the hot tub, which showcased the definition of his arms and chest. My mouth went dry and butterflies erupted in my belly. He continued, apparently unaware of his effect on me.

"I'm only kidding. We already know I'm too much of a lightweight for the party scene, and you're the only girl I want to see in a wet tee shirt." He waggled his brows, drawing a reluctant curve to my lips.

"So what's keeping you awake tonight?" I asked.

"I have visions of oversleeping and missing my flight. Then where would we be?" He laughed.

"You could always get a job on the ship. I hear your stint as a Bingo caller is legendary."

"Only if you stayed on board with me and became a lounge singer." Ethan's dimples deepened and the edges of his eyes crinkled, sending another wave of affection to my heart.

PJ Sharon

It was fun to imagine floating off into the sunset together, but both of us knew that life had other plans for us. "Wouldn't that make our parents happy?" Sarcasm being preferable to the alternative, which was to accept that our time together was nearly at its end, I closed the distance between us and slipped into Ethan's ready embrace. Bubbles swirled and splashed up over the edge of the tub onto the deck.

"The only person I care about right now is you," Ethan whispered, his lips dangerously close to mine as he ran his fingers through my hair. A brush of his lips sent a spike to my pulse and then he pulled back. His gaze shifted back and forth with mine and when I smiled, he drew me into a deep kiss.

A fire ignited inside me. The sensation of our bodies pressed tight, skin on skin, was more than I could take. If he'd wanted to in that moment, he could have had all of me and I wouldn't have had the strength to say no, but before I could do or say anything to push us in that direction, he withdrew from the kiss. His steamy gaze met mine and his voice came in gravelly stops and starts.

"I…we can wait." He pushed wet strands of hair out of my eyes and a serious look of admiration took over. "What you did earlier—tossing your sister's bracelet into the sea—took a lot of strength and courage, Lexi."

The words sank in, and finally, I believed them. Whatever had spurred me to make such a bold decision, I realized I had more strength than I ever thought possible. In that moment, I knew I had the power to say yes or no—to take control of my life, and to let go of anything holding me back from being the best person I could be, whatever life had in store for me next.

Chapter 41

On our last morning, I dragged myself out of bed and climbed into the shower, my eyes barely open. Ethan and I hadn't lasted long in the hot tub. Fortunately, or unfortunately, the heat of the water combined with the combustible rise in temperature between us had driven us out and back to our respective rooms before any real damage was done. I stood under the hot water for a long time, waking slowly and dreading stepping onto another plane and having to leave Ethan.

We were already docked in Civitavecchia and the shuttle would be waiting to take us to the airport. Then it would be goodbye, not knowing when we would see each other again. It was easy to talk about plans to stay in touch when we were stranded together with no outside influence. But once Ethan returned home and started college in a few weeks, he could just as easily forget all about me. A new and deepening sadness seeped into my chest.

I threw on my comfy jeans and the baggy tee shirt I'd arrived in and packed my bags. I'd already sent Maddie's things down with the steward and taken care of ensuring their passage back to California. All that was left to do was to say goodbye to the ship. I stepped out onto the balcony and looked past the port to the open sea beyond. An instant flood of sorrow mixed with gratitude cascaded through me. A satisfied smile curved my lips even as I fought back tears. I opened the small baggie that held what was left of last week's joint, and memories of that night rushed back.

I'd grown up so much in such a short amount of time. I hardly felt like myself anymore. But then, I really hadn't felt like myself since Amanda died. Or for that matter, maybe I'd lost myself when I was six and Dad crashed into Jake Connelly, thrusting all of our lives into a tailspin. I took in a deep breath of salty air. The balmy warmth filled my lungs and hope sparked inside me, pushing away the sad memories. Maybe this was the start to finding the me I'd lost so long ago. In a moment of clarity and determination I dropped the roach overboard and crumbled the baggie into a tight ball.

A soft knock at the door drew me back into the room. When I answered it, Ethan stood waiting, a medium sized suitcase on wheels at his side and a backpack over one shoulder.

"You ready to go?"

"Ready as I'll ever be." Facing the next few weeks of being a caregiver to Maddie seemed a mixed blessing. It would keep me away from home and my friends that much longer—a prospect that had my head spinning with thoughts about how it would all work out. But it would also give me time to process everything I'd learned and all that had happened on our trip before going home to face Mom and Mitch. I owed them both an apology, and I wasn't looking forward to sucking it up and dealing with all the fall-out of my legal troubles. Completing my drug and alcohol classes before my next court date would be the least of my worries.

We disembarked with all the other passengers and climbed aboard the shuttle to the airport. I looked back at the cruise ship one last time.

Ethan must have noticed my sad expression. "So now that you've cruised the Mediterranean, I bet you'll want to see more of the world."

I grimaced. "Not if it entails flying, boating, or otherwise stepping off of solid ground."

"You managed your motion sickness pretty well on the cruise."

"Thanks to you and those magic pills. If I wasn't taking them every night like you told me to, it might have gotten ugly out at sea."

He grinned and wrapped his fingers around mine, resting both of our hands onto his thigh. "Hopefully the flight home will be better than the flight here."

My cheeks heated at the memory of throwing up on him on the plane before we'd even met. "Be glad you won't have to fly back with me."

"Honestly? I wish I was." The longing in his voice let me know he meant it. Then he smiled again and my heart jumped. "Aside from the puking thing, you're a pretty fun travel buddy."

We laughed and spent the rest of the ride to the airport talking about all the cool places we'd seen. It seemed neither of us wanted to dwell on the fact that it would be a while before we saw each other again.

When we reached the airport, Ethan walked with me, checked my bag, and made sure I had my ticket. His plane wouldn't be leaving for at least an hour after mine. As we passed through the security line, my palms began to sweat and my anxiety built to a crashing roar in my ears.

Ethan led me to an area away from where first class passengers were already beginning to board the plane. He turned me to face him and laid a hand on my cheek, his palm warm against my skin and his eyes filled with emotion. "I'm going to miss you."

"Not as much as I'm going to miss you," I said, certain it was true.

"I want you to call me once you're settled in at Maddie's place."

"I promise. Although won't you be busy moving?" He shrugged but I couldn't let him off the hook so easily. "Are you cool with living on campus?"

"Who wouldn't be?" He leaned against the wall, glancing at the clock counting down my departure. "I'm used to living away from home and my dad's never there anyway," he added, his expression strained.

"There's always the holidays, right? And if he's not around, you can come spend them with me." My attempt to lift the mood felt forced, but I hated seeing Ethan unhappy—a fact I was sure would be my undoing someday. I ran a hand through his hair, which had grown out some and made his features softer somehow. He tugged at his lower lip with his teeth, an awkward silence falling between us. "Unless it's going to be too hard—trying to see your dad and come see me too?" My hand slid down his cheek, and I tucked my thumb into my belt loop, unwilling to lose control over my emotions just because I didn't want to let him go.

"I'll make time for both," he said as he stepped closer and retrieved my hand once more.

My heart kick-started into overdrive. That one small gesture and his words of reassurance meant everything. If only I wasn't already missing him. "I want to thank you again."

"You don't have to." A tinge of pink spread up Ethan's neck to his cheeks and his gaze fell to his sneakers.

"I want to." I clung to his hand, trying to find the right words. "I could never thank you enough for what you did for Maddie. As for me…" I faltered, warmth radiating up my cheeks. "Meeting you has changed my life—has changed me."

"I didn't want to change you, Lexi. I only wanted to help you see how special you are."

"I just wish I hadn't been so afraid."

"Of me?" His eyes widened in surprise.

"No. I was afraid of me. Afraid of who I was becoming—maybe even a little afraid of living. Most of all, I was afraid of letting go of the people I'd lost because I thought it meant I didn't love them anymore. As if somehow I would forget them, and it would be like they had never been a part of my life at all." I thought of Amanda and about my dad and my chest ached with love and longing followed by a warmth that told me they would both always be with me. "I'm not afraid anymore," I said. Then I leaned in and kissed Ethan's cheek, turning the pink in his ears to a deep red that made me smile. I captured his gaze and our eyes met and lingered. The feelings overflowing my heart were reflected in the expression on Ethan's face. "I love you, Ethan."

"I love you, too." Ethan laid a tender kiss on my lips and wrapped me in his arms. We lingered there for a long moment until I heard the call for final boarding. When he pulled his lips away from mine, his green eyes glistened. "This isn't goodbye." He planted a gentle kiss on my forehead. "Let's just say, *À la prochaine.*"

I gave him a quizzical look.

"It's French. It means 'until next time.'"

"Let's hope that next time is very soon," I said, my heart overflowing with love.

"Count on it." Ethan kissed me again, and anything seemed possible.

Epilogue

The doorbell rang and I flew down the hall to answer it, running headlong into Mitch.

"Where's the fire?" He pulled up short and let me pass in my mad dash to greet our guests.

I yanked the door open.

Ethan and I stared at each other for about two seconds as if we were both in disbelief we were finally seeing each other in person after two long months. We'd only seen each other once a few weeks after school started when I'd taken the train into New York and spent the weekend at his house, chaperoned by his dad of course, who was spending more time there of late, according to Ethan. Since then, we'd been in constant contact through texts, phone calls, and e-mails. I flung my arms around his neck and nearly tackled him.

"You missed me, huh?" He squeezed me tight and lifted me off the floor, still carrying me as he stepped into the foyer. I could see Mitch to my side waving in Doctor Kaswell and heard him apologize in greeting, but it barely registered over the thundering beat of my heart. Ethan lowered me slowly to the ground and pulled back, studying my expression before planting a sweet kiss on my cheek. "I missed you, too."

I wrapped an arm around his waist and led him toward the kitchen, certain the perma-smile on my face was as bright as a hundred-watt bulb. "Maddie's here visiting and you have to meet my mom," I said, trying to act natural and not acknowledge the fact that my feet had wings.

Mom met us coming around the corner. "It's great to finally meet you, Ethan. Ali has told us so much about you."

"Mom, its Lexi now."

"So you keep reminding me." To my utter mortification, she patted my butt as we passed and turned into the kitchen. "You'll always be our little Ali Cat." As much as I wanted to be annoyed with her embarrassing display, it was good to see a spark in her warm brown eyes. The fact she'd adopted the nickname from my dad gave me hope she was well on her way to forgiving him. She'd been released from the hospital a week before I returned from Maddie's and since I'd been home, she seemed to be better—more alive. The family therapy sessions were still painful, but I figured we both had come to some kind of peace with Amanda's death. Moving forward would be a slow process, but together we would take it one day at a time.

When we entered the kitchen, Maddie raised her arms and all but plowed me out of the way to get to Ethan. "Oh, my darling boy, I can't tell you how good it is to see you!" She hugged him robustly, and Ethan wrapped her in a snug embrace in return.

"You, too. It's good to see you on your feet."

Maddie tipped her head back and rested a hand on Ethan's face, a sincere look in her eye. "Solely because of you." She released Ethan and addressed Doctor Kaswell. "And of course, you too, Martin."

The doctor took his son's place and hugged Maddie as if the two were old friends, which from the looks on both their faces, they were. The sudden blush in her cheeks insinuated she had formed a crush on the good doctor. No wonder, since he had invested a considerable amount of time, money, and effort to ensure her swift recovery. "I'm happy you're feeling better," he said. "Are you still doing your cardiac rehab?"

Maddie looped her arm through his and led him toward the living room, laughing theatrically. Ethan and I exchanged a quick glance and grinned.

Mom and Mitch shooed us out of the kitchen, insisting they could finish preparing the turkey dinner on their own and that I should go entertain our guests. Since Maddie had Doctor Kaswell spellbound with the details of her rehabilitation, Ethan and I escaped to the screen porch.

I pushed the slider shut and found a seat on the futon, a lumpy old beast from Mom's apartment before she and Mitch bought the house on Thompson Lake. It was hard to believe we'd lived there for the past four years. So much had changed since those days when it was just me, Mom, and Amanda, trying to recover from Dad's loss and pick up the pieces of our lives. Except that Amanda never did. She'd lost herself to her grief and anger and had let it destroy her. I shivered, determined I wouldn't make the same mistake.

Ethan grabbed the blanket off the back of the couch, wrapped it around my shoulders and snuggled in next to me, his arm tugging me into the warmth of his body. I rested my head on his chest, stretched my arm across his waist, and squeezed in closer. A cool breeze coming in off the lake carried the scent of dry leaves and apples from the apple tree out back, the screens not yet replaced by solid windows for winter. The brisk November air raised a chill on my skin. Ethan played his fingers through my hair.

"How have you been?" he asked softly when we were all settled.

"Okay," I said honestly. "I think I made honor roll this semester. I'm almost done with the drug and alcohol program, and Mitch has me set up to do my community service teaching guitar to kids at the Rec Center."

"That sounds like fun."

I heard the smile in his voice.

"I actually think it will be kind of fun. It hardly feels like punishment, although, Mom and Mitch barely let me out of their sight these days. I'm lucky they've been letting me go to band practice."

"Yeah, how's that going?"

I snickered. "Well, D.D. and Sami weren't too happy when I refused to hang out with the partiers and joined a band at the Community church instead, but I think they get why I needed to make the change. My legal troubles aside, I never liked the music they wanted to play, and I needed to get away from the whole scene if I was going to make this sobriety thing work out. The youth group at the church plays a lot of contemporary Christian music that's pretty cool. I still see D.D. at school and Sami has plenty of other friends to keep her from missing me. They'll get over it."

Ethan planted a gentle kiss on the top of my head. "I'm really proud of you. I'm glad you're turning things around."

"Don't get me wrong. It wasn't easy to say no at first. Some days, it's still not." Eyeing him sideways, I added with a half-smile, "But it's getting easier and it seems worth the effort. Just don't expect me to be good all the time."

"Me either." Ethan raised a mischievous brow and pulled the covers over our heads. He descended on me with an evil laugh. "Mwahahahaha!" As he tickled my neck with kisses and soft bites, I giggled, every cell of my body lit up with joy and happiness. Ethan and I were finally together. I'd missed him so much my body ached for his touch. With him so close, and so full of life, I soaked in the miracle of it all. I loved him and I wasn't afraid.

Whatever happened next, I knew we'd be okay—that I would be okay. Life's forward momentum was unstoppable, unpredictable, and sometimes ruthless. But every moment of it was a gift to be cherished.

∞∞∞∞

A short time later we all sat around the table, Maddie still mercilessly flirting with Doctor Kaswell, who didn't seem to mind in the least. Either he had a world-class bedside manner with patients, or he was sweet on my grandmother. Ethan and I exchanged a quick grin. Mitch was slicing up the bird while Mom set the bowl of mashed potatoes next to the asparagus and settled into her seat.

"I know we don't do this all the time, but I think it's a nice tradition to at least take a minute on the holiday to give thanks. Who would like to say Grace?" asked Mitch, pulling in his chair.

"I'd like to do it," said Maddie.

We all held hands, Ethan on one side and Mom on the other. I lowered my head and gave my attention to the deep sense of thanksgiving that filled my heart.

Maddie's words came strong and clear.

"Dear Lord, we appreciate the many blessings you have bestowed upon us. For this family, these friends, and for this wonderful feast, we give you thanks." Her voice grew softer, a slight hitch taking over. "And Lord, please watch over those who've greeted you ahead of us. We know that our loved ones"—she nodded to Ethan and then his dad, honoring the woman they'd both lost so long ago—"my dear Henry, our sweet Amanda, and our beloved Nicholas, who we hope has found peace in your loving arms and has been reunited with his father and his daughter—that they may care for one another in heaven."

279

Tears welled in my eyes and Mom's grip on my fingers tightened. Maddie's words gave me comfort as I imagined Dad and Amanda with Grandpa Henry fishing at the edge of Thompson Lake, the three of them smiling and happy. Amanda would lie back on the beach with her face lifted to the warm sun, Dad and Grandpa Henry discussing the merits of worms verses corn for bait, and the water would sparkle with dancing sunbeams as far as the eye could see.

"Amen," we all chimed in, bringing my focus back to the present.

"I'd like to add one more thing," I said. I waited until all eyes were on me and for my heart to slow with the deep breath I'd just taken. A technique I'd worked on with the Medusa Lady, a.k.a. Doctor Reynolds, for the past few weeks in preparation for springing the news on Mom and Mitch. "I've applied to music school for fall semester next year," I said, expecting an immediate negative response from my mother. I didn't give her a chance to speak. "I don't even know if I'll get in, but I need to try. I think Dad would have wanted me to." I glanced at Maddie who was beaming and much to my surprise, offering no argument. Mom's eyes flooded over with tears. "Don't cry, Mom. It's local, so I won't be moving away…and it's not for another year."

"I'm not crying because I don't want you to go to music school or because I'm afraid of you moving away someday. I'm crying because I'm proud of you. Your father would have been too. You're right. He would have wanted you to pursue your dream of music if that's what you love." She touched my hand and pulled herself together, her expression turning serious. "But I still think you need to have a back-up plan in case you decide later it's not the life you want." She eyed Maddie, no doubt looking for support for her coming argument.

I cut her off again. "I've already thought about that. I plan to take courses in architectural design at the same time. I even added art history to my spring class schedule."

"Are you sure you can handle all of that, sweetie?" Mom asked, her expression full of concern.

"I won't know unless I try, right Grandma?"

"That's right." Maddie grinned. "And don't call me Grandma," she added, her sharp blue eyes leveled in my direction.

We all laughed and it felt so good to have my plan laid out before me that suddenly, a few years of school didn't seem like forever. I would handle whatever challenges came my way and I'd do my best to make choices I could be proud of. Ethan and I would see each other whenever we could. We'd stay in touch by phone, or text, or Skype, or train. It didn't matter. Because the future was ahead of us—ours to live.

As everyone dug into their Thanksgiving feast, I looked around the table at all the people who meant so much to me. When my gaze landed on Ethan beside me, I caught him staring at me, a crooked grin edging his lips.

"What are you thinking?" he asked below the chatter of conversation around us.

"I was thinking it might be possible to put the pieces of love back together—even if all the pieces aren't here." I studied the smiling faces of my family and saw the truth. That maybe with time, the love would take over and fill the spaces until we were all whole again.

Ethan leaned in and gave me a brief, tender kiss. "In case I forget to tell you a thousand times today, I love you."

Another crack in my heart smoothed over. I whispered back, "You could say it a thousand times, but I can't imagine feeling more loved than I do in this moment."

PJ Sharon is the Award Winning Author of contemporary young adult novels, including SAVAGE CINDERELLA, winner of the 2013 HOLT Medallion Award. She is excitedly working on The Chronicles of Lily Carmichael, a YA Dystopian trilogy. WANING MOON, Book One, was a 2013 finalist in both the National Excellence in Romance Fiction Awards and the Colorado Romance Writers Award for Excellence. Book Two, WESTERN DESERT is now available. Look for book three, HEALING WATERS in 2014.

Writing young adult fiction since 2007 and following her destiny to write romantic and hopeful stories for teens, PJ is a member of Romance Writers of America, CTRWA, and YARWA. She is mother to two grown sons and lives with her husband in the Berkshire Hills of Western MA.

Connect with PJ Sharon

I love hearing from readers! Please feel free to connect with me via the following sites.

If you enjoyed PIECES of LOVE, please take a moment to leave a review on Amazon, B&N, and i-Tunes or go to **Goodreads** and share your thoughts. Any help in spreading the word about my books is greatly appreciated. I hope you'll check out my other books. You can read HOLT Medallion winner, SAVAGE CINDERELLA for FREE for a limited time on www.wattpad.com

Find out more about PJ and her books by visiting her website, and sign up for her newsletter for bonus content at www.pjsharon.com

"Like" PJ on Facebook at www.facebook.com/pjsharonbooks

Follow PJ on Twitter at www.twitter.com/pjsharon

PIECES of LOVE theme song available on i-Tunes at: https://itunes.apple.com/us/album/pieces-of-love-single/id848325918

11984785R00164

Made in the USA
San Bernardino, CA
04 June 2014